The Freemason's Family

By the same author

Non-fiction
Investing in Antique Silver Toys and Miniatures (2011)
Masonic Memorabilia for Collectors (2002)

Fiction
The Freemason's Daughter (2009)
The Hurtley Sisters (2011)
The Naked Corps (2013)
Playing Away (in preparation)
The Elusive Mr Hooper (in preparation)

Poetry
Poems of an Old Soldier (2012)

The Freemason's Family

Bill Jackman

Jackman Publications

Contents

Dedication

I dedicate this book to three beautiful granddaughters, Sophie, Kate, and Chloe

Author's note

The Freemason's Family is the sequel to *The Freemason's Daughter*. Beatrice has married her friend Charles and the family of four have emigrated to Australia, where, along with other members of the family already there, they each become involved in a variety of adventures including, piracy, war, rustling, murder and love.

Main family characters

Beatrice	A former nurse
Richard White	Beatrice's first husband
Charles	Beatrice's second husband
Ann	Beatrice and Richard's daughter
Norman	Beatrice and Charles's son
Bruce	Beatrice and Charles's son
Alex	Beatrice's stepbrother
John	Alex's natural father
Clare	Norman's fiancée
Sheila	Bruce's wife
Harry	Bruce and Sheila's son
James	Ann's husband
Arthur	Ann and James's son
Mary	Ann and James's daughter
Ray	Mary's first husband
Archie	Mary's second husband

1 *Beatrice*

*T*HE UNEXPECTED BLAST on the ship's horn nearly caused Beatrice Redlock to jump out of her whalebone corset with fright. She was a first-class passenger on the *SS Great Britain* on her way to Australia, with her new husband Charles and her children. She was deep in thought, thinking over her past life, and those people she had loved, many of whom she would see no more.

The ship had called at Gibraltar many times before. But this was the first time it was going to Australia, via the newly opened Suez Canal. The ship was packed with over six hundred passengers, some getting off at stops en route. The Australian Gold Rush had started, and a over a third of the passengers were fortune hunters, many unable to pay their fares and working their passage to Australia. The combination of various classes of passengers was quite remarkable. Space was at a premium, and naturally those that had paid the first-class fare had the largest share of it. Even the first-class passengers were mainly confined to a single cabin with one bunkbed, or one with two beds. They were dark, very hot and cramped.

The worst space on the ship was in steerage, which was at the rear of the ship down below where the rudder and propeller were housed. It was noisy, smelly and very hot. This was the area where horses, cattle and other farm animals were stored together, with their feed and other stores. Despite the terrible conditions it was packed with passengers looking for a cheap passage to Australia.

Beatrice had been on the *SS Great Britain* before. The last time she travelled on it was when she was returning from the Crimea, where she had served with distinction as a nurse under Florence Nightingale. The ship was being used as a troop carrier in those days, and had very little of the fineries and comforts she had today after her refit. There were four in total in her family, including Charles, her new husband. There was Norman who was twelve, and Ann aged ten, not forgetting herself.

The hot morning sun blazed down on all the passengers on deck. Beatrice, dressed in a summer dress was still too warm and her straw bonnet did little to keep the sun off. She opened her floral parasol which did at least place her in some shade. She looked over the side at the crowds gathered on the quayside.

They were waving madly at the passengers, some trying to pick out those they knew. A small military band had started playing a medley of marching tunes to celebrate the arrival of the *Great Britain*. The poor bandsmen were feeling the heat in their uniforms of blue and red serge with button-up-to-the-neck jackets.

It was after all midsummer, and conditions below deck on the ship were just unbearable. The portholes let in only warm air as there was no breeze, and although there were some electric fans there weren't enough of them. The thought of travelling via the Suez Canal was another reason the ship was so full. None of those on board had experienced this adventure before and even the captain and crew didn't quite know what to expect, though they had all been assured it would be *plain sailing*. The journey would knock weeks off the time it normally took to reach Australia via the Cape of Good Hope.

Beatrice returned her thoughts to her life before she had married Charles. She had never imagined for a moment that the future held many more adventures for her family when she arrived in Australia. Plus, it wouldn't have the restrictions of the staid Victorian life she was leaving behind in England.

*

Beatrice's memories were interrupted when she felt a pair of hands covering her eyes, and Charles's seductive tones offering her a penny for her thoughts. She turned and faced him. He really was the most attractive man she could have married. He was six foot tall, bronzed by the Australian weather, hardly an ounce of excess fat on him. His muscular arms held her gently like a baby in his arms as he bent down to kiss her lightly on the lips.

'Don't Charles. What will people say?' she reprimanded him.

'To hell with those Victorian pomegranates, we're not in England now,' he chuckled.

'And we're not in Australia yet, my dear. I think you ought to show a little tact until we get there, and curtail that sort of language. After all, we don't want to be the butt of everybody's conversation.' she said, trying to be serious.

'Yes you're right, I'm sorry. It's just that the freedom of speech and the way of life is so casual back home in Australia, not toffee-nosed like England. I just yearn to get there again, fast.'

Charles had grown out of the manners of Victorian England. Even his parents found his attitude unbecoming at times, and had to correct him. He had truly taken on board in the years he had lived in the country the ways of the Australian sheep-herders. In fairness he never let out one of their profanities, though he had come pretty close to it.

He grinned at her. 'I could just do with half an hour of you and me alone in our cabin.'

'There is no chance of that, dear husband. You will have to wait till we get settled in Australia.'

'It's this sun that's having that effect on me. I think I'll go and have a beer,' he said, releasing her and heading for the cabin.

'Hurry up because we will be going ashore soon. Get the children for me, Charles. I left them in the cabin reading books.'

He waved in acknowledgement as he disappeared below decks. Beatrice felt so happy. It was as if she were having a second chance, a second chapter in life.

It came as a great surprise to Charles to find out that Beatrice's son Norman was actually his boy, and not her first husband's, as everyone thought. He had been conceived because of an afternoon love romp in the meadows, a flirtation in which Beatrice should take all the blame because it was she who had taken the twenty-three-year-old Charles and given him his first introduction to what the physical side of love was all about. Unfortunately for Charles it all ended there, as a month later she married Richard, and although she knew the truth she made Richard happy in believing that Norman was really his son. He died never knowing the truth.

When Norman and Charles stood side by side there was no mistaking the similarity in their features. Norman was nearly thirteen with dark brown hair and matching colour eyes. He was a quiet boy and preferred to spend his time reading than joining in the boisterous games of the boys of his age. When told his mother and Charles wanted to marry he was happy, and the only concession he asked was that he could call Charles *father*. If only he knew the truth, and how happy it made Charles.

Ann, who was Richard's and Beatrice's daughter, took after her mother in looks and character. She was eleven with long, light brown hair which hung down her back. She had a melodious voice and said she would like to be an opera singer when she grew up. She too liked Charles, and found him a fine replacement for 'her real father who she had loved dearly. Both Beatrice and Charles agreed that no one but themselves would ever know the truth about Norman's parentage.

Charles was a self-made success story. He had gone to Australia penniless, yet within two years had opened a sheep farm and had successfully built it up, overcoming many obstacles on the way, so that it eventually became a profitable business. Beatrice's family, though very adept at farming, had never been to Australia before, but Beatrice had handled sheep on her father's estate, so she was thrilled to think she would be back farming again.

They had left behind in England her dear friends Betsy, Sally, and Dory, all of them widows.

Charles came up from the cabin with their two children. They were very excited at the sight of a new country, even though it was only an island.

'Can we see the apes, mother?' asked Ann.

'I want to see the Changing of the Guard,' said Norman.

'Be patient, children, there will be many exciting and new things to see. Stand close by as we disembark,' said Beatrice, ushering them before her. The whole family needed to stretch their legs as conditions were very cramped on board: even though they had first-class accommodation, space was at a premium.

Their tour of the island had to be shortened once they had seen some of the sights as Ann had blisters come up on her heels which meant an early return to the ship.

'How long will it take to get to Australia, father?' asked Norman, as he scanned an atlas of Australia.

'It's usually a three-month trip, but as this ship has a propeller it could reduce that sailing time by two weeks or more. Our next stop is Malta and then Suez.' Charles looked at the proposed route.

Later that afternoon the iron ship made its departure from Gibraltar and the family once more settled down to the pleasantries of sailing through the Mediterranean and watching the dolphins racing alongside the ship.

Malta, like Gibraltar, they found wonderful and this time the whole family were able to spend plenty of time enjoying the island. In fact Ann was so impressed she wanted them to stay and not go any further. Beatrice, who had been to Malta before, found pleasure in showing the family the sights. She had some very pleasant memories of her own of the fantastic week she spent making love in Malta with her friend and future husband, Richard White. She had too had fallen in love with Malta. Soon after leaving the island they arrived at Port Said, in Egypt.

Beatrice was fortunate in that her family had first-class accommodation. The conditions were so cramped on board. They had a room or lounge, to themselves. Most of the other cabins had just enough room for one or two narrow bunkbeds side by side; any luggage had to go under the narrow bed. There was very little headroom above the bed and no shelves – just a small bedside table between the two for a candle to stand. It was so hot and stuffy that one couldn't wait to get on deck. There was just the main top deck and this was principally for the first-class passengers. The huge steam engine gave off unbearable heat.

Once they had entered the Suez Canal everybody wanted to be up on deck to admire the view of Egypt on either side of the canal and hopefully to catch some breeze. The sun blazed down. It was so bad that the captain had the top deck covered along its length with a long parasol supported and strung together so that all on the deck were protected against the sun; even the poultry and cow, reserved for milking, enjoyed this luxury.

'Look, Father, there's the pyramids,' shouted Norman gleefully, as the long iron ship made history, being the first of its kind to sail along the canal. The ship's speed was very slow, as the width of the canal was nearly the same as the ship. The captain knew he mustn't make any waves. The children, like many other people, were dashing from side to side to take in as many views as possible. An Arab, walking along the canal side leading an ungainly camel, waved at the passengers, who politely responded, though some did shout out greetings. It was the first time most of them had seen anything of Egypt.

It was such a wonderful feeling sailing through the Suez Canal. Very few boats had passed through since it was opened in November, but numbers were increasing. The first stop had been Port Said. The family gazed in wonder at the panoramic view of the harbour, and the hustle and bustle of little boats.

These little boats, manned by two men in each, scurried around the bigger ships trying to sell them fruit and souvenirs. The sides of the ship were thronged with fascinated viewers all wanting to take in the splendour of Egypt which had not been available to travellers before then because there was no Suez Canal, and those travelling to Australia had to go via the Cape of Good Hope.

The captain thought it better not to let his passengers ashore at Port Said as he had been warned there could be complications between his passengers and the Egyptian authorities.

'Where does the Suez Canal finish, Father?' asked Norman, who was the most inquisitive member of the family.

'It joins up with the Red Sea, my son,' his father replied, as he tried to shield his eyes from the glare of the fierce midday sun.

'Look, Father, we are coming into a lake,' said Ann, bewildered.

'Yes my dear, it is called "The Bitter Lake" and has been built so that ships can pass each other, which they cannot do on the canal. Each ship will have to wait its turn to proceed further, and then only when the canal is clear.

'It's all very exciting, Father,' said Norman, who was taking it all in.

'Tell me some more details about the sheep farm, darling,' Beatrice asked him.

'I've told you lots before when we were in England.'

'I know, but it's different now. I am actually going to be part of it. Did I tell you I dreamt about your sheep farm more than once when I was a nurse in Crimea?'

'Alright, let's sit here where there is a little shade.'

'I'm going off with Jennifer, my friend, for a walk around the ship,' said Anne. 'Come on, Norman, come and join us.'

'No thank you,' said Norman. 'Mother I'm bored. Did you bring any books with you?'

'I have some books on sheep farming,' answered Charles. 'I don't know if they will be of any interest to you. However, you are welcome to read them. I can do with all the help I can get when we get to Australia. I hope you will help me in the running of the place. Do you want the books?'

'Yes please, Father. I am interested, although I have already studied the climate and conditions out there a great deal.'

'Fine, they're under my bed in our cabin. There are three of them. Go and help yourself.' Norman dashed off to find his books.

'It's nice to know he's interested. I know he will grow up to be a son you can love and respect,' said Beatrice.

'I do already,' he said, giving her a gentle squeeze round the waist.

Beatrice wouldn't let the matter drop as to her role on the sheep farm

'What will I be doing, Charles? Can I work with the sheep? Remember I worked on my father's estate and helped at lambing time?'

'Of course you can. That's why I married you so I could have an extra unpaid hand on the farm,' he grinned.

'Who does the cooking and house cleaning?'

'Not you. We have a team of Aborigines who do all that. Murky is the cook, and Scrumpy is the housemaid. She's a little darling, you will like her.'

'Have we got neighbours?'

'Why of course. The Kingston family aren't far away.'

'How far?'

'Only about a hundred miles or so,' he said with a grin.

2   *Rough Seas*

THE QUIET was shattered by the ship's alarm system giving out three blasts over the hooter. Everyone was amazed. What could be wrong? The ship's bows swung sharply to the port side; there was a loud crunching noise and the ship came to a halt, very suddenly. Standing passengers who were not holding on to a rail were flung forward. Charles and Beatrice were lifted from their seats at the force of the impact.

'What's the matter?' shouted Beatrice. 'Are we sinking? What was that bump, Charles?' She wasn't alone in her concern; all the other passengers looked worried and scared; there were some casualties among the elderly and infirm. Passengers hurried to the side of the ship to see the reason for the impact for themselves.

'We have hit something,' said Charles. 'I don't know what. Wait here.' He went to the rail to see the reason for himself. As he could see nothing on the port side he crossed over to starboard. The ship was at angles across the Suez, its nose stuck in the river bank. Several elderly people were hurt in the collision.

The nurse's training Beatrice had acquired in the Crimea surged once more through her body. She knew she must help anyone who was injured, and defying Charles's instructions to stay put, she dashed over to an elderly lady who had fallen.

'What's the matter?' she asked. 'Can I help?'

The woman looked at her, astounded. 'Who are you?' she said. 'I don't want a posh woman who is a nosey busybody. I am in pain. I need a doctor.'

'I am not a doctor, but I served in the Crimea with Florence Nightingale and am used to all kinds of wounds,' said Beatrice, feeling her pulse. The woman paused for a moment, taking in what Beatrice had said.

17

'Oh very well then, as there is no doctor available. It's my ankle.' She was crying, clearly in pain.

'May I look at it?' said Beatrice. 'I can tell if it's broken.'

'All right my dear, but ask the men folk to look the other way,' she begged.

'Will you men turn your backs please as gentlemen whilst I undo the lady's boot and look at her ankle?' They did as she asked. She untied the woman's boot, and soon ascertained that the injury was not a fracture but a sprained ankle.

'I'm pleased to tell you it's not broken, but you have sprained it.'

'Are you sure?' the woman asked, surprised.

'Yes, I could tell when I examined it. You need to rest. I would suggest a cold wet bandage tied tightly round the wound, and try not to walk on it for a few days.' The old lady looked up to a gentleman who appeared to be her husband as it was he who was fussing over her.

'Let me be, Herbert. Get me downstairs so I can rest,' she commanded. 'Thank you my dear,' she said to Beatrice. 'You are a credit to the nursing profession.'

Beatrice thanked her and turned away to find Charles. He had been standing watching the whole incident and greeted her with a smile when she saw him.

'Well done, Beatrice. You will be a great asset on the farm. We are always having accidents.'

The ship's crew were running everywhere, trying to pacify passengers and answer questions from irate colonists, who arrogantly demanded the reason for the collision, which they concluded there clearly must have been. Charles grabbed the arm of a passing sailor.

'What has happened? I want to know.'

'It appears we have run into the bank, sir. A small fishing boat cut right in front of us. We had a choice either run it down or take evasive action. That's why the captain blew the ship's hooter.'

Charles thanked him and went and looked over the side to where the bow of the ship had embedded itself firmly into the canal bank. The captain was trying in vain to release his ship by continually putting it into reverse gear, but with no success.

'Ladies and gentlemen. Don't be alarmed. We have run into the bank and are jammed, the reason being that we tried to avoid an accident with a fishing boat. I don't think there is any serious damage and assistance is on it way to get us free from the bank. Please don't worry. I will keep you informed.'

Gradually normality resumed and the interest in the accident of their ship subsided as passengers continued their various relaxations. Ann came running up to Beatrice.

'Mother, Father, are you alright? Isn't it exciting? Where's Norman?'

'I don't know,' said Beatrice. 'In the cabin I assume. Charles, go and see that he's alright please.'

Charles and Ann went to find Norman. They opened the cabin door and saw Norman lying on the floor with a big wardrobe that had become detached in the collision and had come crashing down on him, pinning him beneath it.

'Norman! Norman!' Charles called. There was no reply. 'Ann, go and tell Mother what has happened, and tell her we need a doctor here quickly.'

Ann rushed off without a word to find her mother. Charles lifted the wardrobe back to its position. The boy stirred and moaned.

'Hold on, son. Help is on the way. Are you hurting?' It seemed a silly question, but he was anxious and wanted Norman to speak.

'It's my leg, Father, that's where the pain is,' he said, trying to nurse it, but it was too tender to touch. It was twenty minutes before the ship's doctor arrived. He seemed a very old doctor by modern standards of the day. Dressed in a tweed suit and waistcoat and hat, with a gold watch and chain, he looked completely overdressed for the tropics. He was a chubby fellow with grey hair and watery blue eyes.

'I'm sorry I'm late,' he said, looking around the cabin, 'but the collision has given us a great many casualties. Is this your son?'

'Yes, he's in great pain,' said Charles. 'That big wardrobe fell on him and has damaged his leg.'

'Yes! I see!' He opened his medical bag and took out a stethoscope. Having checked the boy he agreed that it was not serious, only a broken leg.

'Don't worry young man, we will soon have you in splints,' he said, smiling at Norman and turned to Charles.

'Wait here with your son and I will have some deck hands bring him to the medical bay.'

He touched his hat and bade Charles good day. Ten minutes later two crew members came and took him to the sick bay, with Beatrice running at his side, constantly reassuring him that he would be alright. Later that afternoon a tug ship appeared from Aden. The passengers were told not to go to one side altogether, as it would make the unwedging of the ship more difficult and could even result in it capsizing.

Norman was to spend the night in the sick bay and rejoin the family the next day. He seemed happy enough, surrounded by books.

It was while they were having their evening meal that the captain made his announcement.

'Ladies and gentlemen, I am sorry to tell you that we will have to evacuate the ship. We cannot refloat it while there are so many people on board, so at eight o'clock I want everyone to leave the ship. The crew will be there to help you. Take with you blankets and whatever you need for the night.'

They manned their boat stations at eight o'clock and an organised disembarkation proceeded. One old lady fell into the canal trying to save her dog; otherwise there were no further incidents. The night was dry but very cold, and they all needed their blankets. Just before dawn a patrol of Egyptian police came on board the ship and spoke to the captain.

'Captain Smith?' asked the Egyptian police officer.

'Yes, who are you?'

'I am Captain Barrack of the Egyptian police and I have come to arrest you and your crew and take your ship as security.'

'What the hell for?' asked the captain of the ship.

'The reason is simple. You have landed illegally in Egypt, therefore you will be taken and be placed in prison until this matter is sorted out.'

'But we can't move,' said Captain Smith. 'I'm hoping that we will be free in a few hours and able to proceed. Surely in God's name you can allow us that time. Then we will be gone and will bother you no more.' Suddenly he realised that the only way out of this was to please the police captain. He thought he would try that approach. The workmen and natives had been working hard to free the Great Britain.

'Is there no other way this can be sorted out. We have the ship free from the canal bank, and are ready to sail. We can be away in an hour at the latest,' said the captain, who, having removed his cap, was scratching his greying head of hair trying to find a solution which would save face for both parties.

'This is most unusual, Captain Smith. However, rather than put these poor people through another cold and uncomfortable night, I will accept £500 English sovereigns for their release.'

The captain was fuming: he could see that this was illegal but with so much at risk he was not inclined to argue, and instructed his purser to arrange the payment. True to his word, once he had been paid the police man disappeared with his men into what remained of the night.

'What an opportunist,' said Captain Smith. He was hopping mad. That was an enormous sum of money to pay, but what could he have done? He hoped the ship's directors would understand.

Within an hour they had sufficient steam to move the ship carefully along what remained of their journey along the Suez.

Before moving off, the ship was checked over for structural damage but nothing of any importance that would delay their departure was found so the journey continued. Their next stop was Aden where the ship took on water and coal. No one went ashore as there was nothing of any consequence to see. However, the ship was given a thorough inspection for safety to enable her to continue to Australia.

The bow was a little dented, but the soft sandy bank had cushioned most of the impact.

Their next port of call was at Colombo, the capital of Ceylon. It was very hot and Beatrice dressed the children as best she could so that that they didn't overheat and become ill. Charles went and changed a little money with the ship's bursar and they all went ashore.

When the children saw the Indian people and cows walking together in the high street they thought it very strange. Norman was not able to join the family ashore and had to content himself with the view from his cabin window. There was so much for the young family to see and learn about. Charles and Beatrice were both blissfully happy together. Their marriage had been a long time in coming, but it appeared to be a good solid relationship. Little did they know how much they would need each other in the trying times ahead Charles was in his element in his new role of being a father, and relished in it, advising them about all aspects of life and travel to help to broaden their education.

They stood together looking over the side of the liner as it very slowly made its way through to the Indian Ocean. It was a very quiet evening, with just the thud, thud of the engines as they slowly nursed the liner through the calm waters of the ocean. It was so pleasant and cool after the sweltering heat of the day. Apparently, it was permitted to sleep on deck when the weather was like this, though hardly anybody did as it wasn't the done thing. Those that did sleep on deck were single male passengers, but no ladies.

Norman was getting better and was now hobbling about. It would only be a matter of days before he was well enough to have the splints removed.

Suddenly Beatrice felt a change in temperature. She pulled her shawl closer round her shoulder.

'My! It seems to have got a lot colder, and look there are dark clouds scudding across the sky. Do you think we are in for a storm dear?'

'Quite likely,' said Charles, putting his arm around her waist to comfort her. 'They can be sudden and very fierce out here. Come on, let's go downstairs to our cabin.'

It was the monsoon period and sudden storms were very much a way of life. It was at night that the squall hit the boat. First there were high winds. They were so fierce that the captain had to drastically reduce sail and just stay on the engines. It was in stormy conditions like this that the ship proved the value of having both sail and steam. The big propeller made the ship very unstable and that along with the constant thud of the massive engines gave Beatrice a constant headache.

The ship swayed from left to right and up and down at the same time. These gyrations caused most of the passengers to be violently seasick. Water came down the hatchways and flooded the corridors. Everything that wasn't fastened down fell on the floor. The lights went out and nobody could see where they were going. The storm raged on. It was like riding a bucking bronco, thought Charles, who had done his share of that in the past. Suddenly there was an almighty crash that could be heard throughout the ship.

'Mother! What was that bang. I'm frightened!' squealed Ann.

Norman hobbled out of bed and put his arm around his sister to comfort her.

'Don't get upset, little sister .No harm will come to you. I will see to that.'

'I think that was a mast that has broken. It happened to me when I first went to Australia,' said Beatrice, trying to act brave and reassuring. No one was allowed on deck even if they wanted too,

'Oh dear, this ship does seem unlucky Charles. Do you think it will make it to Australia?' asked Beatrice.

One could hear passengers running up and down the corridors, many of them frightened of the storm and its consequences.

'Of course we will, my dear. You have experienced worst storms than this when you sailed to the Crimea; or have you forgotten?'

'I know Charles it was like this, in fact even worse, we had to throw the guns overboard to stop the ship sinking, but I didn't have to worry about my family in those days,' she reminded him.

'Have you been to sea in worst storms than this, Mother?' asked Norman.

Before Beatrice had time to answer his question the few lights that were on board went out. The children gave a cry of alarm. Beatrice kept her voice calm as she replied.

'Yes dear, a lot worse, I'll tell you all about it one day.' The storm seemed to be getting worse. The ship was banging down hard on the waves making the thing shudder.

'I feel so ill. How long is this going to last?' sobbed Ann.

'I don't know. Ann, be a brave little girl. It's what is known as seasickness. I know it's unpleasant, but it will pass. I have it as well, but I must be brave.' Beatrice cuddled her frightened little girl. 'There is no cure for it I'm afraid my dear.'

'What shall we do? Are we going to sink?' Anne cried, looking as white as the boiling sea around the ship.

'Don't worry, my darling. You will be safe. These ships are made to fight their way through big storms,' said Beatrice, looking at Charles for confirmation. Norman just lay on his bunk facing the wall, saying nothing. The lights came back on and the children looked around blinking. The wind was still howling and the boat wallowing in the heavy sea making little progress. There was another crash of thunder and the lights went out again. Beatrice reached out her hand and grasped Charles. She wanted reassurance and also wanted to show him she wasn't afraid as long as she had him with her. He leaned over and kissed her.

'Come on family, there is nothing we can do. Let's go to bed and try and get some sleep. Remember, God is watching over us,' said Beatrice, tucking her children into bed. No one slept much, and the conditions stayed that way all night. The dull dreary light of dawn filtered through the water-covered portholes. One could see nothing but the high seas. One moment the ship was in a hollow, the next on a high and the passengers could look across the tormented waters; many of them hoping to see land. However, the wind had dropped and the sun was beginning to shine again

They washed and changed out of their nightclothes.

'Anyone for breakfast?' Charles asked, with a grin. 'I'm going – who's coming with me?'

'Not me,' said Anne and Beatrice together.

'I'll come with you, Father,' said Norman. The two of them made their way to the dining room. The waiters were trying to lay tables. There were very few passengers in sight. Usually there were hundreds.

'What's the damage like up top?' Charles asked a steward.

'Very untidy, sir. A mast broke in the night and caused a lot of damage. There are ropes and sails everywhere and the kitchen area has been partly demolished. So it's a cold breakfast and lunch, as well, I expect, sir.'

Charles thanked him. The heavy seas and the wind blew all that day. As evening approached things gradually returned to normal. Within an hour the evening sun was shining through, and the seas became comparatively calm. It was as if nothing had happened.

They were approaching Singapore, where the ship was due to call for re-provisioning. The captain announced the ship would stay for five days, instead of the scheduled two days. The family went on deck later. Part of the deck had been cordoned off for safety reasons.

'What a night, wasn't it?' said Charles, to a couple of a similar age to themselves, who were viewing the damage of the night before.

'Yes, we didn't sleep a wink. Wendy kept thinking the boat would sink. We don't want many more like that. Are you going far?'

'Yes, we're going to our sheep farm in Australia. How about you?'

'We're getting off at Hong Kong. We have a house there and a small plantation. My name is Michael Harptree, and this is my sister Wendy.'

Charles introduced Beatrice and Anne who had just arrived on deck looking as green as the sea. Wendy was a small woman and a little tubby. She was dressed in a black ankle-length dress and button-up boots. Michael was tall and stout. He had a reddish chubby face, rather like a farmer and straw-coloured hair which curled at the edges.

'We were just going into the lounge for a glass of beer. Would you like to join us?' said Michael.

Charles looked at Beatrice for confirmation. She nodded.

'I'll join you, but I don't want any alcohol,' said Beatrice.

'Yes, that would be fine, lead on,' said Charles. They found a table and ordered drinks while Anne went off to find her friend. The men were talking away about travel and prices of goods at home, so Beatrice turned to the lady who had been introduced as Wendy.

'Please excuse my curiosity, but did I hear you are Michael's sister?'

'Yes, that's right. I was until recently an Anglican nun, but I have finished my time with them and am coming home to lead a little more normal life,' she smiled.

'Yes, I know what you mean I was in Crimea with some Anglican nuns. They were very hard and conscientious workers. I admire them greatly.'

'I was in Crimea as well. I came out in March '55.'

'That was the month I came home,' volunteered Beatrice.

'I don't suppose your name was Beatrice Cushingham, was it?' Beatrice smiled and nodded her reply.

'Oh, I am pleased to meet you. Miss Nightingale has been a wonderful leader, and I am not taking anything away from her when I say that in Sebastopol hospital you are a legend. They think the world of you.'

'That's nice to know. Thank you, Wendy.' She sipped her drink. 'What do you intend to do with yourself now you have finished as a nun?'

'I think I would like to look after the poor and sick of Ceylon.'

'That's certainly commendable,' said Beatrice. Apart from Crimea, the two of them hadn't a lot in common.

'Come on you two, let's have some more drinks,' said Michael.

'Not for me, Michael. I'll stay on fruit juice,' said Beatrice.

'He's always drinking. His doctor told him to ease up,' said Wendy.

'What shall we drink a toast to?' said Michael, raising his newly charged glass.

'Let's drink to the future,' said Charles. This was agreed upon and they all raised their glasses and drank a toast to that.

*

They were allowed to disembark at ten in the morning next day. Michael insisted they all come to his village for drinks and lunch. Charles begrudgingly accepted, though Beatrice and the children were in favour. A carriage was already waiting, with Michael and Wendy seated in it, when Charles and his family disembarked.

'Come on, Charlie. I'm gasping for a cold bottle of champers. Eh, what say you?' he said, slapping Beatrice lightly on the knee. They drove high up into the hills to a magnificent little hideaway villa, surrounded by palms and equatorial greenery. It kept a lot of the scorching sun off the house.

'What's the big pool of water for?' asked Charles.

'That, my friend, is for us, to lie in and cool off.'

'What a wonderful idea. What do you wear?'

'Well, it depends who I'm with. If it's a pretty maiden, then hardly anything,' he chuckled loudly.

The ladies, within hearing, blushed except Beatrice. She quite approved of the idea and wished she could strip to her bare essentials and lie in the pool, which was only about eighteen inches deep.

Lunch was lobster and crayfish salad, with sliced oranges in brandy. All of this was consumed with chilled Krug 1850 champagne. The children took their socks off and paddled. They loved it. Michael disappeared after lunch saying he was going to get a cigar, and some pictures to show them. They waited nearly forty minutes, but there was no sign of him.

'Whatever could have happened?' Wendy asked, very agitated.

'Wait here and I will go and look for him,' said Charles. 'Michael ... Mike ....are you alright? Oh my godfathers,' he exclaimed, in horror. Michael was lying quite still in the hallway.

Seeing Mike lying there convinced Charles that the drink had eventually caught up with him, and unless urgent medical attention was on hand he would be dead within minutes.

'Beatrice, come quickly. Wendy come too, it's Mike, and he's out cold.' Beatrice hurried to his side and tried to find a pulse. She leaned over him and, placing her mouth over his, she blew. Wendy grabbed her collar.

'What do you think you are doing? He needs help, not affection. This is no time to kiss my brother when he can't help himself,' she said, very annoyed.

'I'm not kissing him. I am blowing air into his lungs hoping to get his heart started again.' She tried again and again, keeping it up for ten minutes.

They all stood around in silence, firmly convinced that Michael was dead and that Beatrice was wasting her time with this voodoo type of cure she was practising. Suddenly he coughed and opened his eyes.

'Well done, Beatrice,' they all cheered.

'Where am I?' he asked.

'Lie still, we will get a doctor.'

'I don't need a—'

'Lie still. You nearly died. In fact you may have done,' said Beatrice sternly. Wendy had gone for the doctor.

'Where on earth did you learn to blow into someone like that?' asked Charles. The two children stood looking on amazed.

'In Crimea there was this young soldier. He just passed out and stopped breathing. Normally they would have taken him out and buried him. God knows how many might have been buried alive when they're not actually dead. Anyway this boy looked so young and helpless. So I pushed the orderlies aside, opened his mouth and blew like I did then. After five minutes he came to. Everyone was amazed. The military just didn't want to know. They said it was witchcraft. They forbade me to ever do it again.'

'Where did you find out how to do it?

'To be honest with you it was partly witchcraft. You see, when I was studying to be a nurse for Crimea; I read every thing I could find. One of the magazines I found was *Medicines of Tribal Africa*. Most of the contents were beyond my comprehension, but I distinctly remembered reading about how they brought this girl back to life that had drowned in a river. I had never tried it before.'

Michael was sitting up now. Colour had returned to his cheeks. He wanted to get up, but Charles wouldn't let him.

'You owe your life to Beatrice,' said Wendy.

'I know. I'm eternally grateful, Beatrice. Thank the Lord you were here. How can I repay you?'

'By cutting right down on your drinking and taking life a lot easier. That's how you can repay me,' she said with a smile.

The doctor came and gave him a dose of laudanum and sent him to bed to rest for a few days. Beatrice and the family returned to the ship, leaving Wendy to look after her brother.

Two days later the *Great Britain* continued her voyage to Australia.

3   *Convicts*

*I*T WAS SOME DAYS later when they were sitting on the deck enjoying the sunshine that Norman said:

'Mother! Do you know, as long as I can remember you have always attracted some sort of adventure? There is never a dull moment when in your company. I find life very exciting not knowing what is going to happen next.'

Beatrice was stuck for words.

'The boy's right. You do attract adventure, and yes you are fun to be with,' said Charles.

Beatrice smiled at the family. On reflection she had to agree with them.

Apart from a few more gales the rest of the journey to Australia was uneventful. Every day when they woke up, the sun was shining.

'What a difference from England, mother. It is warm and brilliant sunshine here, and in England when we left there was snow on the ground,' said Norman, taking in all the sights of Sidney Harbour. 'They speak differently too, don't they Father, the Australian people?'

'Yes son, they have a sort of twang to their words. I'm sure it won't be long before you're speaking like a native?'

'And why do they call us Poms, we are Englishmen?' Norman, still had more questions for his parents.

'I know my dear, but they think of us as emigrants and the nearest rhyming word they can find is pomegranate.'

'It doesn't rhyme, Mother,' the boy said.

'Don't let it worry you son, there will be other and bigger differences you will come across. You must learn to accept them. Remember, this is their country, we are the visitors. '

The next morning when they awoke they could see they were approaching the continent of Australia, which was to be their new home. The children were excited and wanted to stay on deck and watch the ship enter harbour and dock.

'Are you packed ready to disembark dear?' asked Charles, appearing on deck, where the family were watching the goings on of soldiers and convicts working on loading and unloading the ships

'No I'm not. I still have breakfast to finish yet. There's no hurry is there, Charles?'

'No but I don't want to hang around when we get into harbour. I have Alex waiting for us with a pony trap.'

'Alex... You mean my Alex? My stepbrother – the man who tried to rob us?'

'The very same. He's a changed man now. He's the ranch foreman, and he can never do enough for me.'

'Does he know I am his sister and have married his boss, and that we are coming out here?'

'Yes he does.'

'Oh how exciting,' said Beatrice, her face aglow of happiness at what she had heard.

'What's that mother?' asked Norman, seeing the excitement on his mother's face.

'You're going to meet my brother. He is your Uncle Alex, and has come out to Australia to help father with his sheep farm.' Norman looked a little confused, but did not ask his parents to elaborate on the subject.

They arrived at Queensland Harbour two hours later. Norman looked down on the quayside at all the shouting and traffic going on. There were soldiers with rifles dressed in red and white coats with plumes in their hats. They looked very untidy and slovenly as if they didn't care. They lounged against stacks of bales, talking and smoking. Their rifles stood unguarded next to them as they chatted with their friends.

They were supervising a workforce of poor white wretches who were hardly clothed. Their ankles were shackled to each other and they walked with a shuffle, heads bowed, as if all interest in life had been extracted by the use of the overseers' whip, which he generously applied to their bare backs.

Many of them already showed the scars of previous beatings. The overseer seemed to apply the whip despite a man doing his best to lift a heavy bale. Although Norman was fascinated, it sickened him to see human beings treated in this fashion. He wondered what sort of a country he had come to which allowed such atrocious goings on. His father came and stood next to him, watching the traffic on the quayside.

'What is it, Father? Why are they beating those poor men, and look at the condition of them?'

'I know what you mean, Norman, but this has been a way of life out here for nearly one hundred and fifty years. You must have heard talk of the shipping of convicts to Australia? Well, the practice of sending prisoners out here has stopped but they are still convicts serving their time, and there will be other people who have done wrong and live out here so we will always have convicts. They get better treated now than years ago. There is nothing you can do about it. It's a way of life out here. Remember we were the ones who sent these poor wretches to live in Australia for some very petty crimes. Now come on downstairs and help your mother. We will be disembarking shortly.'

The chain gangs were coming on board now to assist in getting the ship unloaded.

'Look, Father, there are small children running around dressed in rags. What are they doing?'

'Some of the prisoners have children. They lead the life of a convict themselves, though they are not beaten. Once they are past ten they are expected to earn their keep and do simple jobs. On board this ship you will find them cleaning the accommodation.'

Norman couldn't believe that adults treated children like that. 'I think it's shameful, Father, I really do.'

'That's the way it is Norman. You can't change it, so don't try.'

The convicts had been unshackled for the purpose of going on board the *Great Britain* so they could manoeuvre their way round the narrow steps and staircases. Norman noted the female convicts with their children; some even had babies. He was amazed at what he had seen. It was unbelievable. Deep in thought he went downstairs to his family cabin.

As he walked along the corridor he saw what appeared to be a mobile bag of rags enter a door marked STORES. He stood outside wondering what he should do. He guessed it must be one of the child convicts. As he stood there quietly, the store door opened a little and a frightened face peeped out. It was small, very dirty and had long, unwashed curly hair, which must have been light brown on a good day. Today it was covered in blood, dirt and sweat. Their two faces looked at each other for what seemed ages, but were no more than three seconds. Without a word she went back inside the store, pulling the door shut behind her.

Norman's curiosity was alerted now, so he pushed opened the door and entered the darkened store room. There was a little light filtering from a vent in the roof and he could just make out the figure crouched in the corner. It was sobbing. It couldn't harm him, thought Norman, if it was crying so he spoke.

'Don't cry. What's the matter? Who are you?' he whispered.

'Don't give me in, master. Please don't tell them I am here,' the little wretch said. 'Poor boy,' thought Norman.

'What's your name?' asked Norman, attempting to get closer to the boy.

'Mary Brooks,' she replied quietly.

'Mary? Then you're a girl? What's a girl doing here?'

'My father is a prisoner, and has been for ten years, so I have had to stay here with him,' she said, hardly audibly. 'I am trying to hide, to escape from this terrible prison. I have been here a year and don't think I will live two years. It's hell on earth. My dad says its God's dustbin of humanity. Have you got a crust of bread sir?'

'No, I haven't. How old are you, Mary?'

'Ten, sir.'

'Don't call me sir. I am only two years older than you. My name is Norman. Wait here and I will see what I can do. Hide under those sacks in case anyone one finds you.' He peeked out the door. Seeing it was all clear he let himself out, and went to his cabin.

'Where have you been, Norman?' said his mother. 'We have all been looking for you. There is a glass of milk, and some bread and meat and an apple for your lunch. Now hurry and eat up as we have to be off the ship in half an hour.'

He wondered, dare he tell her about Mary? It would be difficult to help the little girl without his mother's help. He decided to pluck up courage and tell her.

'Mother, don't be mad at me but I have something to tell you.'

'Yes dear, what is it?' she said as she hurried about doing last-minute packing ready for disembarking. There were no lights on. There was no generator running as the ship's engine had stopped. One had to rely on sunlight, which barely entered the tiny portholes on the ship.

'I have found a poor wretch of a girl who is starving and is a prisoner. She is trying to hide so she won't go back to prison. She is only ten, mother and she has been beaten. She is a prisoner, mother; can we help her, please?' he pleaded

His father was out of the cabin seeing to the unloading of all the household effects brought from England. Beatrice listened attentively. She was a lady who never took long to make a decision.

'Go and get her and bring her in here, son, quickly. I have an idea.' The passage way was still empty. Norman went into the store.

'Mary,' he whispered. Her head appeared from the pile of sacks. 'Come quickly, we are going to help you.'

She was hesitant at first, not knowing if it were a trap, but she decided she had nothing to lose and stood up. Norman took her clammy soiled hand in his and opened the door a little. Two men were coming down the corridor.

'When I find the little bitch I'll tan her arse for her,' said a burly sergeant, with a wart on his nose. He was leading a search party. 'Search the empty cabins, she can't be far away.'

Once the pair had passed Norman tugged urgently on her thin arm. 'Come on, quick,' he said, pulling her along after him, into his cabin.

'Mother, this is Mary,' he said.

Beatrice looked at Mary and felt immediate sympathy, understanding why Norman wanted to rescue her.

'We must waste no time, Mary. Do you want to come with us?' said Beatrice, Mary hesitated. She knew these people would be in terrible trouble if they were found out helping a prisoner to escape. But that was what she wanted. Besides she wasn't a convict, it had been her parents who was convicted, and her mother had been dead a year.

'Quickly, yes or no?' demanded Beatrice, who realised that time was not on their side.

'Yes … yes please,' said Mary.

'Alright! Quickly, get washed, undress completely and face me. Norman, go on deck and tell Father he is to take Ann off the ship and leave her with Alex. Then come back here quickly. Tell him what we're doing, hurry.'

Beatrice gave Norman's lunch to Mary. She knew the child was famished. Mary crammed the food down her throat – she was starving hungry. Beatrice got scissors and quickly trimmed her hair to length. Already there was a big transformation in her. She had sorted out a few of Ann's clothes. Mary was a tall girl, and a pair of Ann's shoes fitted her.

The transformation was unbelievable. Beatrice felt sure she could be smuggled off now. She didn't look the same scruffy, dirty child Norman had brought in twenty minutes ago. Norman ran all the way up on deck. There were soldiers and other men searching under sacks and boxes.

'What's the matter, Father?' he asked, though he guessed.

'A young woman has escaped from the prison gang and they think she is hiding on board as a stowaway, hoping to get back to England.'

'That's impossible, Father!'

'I know son, but people do the strangest things and take great risks when they are desperate.'

'Father. Mother wants you to take Ann ashore and leave her with Alex. Because she wants to smuggle the girl they are looking for off the boat as one of ours.'

'Impossible, your mother's mad,' he blurted out in astonishment. He thought for a moment or two. 'Come with me son, I have an idea.'

The two of them hurried back to the cabin. Mary was sitting very composed on the bunk. The difference from twenty minutes ago was unbelievable. She was, underneath that dirty grimy exterior, a pretty girl.

'Norman's told you?' said Beatrice, seeing the concerned look on Charles's face.

'Oh yes, he told me. What do you think you're doing? You can't interfere in controls of the State and the prisons, Beatrice.'

He looked at Mary. Her sweet face was already shedding tears at his outburst. There was silence for a moment. Nobody knew quite what to do; and there were only five minutes left before they disembarked.

'I've got it,' said Charles. 'The two girls should walk together, talking and laughing like sisters, not looking at the guards or anything else. You're just two happy sisters. Understand? Can you do it? I will be watching, don't be afraid, just be natural. Have you another doll for Mary?' Ann took one out of her bag and gave it to her. 'Remember we are just one happy family. Alright let's go, and may God watch over us.'

'Amen,' said Beatrice, as they trooped up on deck. The bright afternoon sunshine caught the girls by surprise: they shielded their eyes as they walked down the gang plank, which helped enormously in hiding their faces.

'What about the luggage?' asked Beatrice, as she ushered the children along.

'Don't worry, that's all in hand. I have arranged for the luggage apart from what we are carrying to be delivered to the ranch. They know our address,' said Charles. He was well aware that someone could be suspicious as he only had one daughter, but on the other hand, he reasoned, who on earth would suspect a family travelling first class to abscond with a young prison girl when they already have a family of their own? It was this thought that gave Charles the courage to face the officials lingering on deck watching the passengers disembarking. He deliberately stood in their line of sight so that he blocked the view of the passengers getting off the ship.

'My! It's good to get back home to Australia. I have missed it,' said Charles to the two soldiers.

'Have you, sir? Welcome back, the tucker is better back here ain't it?' All three of them laughed, heartily.

'They're two fine girls you have there, to be sure,' said the overseer in his thick Belfast accent.

'Thank you, sir,' said Charles, watching the family approach the gangplank.

'And that would be three nice girls including their mother?' suggested Charles, with a wink and a smile. The Irishman took a moment to take in what he was saying.

'Oh yes, to be sure. That's three altogether,' he confirmed with a chuckle.

'Excuse me sir,' asked an officer, 'you wouldn't by any chance have seen a girl, a convict girl? She would be dirty and in rags. She wasn't near your compartments?'

'No, there was nobody of that description on the first-class deck.'

'No! Of course not, how silly of me. Good day sir.' He saluted Charles, who was about to leave the ship and follow the family down the gangplank, when suddenly there was a shouted command from an observant soldier watching the passengers.

'Hey! Wait a minute,' shouted a corporal, who had been paying a lot of attention to those passengers disembarking. 'You, madam, with the two girls. Stop where you are!' Beatrice froze. She realised the game was up and some very astute soldier had spotted Mary for what she really was. Beatrice also realised that to continue could mean arrest.

'Stop girls,' she said as she slowly turned towards the direction where the shout of alarm had come from. The corporal was running towards her. Charles stood there with his mouth open, unable to do anything. As the soldier got near the girls he picked up something. The girls hadn't moved, though Mary had started to weep at the thought of being caught out.

'What is it, corporal?' asked Beatrice, who with her experience in the Crimea was used to the military rank and file.

'Excuse me, ma'am,' he said, taking Mary by the shoulder and turning her round to face him.

'Don't cry, little girl,' he said with a smile. 'I saw you drop your doll, so I picked it up for you.'

'That's kind of you, corporal,' said Beatrice. 'Say thank you, Charlotte.' She knew she dared not used the child's real name. Mary was no fool, and thanked the soldier, keeping her face pointed downwards.

'I have two girls of my own, miss, so I understand.' He smiled at them, turned and returned to his post. The soldier had no idea of the number of revolutions Beatrice's tummy had done in that five-minute period.

Once the corporal had returned to his post on the ship Charles went over to him and taking out his wallet he thanked him and handed him a golden guinea, which was equivalent to a month's pay for the soldier. The corporal beamed a broad smile and thanked him.

'She cherishes that doll. I don't know how we would have got her to sleep tonight without it,' said Charles, shaking the man's hand vigorously.

'That's alright sir, thanks for the tip,' said the corporal, tucking it into his baggy dusty trousers. Wishing them all good day, Charles walked down the gangplank and joined the family who were by now already seated in the carriage which was to take them to the farm.

'Take us home, Alex, and don't waste any time. We will explain later,' he said to the driver. Then without another word Alex had cracked his whip and the carriage leapt on its way to the farm. When they were well out of sight, Charles stopped Alex.

'I think we have pulled that off successfully, Alex. This is your sister Beatrice.'

'I know, I remember how beautiful she was. Hello, my dear sister.'

'Hello Alex. It's lovely to see you,' said Beatrice, as they hugged each other.

'And this little maid is Mary who we have stolen out of prison, with out being detected,' said Charles, happily.

'Father, look. There is a horseman galloping this way. He wants us to stop,' shouted Norman.

'Get going Alex, quickly, they must have guessed it was us who took Mary.' The little girl started to cry, thinking she had been found out. The soldier on his horse was catching them up. Their horses were getting tired and still had a long way to go.

'Stop, Stop,' the mounted officer demanded. He drew alongside, very hot and sweaty. Charles had stopped the horse and trap.

'What on earth is the matter, officer?' asked Charles.

'You dropped your wallet sir,' he said, handing it over.

'So I did. Very good of you to come chasing after me, Lieutenant. Here my good man; Take a guinea for your trouble, and thank you very much.'

They waved him goodbye and a great feeling of relief came over them all. That was all there was to it, much to everyone's relief. They really thought they had been found out. They all started laughing in tearful joy. The hot sun beat down on them as they made their way to the farm.

'I don't believe it, what a way to enter our new country,' said Beatrice.

4 *Disease*

'*H*OW LONG WILL it take to get there, Father?' asked Ann.

'About an hour. I see Alex has brought food and water with him. You can see I have trained him well,' laughed Charles.

'Mary, I haven't introduced you to your new family. Would you like to refer to us as Mother and Father? I know you had your own once, but we will be your new parents, and these will be your brother and sister, Norman and Ann.'

'Oh yes, Mother, I would like that. I can't thank you all enough for your bravery in rescuing me from the jail. My mother died a year ago and my father who was convicted with her is still serving time. They kept me in the prison even though I had done no wrong. My parents stole a sheep. We were starving and nearly dying. They both got twenty-five years. My father is getting very old and weak. I don't know how much longer he will last.'

'Will he worry about you, Mary?'

'I will write him a letter soon explaining all he needs to know,' she said with a smile.

'I can't get over the way we stole Mary away from them, right under their noses,' said Beatrice.

'It was done so quick, Mother, wasn't it?' added Norman.

'I think that's the secret,' said Charles. 'It was the sheer audacity of the snatch. Nobody suspected it could be done. It wasn't as if we knew the child.'

'So you're not really a prisoner at all then Mary?' said Beatrice. 'This throws a different light on the subject. We haven't really committed a crime, as we certainly haven't kidnapped you.'

'That's good news to know we haven't actually committed a crime, like rescuing a prisoner,' said Charles, feeling very relieved. The whole party including the two horses were getting tired after their long drive across the scrub land. There was nothing to see for miles. Norman kept standing up in the cart looking into the distance, whilst shading his eyes from the boiling hot sun.

Suddenly he pointed into the distance. 'Is that the farm ahead of us?' demanded Norman,

'Yes, son, that's it. That's our sheep farm and is your new home.'

'What is it?' asked Mary.

'It's a sheep farm,' replied Norman.

'Remember Norman, Mary hasn't had the chances you have had to see all the wonders of life,' said Beatrice. 'She's been locked in a prison.'

They drove into the sheep farm. The flocks of sheep seemed to stretch for miles – there were thousands of them. They entered a spacious courtyard with flower gardens on each side. A stone-built farmhouse in white bricks faced them. It was two storeys high, with double windows on each side, three steps led up to a large studded door. The windows had coloured curtains hanging from them. The whole atmosphere was of home and comfort. Around the back were more buildings, these were for the staff who ran the sheep farm. Beatrice was most impressed.

'Charles, you have done well. Have you done all this yourself?'

'With a little help from my friends,' he said, grinning at her. He was immensely proud of what he had done. They all alighted from the wagon and were pleased to stretch their legs after the long journey on a wagon.

'Can we go inside, Father?' asked Norman,

'Of course you can, son; it's your home now. See that lady over there, well, she runs the house. Her name is Patsy. You can call her Patsy, she won't mind. If there's anything you need to know about the house, just ask her. She will show you around and where your rooms are.' The three children ran whooping and yelling into the spacious farmhouse.

'As for you, Mrs Redlock, I am going to carry you over the threshold,' said Charles.

With that he picked her up and they laughed together as they entered their new home together. The dining room was laid for a sumptuous dinner. As one might expect, roast lamb was on the menu, but the family were so hungry they all tucked in. Beatrice was knowledgeable enough to know that where Mary was concerned, the operative word regarding her intake of food would be little and often; she just was not used to it.

Beatrice was most taken, not only with the exterior, but the interior of the house as well. As far as she could see very little needed improvement. As the building was comparatively new, all the furniture was likewise. Charles introduced the staff, who had lined up in the hall to greet them. The family moved down the line as they were introduced to each member of staff. When the introductions were complete and they all knew their respective rooms they were eager to explore more of their new surroundings.

'Can we go out for a look around the farm now?' asked Norman.

'Mind the dogs, some of them bite, they're not as friendly as at home; best to stay away from them until they get used to you,' warned Charles.

'Alright, Father,' said Norman, dashing like a madman round to the rear buildings. Some of the barns had sheep and lambs in them. They bleated pitifully when they saw the faces of the children. There was quite a din coming from the hut the men slept in. They had finished their tucker and were enjoying a few beers. It seemed the Australians have always loved their beer. Already they were starting to sing country songs passed down by the early settlers.

'Father said we mustn't go in that hut. It's for adults only,' said Ann.

As the lights went down and darkness invaded the farm the children were fascinated listening to the Aborigines blowing their horns, That deep, throbbing note, so at home in the outback of Australia. When the children went to sleep that night it was the throbbing of the pipes which lulled them to sleep.

The next morning, after a hearty breakfast of steak and fried eggs, the children went for a buggy ride and in the afternoon were given their first lessons in how to ride a horse. The children loved horseriding and within a few weeks could mount and dismount unaided, and to canter and gallop across the green pastures.

However, it couldn't be play and no work. There was no school for a hundred miles so the job of teaching fell on Beatrice's shoulders. She made sure the children all kept up their studies and continued to teach them as they each got older. Besides, it gave her something to do. This worked out fine as the three children were keen pupils. Unfortunately, Mary was years behind the others, but she made steady progress and soon she had mastered reading and writing.

The family had only been in Australia for twelve months when Beatrice found that she was pregnant. She and Charles were great lovers and enjoyed a good sex life but having gone nearly two years without any type of contraception the pregnancy wasn't unexpected, Beatrice was sure Charles would be pleased, so one morning she shocked him with the news.

'Charles, I'm pregnant,' she said to him one breakfast time.

He was lying on the settee and sat bolt upright, looking very surprised. He had never dreamt of this. In fact he thought he was past all that.

'Are you sure, my darling? That's sensational, fantastic. Oh, I am so pleased for us. Don't go rushing around, sit down, and rest yourself we will see to everything. Do the children know? Oh dear, I will have to get the doctor over?' said Charles, all in a tizzy.

The three children were beside themselves with happiness that Beatrice was to be a mum once more. She didn't mind and with all the help around the house she knew she could cope. It was a good confinement, and nine months and two days later Beatrice gave birth to a son, who weighed in at nearly ten pounds.

'My, he's nearly a man already,' said Charles, picking up his youngest son.

'Isn't he like me, a fine crop of curly hair, and handsome. What shall we call him darling?'

'I leave that to you, Charles, you can choose our son's name.'

'Right then. I think I will call him Bruce. That's a good Aussie name. He held his son up in the air. 'What do you think Bruce? Do you like that name?' asked Charles, completely besotted with his new son.

It was soon apparent that those years spent in prison had done nothing for Mary's health. She started coughing up blood, and Beatrice felt sure she was going to be a victim of consumption, for which there was no known cure. Being in the countryside was the best place to be, but it seemed as if the disease had got a hold of the girl and made her very weak.

Norman did not show a great deal of enthusiasm for sheep farming, much to Charles regret. He had high hopes his son would carry on in his shoes and learn all about the farm.

'If you don't want to be a sheep farmer, what do you want to do in life?'

'I think I would like to study law, Father.'

'Law, whatever gave you that idea, my son. It's certainly a surprise to me. You will have to pass exams.'

'I know, Father, I think I can do it. I will be eighteen next year and Mother has done an excellent job teaching us.'

'It will mean you will have to leave home, Norman,' said Beatrice.

'I know, Mother, but it won't be for long.'

'And what do you want to do, young lady?' he asked Ann.

'I want to follow in Mother's shoes and be a nurse. I would like to be a doctor, but they don't have lady doctors do they, Mother?'

'No, unfortunately they don't my dear,' said Beatrice, cuddling her daughter Ann.

'What about, Mary, what does she want to do when she's older?' asked Charles.

'Mary has already said she does not want to leave home and wants to stay here with us,' said Beatrice.

'That's marvellous,' said Charles. 'One out of the four of them is going to stay here, and hopefully look after me when I get old,' he said with a smile. 'Oh I forgot Bruce, he's going to be his dad's right-hand man, aren't you, my son?' he said, picking him up. 'My, you're a heavyweight, Bruce. How old are you now?'

'Nearly six, Dad. I'll stay and help you with the sheep. Me and Mary will, won't we, Mary?'

'Of course, Bruce, we'll look after Mum and Dad,' she said, hugging him.

The younger children had dropped the formal terms for their parents; they didn't seem to mind.

Suddenly, there was the sound of running feet on the veranda and the Aborigine, whom they had nicknamed Mikano, came to the door, very excited. Norman and Ann, and indeed Beatrice, had never spoken to an Aborigine, let alone seen one. He was so like the picture one had seen in the books with frizzy, unkempt hair, very brown with flared nostrils. Not many of them spoke English. It was only because of a missionary school which opened up for a year before disbanding, that some of the children learnt English.

This young man showed an interest in the farm so Charles took him on. He was so good with the animals that Charles had come to respect him and his views. He wore a check shirt, and ragged brown trousers, but his head and feet were bare.

'Boss, come quick, some them sheep really sick, they can't stand up. Two sheep dead now,' rambled Mikano, who was acting as his head shepherd

Charles was very alarmed at this news. He had been lucky for a number of years because he had had no serious diseases with his flocks. Some of his neighbours had not been so fortunate and had lost everything. He ran after Mikano who was leading him to where the sick sheep were. He recognised the terribly infectious condition within a few moments of their arrival.

'It's *scalies.*' he said resignedly. This was one of the worse things that could happen to a sheep farmer.

'Right, Mikano, you must not let anybody come on the farm. If people want to come they must wash their shoes and boots first.'

Mikano looked at Charles bewildered. 'What you mean, boss? They have to wash all over?'

'No, just the boots they walk in, that's all.'

'Why, boss?'

'Because, they bring this disease from another farm. We must stop it spreading. We have to keep these sheep away from the good ones. Then we wash them with coal tar to help kill the diseased. You understand, Mikano?'

'Yes, yes boss I think so.' He looked at Charles and repeated his instructions to make sure he had got them right. 'So if you go off the farm you must wash boots when you come back?'

'That's right, you got it.'

They set about sorting out the sheep that appeared sick from the fit ones, but found the number infected were growing and growing.

'What we gonna do, boss?'

'I don't know the answer. These sick sheep won't get better. Round them all up, drive them away off the farm and we will shoot them all. Don't let them get on grass used for grazing. Get the boys to help and be quick. Make sure you take everyone, no matter how many. Get going.'

Charles went to get the rifles. His mind was in a state of panic. Up to now he had always managed to avoid getting this terrible disease on his farm. Some of his friends lost everything when this plaque had struck their farms. He was determined to take all preventive measures to save as many of his flock as possible.

As soon as he entered the house Norman looked up from the history book he was studying. He could see the look of anguish on his father's face and knew something was wrong.

'What's the trouble, Father?'

'Half the flock are sick. If we are not careful we will have none left. Come on Norman I need your help. We have to shoot the sick sheep.'

Norman, who was against killing animals of any kind, realised right away that this was a life or death predicament, and it was no time to stand on silly, outdated values. The livelihood of the family was at stake. He dropped his book and took the rifle his father gave him. They grabbed their horses and raced after the sheep, taking care not to scatter them.

'This will do, Mikano. Pen them in, otherwise they will run when we start shooting.'

All the men were lending a hand. Beatrice had learnt over the years at her own insistence, how to handle the sheep. She already knew a lot from the days spent on her father estate. The work on this farm was so different to back on her father's farm twenty-five years ago. It was much harder here, but she enjoyed it, and worked with the farmhands late into the night when the lambing season started.

By working as a team they managed to get the sick animals isolated. Having ensured the pens were secure, Charles gave the order to start shooting the sheep. It was not a pretty sight. How he wished there was an alternative to shooting them, but he couldn't risk infecting the remainder of his sheep. Tomorrow they would have to visit all their flocks and kill off any that were sick. They were shooting and shooting and the guns were getting too hot to handle.

The dead sheep were piling high and the noise was deafening, from the sheep and from the farm hands.

'OK that's enough for tonight,' called Charles, signalling for the men to stop shooting and secure the pens for the night. Suddenly a big ram jumped up on the back of another and leapt over the pen. It started running towards the animals that weren't sick and would infect them. Norman was about to chase after the ram.

'Leave it, Norman, I will get it,' shouted Charles, and with that he chased after it. His horse didn't see the rabbit hole and stuck his hoof in it, at the same time throwing Charles onto his head. He lay there unconscious. All who saw the accident ran to Charles. He just lay there out cold.

'Get mother, quick,' shouted Norman to Mikano. He jumped on his horse and sped across the grass lands to the house. He leapt off his horse before it had come to a halt

'Miss Beatrice, come quick, the master boss has fallen off of his horse. He hurt badly. Come quick.'

'Oh no not again,' she said as she removed her pinny and jumped up behind Mikano.

'Hold tight. I in a big hurry,' he said, galloping off. She jumped off the horse and ran to his side. He was still unconscious.

'Get the wagon, and get him back to the house quickly,' she ordered those around her.

Charles was gently lifted onto the wagon.

At the house many willing hands offered to take Charles inside.

'Handle him gently,' commanded Beatrice. 'Lay him on the couch. Norman, go and fetch a doctor.' There was a doctor's practice about five miles away. It had opened up since their arrival six years ago. In fact a small village commune had started there; it was nice to have neighbours who weren't a hundred miles away.

Beatrice sent all the workers away for the night, and attended to her poor husband. She bathed his head in cold water and did a check over his body to see if there were any broken bones. It looked as if her bad luck with men was still with her. She had already lost the best five men in her life, and didn't want to add Charles to the list.

'Oh my head,' said Charles as he came to. 'Beatrice, I can't see. It's like it used to be when I was caught in the fire in that hotel in London. I can't see. That blow on the head has brought back my loss of sight.'

'Don't despair, my darling, things have improved immensely since then. It is surprising what the doctors can do today. You just lie still; the doctor will be here soon.' Charles lay back and closed his eyes, even though it was constant blackness. They heard the doctor stomping on the veranda as he arrived.

Johnny Meadows was the only doctor for miles in any direction. It took a day for him just to get to some patients. Fortunately for Charles the doctor's house was in the next village which had grown up since the family came here seven years ago. Johnny, like most men in the area, didn't dress for the occasion. He wore a large slouch hat, shirt and trousers – nothing fancy. He drove a horse and two-wheeled rig in which was his black bag. The doctor was a happily married man with twin three-year-old girls, and a pretty wife called April. She was thirty that day.

5   *Charles*

1878

'WELL, CHARLES, what have you been up to this time?' he asked cheerily.

'Hi Doc! I have lost my eyesight again.'

'You mean you lost it before?'

'Yes, about seven years ago in London. Funnily enough it was a fall from a horse which brought it back then.'

'Let's have a look,' the doctor said, rummaging in his bag. Open your eyes wide. He struck a match. 'Can you see this light, Charles?'

'I can see a glimmer but that's all.'

'Well, there's nothing I can do. I suggest we leave it for a while. Give the eyes a rest; they may come back to full vision of their own accord. I don't think any serious, long-term damage has been done,' he said, fastening his bag and standing up. 'Just rest. If the sight should return let me know. I will come out and see you in a week's time.'

'Fine, thanks doc,' said Charles, with a smile. After everyone had gone and they were the only two left, Beatrice went to the settee and, sitting down, took Charles's hand.

'Don't worry, my love, remember when you lost your sight last time I promised you I would be your eyes, and I will once again.'

'Thank you, Beatrice. I feel so helpless, especially now we have the flock down with this disease.'

'Don't worry. You can issue instructions, and we will carry them out.'

'The last thing you need now is worry, and anyway there is nothing you can do till morning, so just relax,' she said firmly.

They couldn't wait for Alex to come back from prison. As he was still under sentence the authorities allowed him to work on the sheep farm, but he had to go back to the hardship of prison life one month in every six. This was intended to remind him he was not a free man. He was due back at the farm the following week. If he failed to attend prison as he had been told, he would lose the right – or should one say privilege – to work outside the prison. There were hundreds who would like the chance, and he was made to realise that fact.

The next morning, Mikano and the other hands together with Beatrice and Norman, resumed the shooting of the sick sheep and inspecting the rest of their huge flock.

It was lucky for them that the disease was contained and had not spread. They had caught it just in time, though this did not mean they could become complacent. Charles just could not relax; he wanted to know everything that was going on.

Although Bruce was only six he could ride a pony with the best of them. He loved the farm, and was a natural farmer. If nobody else wanted to take it on in later years then Bruce certainly would.

'Mother, I'm going to the township to see if any post has arrived. It's been ten days since we had a letter,' said Norman.

'Are you expecting anything dear?' she asked.

'Yes I applied to take the exams to be a lawyer and I hope to go away to a university in one of the big cities,' said Norman.

'See if there are any for me, big brother,' called Ann. 'I also wrote away about nursing. Perhaps I have a reply,'

A small town had sprung up in the last few years not far from the farm. Its name was Werribee. It had all the basic necessities, including a store, a church and a pub.

Norman had put on his bowler hat today, to play the part of a young gentleman. He knew he was different from the general farmhands and as his ambition was to be a lawyer, and perhaps one day a judge, he felt it was time to dress the part. He wore velvet trousers and chequered shirt with a tie. He looked and felt distinguished. He called in at the general store and, sure enough, there were plenty of letters, mostly for Charles and his mother, but there was a large brown envelope for him as well.

He did some shopping for the family and, as it was a hot day, he thought it appropriate to go into the bar for a beer. His father had warned him about the dangers of going into bars and that, if he ever did, he should make sure he had a reliable companion with him because of troublemakers, especially drunk ones. The settlement seemed quiet. There were three horses at the hitching rail and as he approached the pub he could hear the tinkling of a piano. It sounded most welcoming. As he entered the bar he couldn't see a thing at first due to the bright sunlight outside.

He walked over to the long, rough wooden bar. It was just a slice of wood which had been rubbed down to prevent splinters. Behind the bar was a huge fat man with ginger hair and a curly moustache. His trousers were held up with a pair of whitish coloured braces, and his moustache was nicotine-stained from an old cigar stub he consistently kept chewing on.

'Good morning, sir, welcome to my bar. What would you like to drink, a glass of milk?'

Everybody had heard the conversation and burst out laughing at the embarrassment shown by this young lad.

'No. I would like a small glass of beer please,' replied Norman; wishing he hadn't come in.

'Does your mother know you're out, sonny?' shouted a ruffian from across the room. This resulted in more laughter and chuckles.

The landlord poured his beer, and Norman paid for it, pocketing the change. As he was taking his first sip, he coughed and spluttered. Well that did it. The remarks and ridicule came thick and fast then. Norman ignored them and stared into the mirror at the back of the bar, letting the laughter subside, and the room return to normal.

He finished his beer and walked out of the bar to more cat calls about him being drunk. It was all good-humoured and nobody was taking offence, least of all Norman. He unhitched his horse and rode home deep in thought, not about his experience in the bar; that was of his own doing. No, it was the farm and his father. How were they going to cope if he went blind?

He remembered when he first met Charles, he was blind then. His mother had taken him to visit Charles in hospital. He had lost his sight in an accident. Luckily he had regained it in a riding accident a few months later. He felt it was his responsibility as the eldest child in the family. Although he didn't like farming he could take it on if he had to, and make a good job of it. Perhaps he should shelve the idea of being a solicitor or lawyer until father was back on his feet and his eyesight restored. He decided to give it some serious thought.

When he arrived back at the farm he gave the reins of his horse to a farmhand who would put the horse away. Norman walked up the steps into the house. It was quiet. There was no one around. He put the letters on the table and sought out his parents. He found them both in Mary's bedroom. Mary was in bed and was having a coughing fit.

'What is the trouble, mother?' he asked.

'It's Mary, she's not well. I fear it's the return of consumption; she's spitting out blood now. Mary lay back on her pillow, her skin as pale as the sheets she was lying on. Her eyes appeared dark as if they had shrunk into her head. Beatrice had seen so many cases of this fatal disease, and she knew there was no cure. She didn't want to lose Mary because she had grown to love her as her own daughter. They were a united family, and already fate was taking a hand in disbanding it.

'What can we do, Mother, to make Mary better?' he asked.

'We will sponge her and give her medicine and cold drinks. The infection is on her chest, that's why she is coughing.'

Beatrice wished she were back home in England. She knew she could call on the skill of the finest doctors in the land who she was sure could come up with a cure. Out here in the outback, she only had the basics, and not many of those. Life seemed so cheap out here. It was a strange situation to come to terms with.

'Will she get better, I mean properly cured?' asked Ann, who was very concerned for her adopted sister. And, to whom she had become much attached.

'I hope so. Come on, she's asleep now, we will leave her to rest.' Charles stood up and Beatrice took his arm to lead him back into the lounge area.

'Alex is due home today Beatrice, will you arrange for Mikano to fetch him from the docks. He had better take the wagon.'

'Leave that to me father, I will tell Mikano what wants doing.' His mother looked up surprised, as if questioning him.

'It's alright, Mother, I have decided to put my plans on hold for a while until the family and the farm is back like it used to be.'

'That's nice of you, son,' said Charles, adjusting his cushions.

Late that evening Alex came home. He looked thin and gaunt; his cheeks were shrunken. He was a complete contrast to the well-fed man who left them a month ago.

'My, Alex, I can see you need a good feed. It seems to get worse every time you go back to prison,' said Beatrice, to her brother.

'Things have changed a lot since I first came here. The prisons are closing down, those for criminals sent from England that is. The wardens don't seem to care if you live or die, as long as you don't escape. There is no organisation. Often we go a day or two without food, or a wash. The place stinks because the toilets aren't working and bodies are taken outside and dumped till they stink, then they are removed.'

'Come and sit down, little brother, and I will feed you,' said Beatrice. They had already discussed with Alex the problem with the sheep, and Charles's loss of sight.

'Tomorrow I will go and look at all the sheep, even those up in the hills. I need to know the situation for myself,' said Alex.

Beatrice was so pleased to be with her stepbrother again. 'Do you ever hear from your sister? She lives in Australia doesn't she, Alex?' she asked later that evening.

'I think she does. She left our home in Newcastle in England ... let me see ... it would be fourteen years ago. I was away from home then. I have never seen her since.'

'She's my stepsister too, you know,' said Beatrice.

'Of course she is, I forgot,' said Alex, putting his arm round Beatrice. He had really taken to her; she was so sensible and efficient.

'I think I'll write to John and find out where she is living.' said Beatrice.

The doctor came that evening to see how Charles was. It had been a fortnight since the accident. He gave Charles another good check over.

'I'm afraid there's nothing for it, old chap. You won't get your eyesight back unless you return to England where they now have much better resources than we do, and are years ahead at fixing eyes. If you want to see again then you must go to England. I will write the report and I know a first-class Harley Street specialist who will perform the operation. Are you game?'

'Have I got a choice?'

'Not if you want to see again.'

'Thank you, doctor. I must first discuss it with my wife. Can I let you know tomorrow?'

'There's no need for that, doctor. We will go to England. Please make your arrangements,' said Beatrice, firmly.

Charles knew it was pointless to argue with her. After the doctor had left, Beatrice called all the family together to discuss the matter. She had obviously already made her mind up as to how it was to be done.

'Right family, and that means all of you, we need to make some decisions regarding your father's health. If we can get him to England there is a good chance he will get his sight back, but we can't all go. So this is what I propose. Charles and I and baby Bruce will go to England. Norman, you will stay in charge here together with your Uncle Alex and sisters. Mary is not well enough to travel. However, I am hopeful of getting the correct medicine for her while I am in England, so that she can be cured.'

'It will mean, Norman, you will have to run the farm. You have two superb advisors in Alex and Mikano. Can I rely on you to take over for six months maximum?' said Charles.

'Of course you can, Father,' Norman replied instantly.

'Right, that's settled. I will arrange for the tickets. I know our parents will be delighted to see Bruce, and I think it will be the last time we see them alive as they are getting very old and infirm,' said Beatrice.

'Try and see our father, Beatrice,' said Alex, anxiously.

'Of course I will. I know he will be delighted to see Charles again. He always said he would make a wonderful husband for me, and he was right,' said Beatrice, squeezing Charles's hand in affection.

'Right, all back to work,' said Norman, taking up the reins of authority.

A fortnight later Charles, Beatrice and Bruce sailed for England aboard the *SS Great Britain*. There wasn't the big send-off which one might have expected when Charles and Beatrice left for England; most of the family who were left were involved with running the farm. Mary was not at all well and Beatrice hoped and prayed she would still be alive when they returned, but secretly she doubted it. So she gave her adopted daughter a special long hug and squeeze. Words weren't necessary as they both knew the end was near.

Nothing had really changed on the *SS Great Britain* since they last sailed on her; except she was older now, and not as clean. They had first-class cabins with portholes so they could see the sights. Bruce was fascinated by it all. Beatrice thought the ship was getting and looking old. It was seven years since they had last been on her. She still pitched and rolled terribly. The journey was, in the main, uneventful crossing the Pacific. There were the usual gales and squalls one associated with sailing the oceans of the world, but they had many fine, sunny days. There was no improvement in Charles's sight.

Bruce was ecstatic at seeing everything on the big ship and the islands they passed. Beatrice was continually teaching him all she could about life; just as she had been taught by her nanny Janet Brown, who had died long ago. They stopped at Hong Kong and Singapore; nothing seemed to have changed in these islands.

One morning Charles and Bruce were very sick in the night. It was sickness and diarrhoea just like Beatrice had witnessed and tried to nurse in the Crimea. It was due to dirty food and water and flies. The human body could only put up so much inbuilt resistance to the horrid germs. She was alright; for the moment anyway. She went to breakfast to find that three-quarters of the ship's crew and passengers had been struck down by it.

She went to see the captain and explained who she was and her past experiences in these matters, and said he must isolate the ship and allow only those on board who had washed their hands. Open all the portholes to let fresh air circulate and scrub the ship right through from top to bottom. And she insisted that all food should be cooked and water boiled.

He looked at her aghast. What did a woman know about such things? He said he would deal with the matter, but in fact he did nothing. None of her recommendations was carried out. It was nearly a week later that the first deaths were announced. First the young and old, and then the members of the crew.

The captain sent for Beatrice, as things were getting out of hand and he couldn't cope. Would she advise him again? Beatrice remembered Crimea and the way the Army authorities would not let Florence Nightingale nurses near their soldiers until they could no longer cope without them. It seemed to be the same with this captain.

Once more she explained how the remedies she had prescribed would help to limit the loss of life. This time her instructions were complied with and the death rate did decrease, and the sick rate also.

Bruce, however, was not well. He wasn't recovering as Beatrice expected him to. He lay there like a limp bag of bones, and he couldn't keep food down. Beatrice was very concerned he would die. She had so much experience and she knew the signs before death. She bathed him in cold water to keep his temperature down and wouldn't let him have any food from the kitchens. She fed him on boiled milk and eggs that she had cooked herself. Slowly he started coming round and saying some words again. She gave him Aspro, which was available in those days, and his colour started returning.

'Oh Charles! Bruce has made a full recovery from the sickness. I thought we had lost him. I didn't want to tell you, and as you couldn't see him. I pretended he was alright, but darling it was touch and go.'

'I am so relieved, darling. I didn't think he would make it.' She sobbed with joy and relief

'I am relieved and happy for you, my dearest. You must have done a good job to save our son. Well done my love.' He held out his hands to feel her, and having done so, he pulled her close to him so he could show his appreciation when he cuddled her. Within a week Bruce was back on his feet and running around with the other children on board.

*

Two months after leaving Australia they docked at Southampton. Beatrice couldn't believe her eyes when she saw Sally and Betsy at the dockside to greet them. All their men folk were dead now.

'Mother, how wonderful to see you here. We never expected you to travel all the way to Southampton, and Aunt Betsy too. Don't you both look well?' she exclaimed, happily. She hugged them both, as did Charles.

'Where is our new grandson, Bruce?' cooed Sally. The little lad was hugging his mother. He found all these strange lady relatives, none of whom he had seen before, very old and musty. He didn't want to be hugged and kissed by them.

'He's very shy,' said Beatrice, making excuses for her son.

'I think it's wonderful that you and Charles have your own child by each other. It always seemed one-sided, the fact that you had two children and Charles had none,' said Sally. 'Though I must admit, the last time I saw Charles and Norman together I couldn't help but notice how much alike they were.' She gave her daughter a very enquiring look. 'Is that more than coincidental?'

'Don't be silly, Mother. You are letting your imagination run away with you,' Beatrice replied, with a wicked smile.

'Hmm! You are obviously not going to give anything away, are you my dear,' replied Sally, who was even more convinced that Norman and Charles were from the same seed.

'Let me see your eyes, my son,' said Betsy, showing understandable concern for Charles's loss of eyesight.

'Don't be too concerned, Mother. I'm sure the specialist will be able to do something to put it right.'

'Let's hope you're right,' said Betsy. 'Come on, we can catch the train back to London. They have improved the service enormously since you last travelled on them, Charles.'

'Come on all of you, you are all staying at my house,' said Betsy.

'Oh Mother, it is so lovely to see you again,' said Beatrice. 'I am so happy in Australia, it's a big country. Norman is eighteen now and Ann a year younger. Do you remember I told you in my letter that we have another daughter? Her name is Mary, we rescued her from a prison party, but she's not well and I don't know if she will recover. I must see if I can get some medicine for her, or she will die.'

'Steady my dear, don't ramble on, you have all the time in the world to tell me the news. Your priority is getting Charles sight restored,' reminded Sally.

'I know, Mother. I will contact Harley Street tomorrow and make an appointment.'

'Come and tell me all the news Beatrice,' said Betsy, calling her over from where she was talking to her mother. 'Have you an appointment?'

'Oh Aunt Betsy. I didn't mean to leave you out. What do you think of your little grandson, Bruce?'

'He is a very smart and intelligent-looking grandson. I am as proud of him as you and Charles must be. I don't suppose there will be any more?'

'No, I don't think so, but who can tell,' said Beatrice, with a smile.

Everybody was chatting away, it was wonderful. The familiar sight and aroma given off by Betsy's house reminded

Beatrice of the many happy years she had spent there, especially when Uncle Bob was alive.

In the morning Beatrice took a carriage to Harley Street with Charles. She had the letter of introduction to the specialist. Stopping the carriage she alighted and knocked on the door. A smartly dressed lady came to the door wearing an ankle-length light-red brocade dress, buttoned up to the neck.

'Good morning, madam, have you an appointment?'

'Not exactly, but I have a letter of introduction from my doctor in Australia who knows Professor Clapttop. Its about my husband's eyes, he's lost his sight.'

'Come into the reception area and I will speak with the professor. He is very busy and won't see anyone without an appointment.'

Charles and Beatrice sat down in the reception area. It was like a little domestic lounge with button-backed chairs, a tiled fireplace that was unlit, and medical pictures on the wall.

'It seems we will have to make an appointment and wait our turn, Beatrice,' murmured Charles.

The secretary had taken the letter with her. Five minutes later she returned, and behind her walked the professor.

'I hear you are a patient of Tony Godbers. He's a fine doctor. Never wanted to specialise; just look after the sick he always said. Is he well? Good. So you have come all the way from Australia? Very commendable.' He approached Charles. 'So you lost your sight when you fell off a horse.'

'He first lost his sight seven years ago in London when he was saving people in a fire.' offered Beatrice, wanting to ensure she made the maximum impact on the professor.

'Did he indeed? It seems what he needs is to get on a horse and fall off again. Unfortunately, there isn't a lot one can do. There is no operation that will restore his sight. Make an appointment and come along and see me in a fortnight's time.'

He bade them good day and retired to his practice. So there was nothing else they could do but wait a fortnight. As they sat in the Hackney carriage taking them home to Betsy's, both of them were thinking the same thing: how were they going to spend the next fortnight waiting for the appointment? Beatrice was the first to break the silence.

'I would like to go up north, Charles, and see my natural father. He is getting very old now.'

'That's a good idea,' said Charles. 'I will be alright here until you return.'

'No darling, you are coming with me. I'm not letting you out of my sight.'

He laughed at her forgivable, unintentional pun.

'If you insist my dearest then I will be pleased to come with you.'

So Beatrice sent a telegraph to her father, John, telling him that she and Charles, together with John's grandson Bruce, would be calling on Wednesday. Betsy was pleased to hear the news about the appointment in two weeks' time and thought the break for the family to go up north would be of benefit to them all.

The three of them caught the train from Kings Cross station. Bruce thought it wonderful as he hadn't been on a train and had only seen pictures of them. He was most impressed, and his eyes were every where.

On arrival at Newcastle they caught a cab to John's home; he was in no state to travel.

John hugged them all and shed a tear of joy. He was particularly pleased to see Charles, who had practically saved his son's Alex life when he volunteered to employ him on his sheep farm.

'This is your grandfather, Bruce. Would you like to shake hands with him?' Bruce wasn't shy this time and shook hands, but once again his eyes were glued to all the hunting trophies on the wall of his granddad's house. There were so many and guns and spears. It would take all day to see them all. They spent the rest of the week up there with John. Beatrice told him all the news, especially about his son Alex. Charles was able to give the story in more detail and he and John would sit down by the fire and chat away for hours.

'I see you are a brother in the craft, John,' said Charles, pointing to the portrait of him hanging on the wall in his Provincial Masonic robing.

John laughed, 'Yes, I don't do any Freemasonry now, though. I am still a member and pay my dues. But I can't get around like I used too. Are you a brother, Charles?'

'Yes. I joined quite early when I went to Australia. If it wasn't for the Masons I don't think any townships would have been built there. Certainly not with those magnificent buildings built by prisoner stonemasons, years ago. It was from this nucleus that the lodges were eventually formed. I was invited to join by the local constable. There wasn't much social life out there at the time and in the big cities Masonic Lodges were starting to spring up; so I went along and joined them.'

'You never told me you were a Freemason,' said Beatrice. 'That means as well as being a Freemason's daughter, I am also a Freemason's wife.'

'That's right,' said John, with a chuckle. 'You could do a lot worse.'

'Alex has turned out to be a good man, John. We couldn't manage without him. He runs the farm; especially now Charles has lost his eyesight,' said Beatrice.

'Ah, well it all turned out for the best after all. Come here Bruce,' said John, the night before they left for London. He handed Bruce a box. 'Here is a present for you my son. Look after them,. Some day they will be valuable.'

Bruce took the box and opened it. Inside was a pair of handmade silver mounted and engraved duelling pistols. The set was complete and they looked truly magnificent.

'Thank you, Granddad. I will look after these, and they will remind me of you.' John was delighted at Bruce's gratitude and enthusiasm.

Next day the Redlocks returned to London. It would soon be time for Charles's appointment. Beatrice so wanted to have another meeting with her friend and mentor Florence Nightingale who had retired now.

She wrote her a letter at her home and asked if they might meet up. Florence invited Beatrice to visit her. It was like meeting a sister you hadn't seen for years. They hugged each other and talked non-stop for an hour about all that had gone on in their lives since they had last met. Beatrice told her about Mary and how ill she was.

Florence gave her two bottles of the latest medicine which should aid her recovery. They all knew that the chance of them all ever meeting again was very slim as the years were taking their toll.

Beatrice had one more visit to make before she returned to Australia: she wanted to visit the graves of her stepfather George Cushingham, and most of all she wanted to visit Fred's grave.

Beatrice had never forgotten her first love, Fred Shepherd. She refused to know the truth about him after he had been murdered by Clive Wainright. She just wanted to remember Fred as he was to her. She remembered how he was her first love when she was twenty-four, and how he was the first man to seduce her and how he had shown her the art of lovemaking, which she had passed on to Charles years later.

What she didn't know, even to that day, was that Fred Shepherd, a smart, dashing young man about town, had originally been employed by her wicked uncle Clive Wainright to murder her. The reason was that she stood in the way of his getting her grandfather's estate, because the solicitors thought that Wainright was the sole surviving relative, which he managed to convince them he was.

As it turned out Fred fell madly in love with her himself, and eventually found out why Wainright wanted her dead. On finding out the truth Fred not only did not kill Beatrice, but told Wainright he wanted £1000 to murder her now that he knew what Clive stood to gain. Furthermore, Fred refused to return the £100 deposit given him on the first contract to kill her.

Clive Wainright was so annoyed at being tricked by Fred that he vowed to kill not only Beatrice, but Fred as well. After a failed attempt at killing them both by running them over in

London, he did eventually trick Fred into a situation where he killed him with two pistols.

All the police in London were looking for Wainright as he was wanted for three murders; but he vanished, never to be seen in England again. He did, however, eventually turn up as a corporal in the Crimea. He had joined the army to escape being hanged for murder.

When Beatrice saw him in the Crimea, she couldn't believe her eyes. She knew of him, and what he had done to Fred. But now he was a patient on her ward. He was unconscious, having been sedated because he had lost an arm, and was now going to undergo an operation with little or no anaesthetic or bandages, to remove both legs, which were rotten with gangrene.

What was more, Beatrice was being employed by the surgeon to lay on the patient's legs while he sawed them off. Hopefully, the patient would be sedated. By the time Clive came in for his amputation there were only a few teaspoonfuls left. As a result of this the patient woke up while his legs were being sawn off.

He screamed in pain, and when he saw this vision of Beatrice lying on his near severed legs, he let out a vile curse; the shock of seeing her, especially in Crimea, killed him. Beatrice felt no remorse at his death, and was pleased that justice had been done.

She and Fred were planning to marry sixteen years ago. It all seemed so long ago now – way in the past. So much had happened since those days. She lovingly placed a posy of flowers on Fred's grave, and blew him a kiss.

The day arrived when she took Charles along to Harley Street for his appointment. The receptionist said to leave Charles in the room and leave his case with his overnight clothes as he would be staying the night. Beatrice kissed and hugged Charles.

'I'll be back to see you tomorrow, darling. Please don't be upset if the operation or whatever he does to you is not a success. There are no guarantees.'

'I know, but if he can do anything to bring me out of this darkness it would be a help.'

Once Beatrice had left, Charles didn't have to wait long for the professor to appear.

'Ah, there you are, Charles. Now as I said before there is no magic cure but the sight can be lost from damage to the nervous system in the head, and as you know, as it has happened to you before it can just as quickly be restored. Come through to my surgery and I will have a look at your eye.'

He looked into his eyes and if he saw anything he didn't say. 'I am going to put you to sleep before I apply my treatment, don't be alarmed – the worst after-effect you will suffer will be a slight headache.'

He ordered Charles to strip off his top clothes and slip into a surgical shirt. Then he lay him down and administered chloroform until Charles was asleep.

'Miss Clancy,' he said to his assistant, 'I want you to sit the patient up and ensure his head is level.'

Together they sat Charles up and Miss Clancy steadied him.

'Now I want you to hold this thick pad over his forehead and I am going to give it a sharp blow which I hope will replicate him falling off a horse and, will restore the patients sight. I am not sure it will work, but it was a blow like that which made him lose it.' He went to a cupboard and took out a large mallet with a big heavy head.

'Right, are you ready Miss Clancy?'

'Yes, Professor.'

'Here we go,' he said, and with that he gave a hefty blow to the pad his assistant was holding, which, when he made contact, pushed Charles's head well back.

'Fine, well that's all we can do. Let him sleep off the chloroform and hopefully his sight will be returned to him.' She looked at him amazed. 'What are you staring at woman? There is no other cure for loss of eyesight. Now help me get him to bed in the small room.'

Charles lay there till morning, in a pitch black room.

Beatrice could waste no time in her urgency to see Charles next day, but knew she had to be patient to let the specialist do his work, so she didn't call on him till 2 pm. When she did call and was admitted, it was to see Charles sitting up in bed with a smile on his face, which suggested the operation had been successful.

'Hello, my darling Beatrice, this clever man has restored my sight, and I haven't a scar or a serious pain to show for it; just a small headache. It truly is remarkable.'

The professor came into the room. 'Yes, the operation I performed is a success. But you must be careful not to take another blow on your head because the next time you might lose more than your sight. You might lose your life.'

'Thank you, doctor,' said Beatrice. 'We will take care. Can I take him home now?'

'Of course. My receptionist will give you my bill,' he said, turning away.

Beatrice got him dressed, settled the bill and returned home to Betsy's where there was a welcoming committee waiting to greet Charles on the return of his sight.

'I wonder what he did to return your sight,' Betsy asked.

'I expect they hit Daddy on the head with a big hammer,' shouted Bruce. They all rocked with laughter at the funny remark made by the little boy.

6 *Alex*

CHARLES WAS delighted at how good his sight was, there was no loss of vision and he could read as good as ever. Two months later, having said what would almost certainly be their last goodbyes, the Redlock family returned home to their sheep farm in Australia. Once more there was a tremendous party laid on to welcome them home, and most important Mary was up and walking about.

'Oh Mary, how happy we all are to see you on your feet. How do you feel?' asked Beatrice.

'A little shaky, but a lot better, Mother. Oh I am so glad to see you home.' She ran into Beatrice's arms and hugged and kissed her.

'I have brought some new medicine from England. It isn't a wonder cure but I am told it's very good.' Charles had gone from the horse and carriage bringing them home to the farm straight, to where the men were working.

'Norman, hello,' he shouted.

Norman looked up surprised. 'Hello, Father, I didn't expect you back yet. How are the eyes?'

'They're fine, son, just fine, but I got to be careful not to bang my head or the eyes could go again. What have things been like on the farm – any disasters to report?'

'Well, we had some more cases of that sickness but we were rigid in weeding them out. I think overall we have lost a third of our flock, but I bought in a hundred fine sheep a month ago, Sam was selling up and returning home so we bought from him. Otherwise there is nothing else to report. Alex is back for his month in prison. He thinks it may be the last time he will have to report.'

'Well, that will be good news,' said Charles.

'Father, I have done what you asked of me and now I would like to go away to study law.'

Ann, who was standing close by listening to the conversation between the two men, decided to butt in and have her say.

'Father, I want to go to the hospital in Victoria to train for nursing. I have been accepted.'

'What does your mother say, Ann?'

'Mother has given me her blessing and said I had to clear it with you, Father,' she said, a little anxiously. The reason why she was anxious was because young ladies were not encouraged to take up professions other than teaching and even that had to be mainly self-taught. To go away to a big hospital and live on one's own was very revolutionary.

'I give my permission for both of you to take up your professions. Please keep us in touch with what you are doing,' said Charles. His children were over the moon, and straight away made the arrangements for their travel and accommodation. Both of them had plenty of money so there was no problem there.

On the following Monday Alex returned from prison. He was very happy because he had proved he could hold down a job and be an asset to Australia.

The prison committee had decided to make him a freeman and allow him to become a fully fledged Australian. This, of course, meant he need not return to prison and would be allocated a thousand acres of land to develop for himself.

Charles was delighted for him, as was Beatrice. However, they didn't want to lose him and made it plain that there was always a home with them.

Alex was forty-five years old but looked nearer sixty; the hard work on the farm, and prison life and food, had all helped to age him. But he was strong and wiry and had many years of useful work in him.

It was a fine day and Alex wanted to develop some ground at the back of the farm. It meant pulling down some sheds and ploughing the ground with grass seed.

He used Mikano and four other men to pull the old sheds down. It was hot, thirsty work. Alex was not a man to sit back and let the others do it all but as well as directing operations he got stuck in with the others.

As the sheds were pulled down, the timber was stacked in piles depending on its condition. It was dirty dusty work, but the men got stuck in, joking with each other and laughing as they went about their labour.

Alex was unscrewing a hinge that was old and rusty. He was not a man to give in, and in trying to dislodge it, he dropped the screwdriver which rolled under the floor of the shed. He could see part of the handle so he bent to pick it up. As he did so his hand received a sharp bite from a funnel web spider that was heavy with eggs.

'Christ!' shouted Alex, as he stepped back in alarm. He knew what had happened, and knew that without immediate and drastic medical attention, the chance of recovery was to be counted in minutes before he was dead.

'What's up, Alex?' shouted Mikano.

'A funnel spider has just bitten me,' replied Alex, spitting the poison from his finger – which he was sucking. Mikano never wasted a moment; he dashed over to where Alex stood nursing his finger and drew a huge knife from his belt. He grabbed Alex finger, laid it on a plank of wood and with one almighty swipe chopped off the finger of Alex that had been bitten.

'Thanks, mate, but that was a bit drastic cutting my bloody finger off, but I guess you may have saved my life, sport,' said Alex, trying to stop the blood flow with his shirt.

'There is no cure for that bite. Good job it was your finger not your leg, otherwise you be dead soon,' said Mikano. 'Maybe we in time and catch the poison before it run in your whole body. You go and lay down, Alex; you not fit for work today.'

Alex took his advice and went to the big house, Beatrice was writing a letter when she saw stagger into the entrance hall clutching his hand which had been wrapped in a neck bandana to stop the blood.

'What's the matter, have you had an accident?' asked Beatrice, leaving what she was doing, and getting up to see to her brother. She could see he was in pain and it took a couple of moments before she realised that his middle finger was missing. Blood was squirting everywhere; not that Beatrice minded the mess. She was more concerned for her brother, who was very ill.

'Oh my dear boy, what's happened to your finger? Come and lay on the settee. I will dress your hand. I wish Charles was here, but he's up on the top meadow.'

Alex's face had gone bright red. Beatrice took all situations like this very coolly. She had seen the worst inhumanities imaginable done to the human body when serving in Crimea. Death was as common as the atrocious weather they had to endure.

'Water, I need water, quick.' Beatrice went and fetched him a glass which he emptied right away.

'Christ, it hurts like hell,' said Alex. 'I've been bitten by a spider. Mikano has cut my finger off. It bloody hurts.'

'What was it – a funnel web?' she asked, very concerned. She knew all about these terrifying creatures and their lethal bite. There was no cure, only the immediate amputation of the limb concerned to stop the poison spreading. If this wasn't done in time then normally it resulted in a funeral. He started to doze off.

'Stay awake, Alex. How do you feel?'

'Bloody groggy.' He lay back resting his hand on his lap and his head on the back rest of the chair. Mikano came to the porch and knocked the door. She looked up, and seeing who it was, asked him in.

'Alex very sick,' stated Mikano.

'Go fetch a doctor, hurry,' she demanded. Alex had dropped off in a coma again. She bathed his brow. There was nothing she could do now but wait for the doctor.

She hoped he would make a recovery, but she had her doubts. There wasn't a hospital within two hundred miles. There was nothing more she could do but pray for Alex. There was no cure and she hoped that Mikano's speedy response in cutting off his finger was in time to stop the poison circulating in his bloodstream.

As the family came in for midday food they all looked at Alex and enquired what was wrong with him. No one in the family, or any one near had been bitten like this; it was very rare, and very unfortunate.

Alex was sweating, his clothes were saturated. He was hot and running a temperature. The hand had become very swollen.

'What's the matter with Alex?' asked Charles, as he clumped into the lounge.

'He's been bitten by a funnel web.'

'Has he! Oh Christ! There's not much hope for him then, poor devil. Is the doctor coming?'

'He should be here soon. Oh I do hope he recovers. Mikano cut his finger off to try and save his life.' Beatrice and Charles looked at him, wondering what more they could do.

'It's in the lap of the gods, my dear,' said Charles. 'We must wait and see what tomorrow brings.'

'I will sleep in a chair by his side tonight in case he needs help,' said Beatrice, as she tucked the blanket round him.

'It's at times like this I wish Norman and Ann were here, but they have been gone a fortnight.' said Charles. 'Ah, here is the doctor; I bet he's seen a few of these bites.'

*

Alex was now in a coma. His mind kept drifting back to his youth. He remembered his hours spent as a cabin boy on the *Tipperary* whaling ship. He remembered the crew and the big seas the whaler fished on. He stuck it for two years before joining the Queen's Navy. He was a powder monkey, running backwards and forwards getting powder for the guns and water for the crew.

He liked that life but then one day he got clipped by a musket ball in his right shoulder and the navy wouldn't let him serve any more. He tried many jobs but couldn't settle. Then he took to drink. He lived with the winos and down and outs in Waterloo, London. He couldn't get enough money to satisfy his thirst and that's when he took to robbing people in the dark streets at night.

It was on one such an occasion he tried to hold up Charles and Beatrice (not knowing she was his stepsister). As a result of that robbery he was sent to a prison in Australia, and eventually came to work for Charles. He realised his life had, in the main, been wasted.

In the distance he was aware of voices; he could just make out the doctor's voice.

'I fear the poison is in his system. It attacks the nervous system, and the Tunnel and the Red back spiders are ones to be avoided. One day, hopefully we will have a medicine to cure these bites; but I have never seen any one recover yet,' he said shaking his head. 'Here are some Aspros. Give him one every three hours. No more, do you understand?'

'Yes doctor, thank you,' said Beatrice. The doctor shook his head in recognition that there was nothing more he could do. He felt so helpless, so inefficient.

'Give me a call if he should get worse or die,' he said, as he left the house.

Alex heard this; he knew only too well what the final outcome would be. He just wished the throbbing pain of his missing finger would subside.

Beatrice sat by his bed on the settee that night. It was very uncomfortable in the chair, but she couldn't leave him. She bathed and changed his wounded hand which had puffed up to twice its size. She looked at it, and felt there should be something she could do. What would she have done in Crimea? she asked herself. Would she have taken a chance at home craft surgery, if she thought it might relieve pain and suffering? She coaxed another Aspro into his mouth with a sip of water. He opened his eyes and smiled at her.

'Thanks,' was all he managed to whisper. Beatrice checked the time: it was two o'clock, and not that it mattered. Alex had gone back to sleep. Charles could be heard snoring loudly from their bedroom at the back of the house. The other members of the family were all asleep.

She bathed his sweaty hot forehead once more. She felt it was decision time. Leaving the room she went into the kitchen and found the sharpest knife she had. She took a clean table cloth from the drawer and started tearing it into strips for bandages.

Next, she sharpened the knife to get a really keen edge on it. She wanted to make sure the knife was clear of infection, so going over to the dying kitchen range fire, she plunged the blade into the hot embers until she was satisfied it was ready.

Beatrice drew her chair up close to the settee. She placed the oil lamp so that it illuminated the area she proposed to work on. She tried to remember what she used to do to the poor wounded, and dying soldiers in Crimea. She decided she ought to wake Alex up and tell him what she intended to do. She rocked him gently.

'Alex, Alex, can you hear me?' Eventually, he managed to open his eyes.

'Yes.'

'I'm going to cut your hand to release the poison, it will hurt. Be brave little brother, it is the only hope I have of saving your life.'

'Go ahead,' he said, falling back to sleep.

She took his swollen hand in hers, and placed it on a clean cloth. Beatrice had a good knowledge of the make up of the human body; where the main arteries were and muscles. Using this knowledge, she made the incision where she thought the most pressure of poison was. She probed a little further down into the hand.

Suddenly there was a fountain of blood and puss shooting from the hand. She knew she daren't stop now. She squeezed the hand until nothing more came out of it. The cut was only small so wouldn't need a stitch. She bathed the wound, and already a more natural colour was returning to the hand. She decided to put a stitch into the finger that had been amputated. Alex didn't stir, but a better colour was coming to his face.

She then got her clean bandages; she suddenly remembered something she had bought on her trip to England. Along with many other medications she had purchased was a good quality healing cream. Beatrice generously applied a good quantity of the cream to a pad, and pressed it firmly down on the incision. She wrapped the hand, and replaced it in a sling round Alex neck. Satisfied she had done all she could she cleared up the mess and fell asleep in the chair, exhausted.

In the morning when Charles came in to see Alex he was still in a coma, and Beatrice had stayed by his bedside all night. He was still running a high temperature and nothing they could do would shift it. The hand she had operated on was much better, but there was no guarantee that the poison hadn't already spread into his body. There was no point calling the doctor out again; he could do nothing more.

'Come away, Beatrice, he is sleeping. You go and get some sleep yourself,' said Charles. He didn't expect miracles. Alex had not only been bitten by one of the world's most poisonous spiders, but he had lost a lot of blood where he had had his finger chopped off by Mikano. By midday he was still asleep. Beatrice felt his pulse: it was very irregular. She opened his shirt and put her hand on his heart; again the beats were very slow.

Mikano came to the door; he had brought the local medicine man with him.

'Mr Charles, he is good medicine man, he has cured spider bites before he said. Do you want him to heal Alex?' Charles looked at Beatrice. She could see he wasn't interested.

'Thank you, Mikano, but tell your man we don't want his services.' The two men left; mumbling together. At three in the afternoon, Alex gave a cough and passed away. Charles went and felt for a pulse but there was none. He straightened his limbs out and drew the blanket over Alex's face and body.

'He's passed away, Beatrice. He never recovered.'

Beatrice was very upset; after all, it was her brother; her own flesh and blood. She raised a cloth to her eyes to cover the tears. Even though she had seen so much death in her life the loss of Alex, whom she had grown to love, hurt her greatly.

'I'm afraid we're going to have to get Norman back. He's young, he has plenty of time to do his studies,' said Charles. 'I can't manage on my own. We do need him.'

7 *Norman*

W ITH CHARLES back home, his eyesight restored, Norman felt justified in following his chosen profession: to be a barrister. Norman got off the train at Victoria and hailed a cab to the Victoria hotel. He just couldn't believe the vastness of the city; how great buildings of magnificent design were springing up everywhere. The wide roads had such a conglomeration of traffic, some pulling wheeled vehicles and some not.

There were horse-drawn buses and masses of pedestrians, all in a hurry to get somewhere. It was so different from the quiet busy life on the farm. He was so taken by the beauty and vastness of the city that he directed his cab driver to take him around and point out places of interest. He pointed out Geelong Town Hall and Victoria Parliament buildings in Spring Street, Melbourne. The majority of the residents seemed to prefer Melbourne for living in. Norman was very taken with the beauty and vastness of the city.

Having seen enough to whet his appetite and give him a good idea of his bearings, he asked his driver to take him to where he was to be accommodated. This would be his new home whilst he did his studies. He paid the cab driver off and climbed the steps of the tall grey-stone building.

The large oak-panelled iron-studded doors were slightly ajar, so pushing them open he walked into a vast hall with oak panelling all around and a large uncarpeted highly polished floor. He looked up at the high ceiling from which hung a multi-lamped chandelier. A broad wooden staircase enabled one to get to the two other levels of the building. Placing his cases on the floor, he rang the small brass bell situated on a polished Portland hall table.

As he stood there waiting he saw a good many young men of similar age to himself pass through the hall, some singly, others in pairs. They looked at him as if he were a piece of refuse blown in from the street. These young men wore dark stripped trousers, white shirts with waistcoat and cravats, and seal-skin top hats when leaving the building.

Norman compared them to himself; he could understand their disassociating themselves with the likes of him who must have appeared to resemble a well-dressed refuse man; of very little consequence.

Eventually a very portly gentleman appeared, similarly dressed to the others he had seen, but wearing a pair of gold-rimmed spectacles.

'Hello, sir. How may I help you?' he asked, adjusting his glasses as he peered at the young man.

'Good morning, to you sir,' said Norman. 'I have come to take up my chambers here whilst I perform my studies.'

Norman pulled the well-read letter of introduction from his pocket and handed it to the gentleman who, having taken the letter, turned towards the light from the open door to read it.

'Ah, Mr Redlock I see. Welcome to our humble abode for that is what it will be to you for a few years to come. I see you have paid your initial fees now there is an additional £200 to pay to cover accommodation for the year.' Norman handed him a bank cheque for the amount.

'Yes, that's fine.' A small boy came into the hall. He couldn't have been more than twelve.

'Come here, Chaucer. Show Mr Redlock to his chambers on the second floor, that's number 21. Take his bags. We like to do things properly here, Mr Redlock,' he said, as Norman went to lift the bags himself. 'Dinner is at eight o'clock in the main dining room, Mr Redlock,' he said, as he turned and disappeared through the same door he had appeared by.

Norman followed the young lad who was struggling with his luggage, but knew it would be wrong for him to offer to help.

He tipped the boy a thruppeny-joey for his efforts and entered his new lodgings, which he knew he would be sharing with another. The room was very large; perfectly adequate for two men sharing. There was a bed on either side of the room and a large chest of drawers for each of them. There were also two kneehole desks for them to study at each, complete with a table candelabra. There were also two wardrobes.

Norman was most impressed with the room and the furnishings; though he had to admit the fees were very high so the accommodation was no more than he should expect. He looked out of the window. The view was on to a green park where children played and mothers and nannies pushed their babies on fine days. He was once again most impressed.

He unpacked and stored his belongings away. And having nothing else to-do that day decided to look up his mothers step sister, or Alex's sister. Apart from Alex, when he was a young man and still living at home, no one had ever seen her. His mother Beatrice had got her address from John when she visited and as she lived in Victoria it seemed ideal that Norman, who was a distant relative, should look her up.

He opened his wallet and saw her address was 5 Waddy Mansions, Melbourne. He had no idea where the house was but guessed a cabby would know. So cleaning his shoes and making himself respectable, he made his way to her house. He didn't realise it was so far, and forty minutes later he arrived at 5 Waddy Mansions. The address appeared far grander than the premises, although the house couldn't be more than twenty years old. It had that neglected drab appearance about it, as if renovation and a lick of paint had missed it out and gone onto the next house.

He noticed a curtain twitch which made him aware that his visiting would not be entirely unexpected. Wasting no more time he walked up to the door and pulled the arm of the bell. A moment or two later it was opened by a very pretty young lady who he thought was about his own age. Doffing his hat he said,

'Good day, madam. I have come to see if a certain Betty Watkins lives here?'

'May I ask why you seek her, sir?'

'I am a distant relation; my mother is her stepsister.'

'I see. Wait a moment.' She left him standing on the doorstep while she disappeared into the gloom of the house.

Within a minute two ladies appeared at the doorway; the second considerably older.

'Hello. I am Betty Watkins. Who are you?'

'My name is Norman Redlock. My mother Beatrice Cushingham is your stepsister.'

'Is she indeed? You'd better come inside and explain,' she said, standing aside to let him in.

Norman felt a sort of chill at the way he was received, as if he wasn't welcome. However, he said nothing and entered the dark, unwelcoming hall of the house. The walls had dark-stained wood panelling and there was a large hand-woven carpet showing considerable wear on the floor. A large candlelit chandelier hung from the ceiling, illuminating several old family portraits of ladies and gentlemen of past generations.

'Come into the lounge,' said Betty.

Norman followed the ladies into an elaborately furnished lounge with a large three-seater soft brocade furnished suite and matching chairs, a large library desk, and several shelves of books; there were two large carpets covering the floor and several candelabras. There was also a small concert piano. Norman took all this in very quickly. If given more time he would have found many more exquisite items adorning the room.

'Sit down, Norman, this is my daughter Clare.'

Norman saw in the light from the window how lovely Clare was, with her beautiful complexion and long brown hair. She wore a high-necked blouse with long sleeves, a light-red cotton skirt and silver buckle shoes.

'How did you find out where I lived?' asked Betty.

'From your father, because he is also my mother's father.'

'That's the first I've heard. Are you saying my father was married before?'

'No, but he was courting my grandmother, Elizabeth Barker, and made her pregnant.'

'Why didn't he marry her?'

'I'm sure he would have had he been able to. But my great grandparents thought it was a disgrace having their daughter made pregnant by a private soldier, so they sent her to live with an uncle called Wainright until she had the baby. In the mean time the great-grandparents had gone to India with their regiment. They never saw their daughter Elizabeth again.

'What happened to Elizabeth?'

'Apparently from what we found out she died in a field of gypsies, and they sold my mother who was her baby to some wealthy people named Cushingham and they brought her up as their own.'

'Would you like some team, Norman?' asked Clare.

'Yes please.' She rang a bell, and ordered the tea from the housemaids.

'So you are what to me?'

'I suppose I am a second-generation nephew. I have never really considered the fact. By the way, your brother Alex is living with my parents on their sheep farm.'

'Is he really? I haven't seen Alex since he was twelve,' said Betty. 'How is he?'

'As far as I am aware he is well. He was happily working on the farm when I left to come here.' He paused to sip his tea. 'Excuse me asking, but why don't you communicate with your father, Betty? He told my mother he would love to hear from you,' said Norman.

'For reasons not dissimilar to your own mother I wanted to marry a soldier and he objected and said if I dared to go against his word he would have nothing more to do with me. So I went ahead and married him and we finished up here. There's a lot more to tell.'

'Is your husband still alive?'

'No he died in the Crimea.'

'My mother served as a nurse in Crimea,' said Norman, reaching for a biscuit

'Did she, what was her name?'

'Beatrice Cushingham,' he replied.

'Wait here,' she went and rummaged through some papers, 'Ah here it is. It's a letter from Gerald, my husband.' She passed it to Norman to read.

My dearest Betty,
How I would love to be with you at this moment I am lying
in a hall full of dying men the smell is atrocious. Hell
cannot be worse than this place. The only thing that has
kept me going is the nurses out here, Beatrice in
particular, she is bloody marvellous and works so hard to
keep them alive I will close now all my love my dearest.
Gerald

He read it through; he knew it referred to his mother.

'My mother was awarded a medal by the Queen for her services in the Crimea.'

'Then it's the same woman. I would like to meet her.'

'I'm sure you will one day,' said Norman, with a smile.

'What are you doing down here, Norman?' asked Clare.

'I am staying at the University where I hope to study law,' he replied.

'Oh a barrister in the family,' she laughed.

'Oh there's a long way to go before that,' said Norman.

'Well it's been an interesting and revealing afternoon. Thank you for calling and please come again,' said Betty.

'Yes please do,' said Clare, rising from her seat as he did.

'Thank you both. I will keep in touch.' He doffed his hat and made his way back to his bedsit.

The sun was shining and Norman felt at ease with the world the future looked very rosy. He liked the thought of the independence he had from sheep farming. He could handle it alright but he felt he needed something more challenging in life, something that would tax his brain, His cab was running alongside the docks and Norman was fascinated by all the activity. He knew he wasn't far from his rooms so he stopped the cab and paid him off intending to walk the rest.

*

He never actually felt any pain from the blow on the head – just sudden blackness. He stopped thinking and wasn't even aware of the transportation of his body aboard the *Sea Vixen* sailing brig. Recruitment of crew for seagoing vessels was usually carried out at offices designed to recruit sailors. The days of press-ganging a man and forcing him to crew a vessel had been made illegal nearly a hundred years earlier. However somebody forgot to inform the captain and crew of the *Sea Vixen* because that's exactly what they had done to Norman.

He came to about an hour after the knock on the head and was soon aware he was at sea. He couldn't see where he was, but could feel ropes and pulley blocks under him, and feeling with his hands he was aware of drums containing what smelt like creosote. He must be in a sail locker room. His head hurt from the blow he had received. He felt around his prison cell and found he could touch all the walls which were of wood.

The steady slopping sound of water as the ship was heading towards the open sea at a steady rate of knots, he wondered where she was bound and would he ever see his family again. He must have fallen asleep because he was awoken by a black man slapping his face to wake him up.

'Come on lad. The captain wants to speak to you,' he said, pulling Norman to his feet.

'Where am I? What's this ship?'

'It's the *Sea Vixen*, son, ain't you never sailed the seven seas before? If not you're in for a treat,' he chuckled, as he took Norman's arm and guided him on to the upper deck. His escort was very black. He had short fuzzy hair with big whites to his eyes. His face bore scars, which Norman found out later, were tribal marks. He wore a gold earring, and smiled with a perfect set of gleaming white teeth.

The crew aboard the *Sea Vixen* were very mixed black, brown, light tan, and white with a sprinkling of Chinese amongst them. They were obviously used to seeing recruits like Norman being taken before the captain, dressed in their smart city clothes. His captor knocked on the captain's door and was invited to enter. His escort went outside and shut the door.

'Welcome aboard, young man,' said the captain, extending his hand in greeting. Norman ignored the handshake. As far as he was concerned they were intended to be a sign between two amicable people who both wish each other well. Norman was not one of those.

'Take a seat,' he said, pointing to a chair on the other side of the table. Norman sat down.

Norman looked at his captor. He was a slightly built man, pinched face, with brown hair, he wore in a pigtail. Most of his front teeth were missing. His eyes from where Norman sat looked green. Despite this he had an engaging smile, and what appeared on the surface to be an honest face, even though he had kidnapped Norman.

'I'm sorry my men had to recruit you in such a harsh manner but we are desperate to sail on this tide as we have to reach South America in six weeks' time or we lose our contract. I have lost three crew members and can find no volunteers – so I had to resort to good old-fashioned press-ganging. Don't worry, you will be fed and paid for your work here. You can't work in those togs – I will find you some suitable clothes. The boatswain is Bert Harrod. He's a hard man, but fair. Just do as you're told and you will be fine.'

Norman hadn't uttered a word up to now.

'I have been assaulted and kidnapped. I demand I be released at the first British port we come to,' he demanded.

'Can't do that, you are staying on here until we find replacements. That might take six months. Mongo,' he yelled.

The black man entered again.

'What's your name, lad?' asked the captain.

'Norman Redlock'

'I'm Captain Vic Masters. Get Norman fitted out with some suitable togs and take him to Bert Harrod for duty.'

'Right, Captain,' he replied, taking Norman's arm and leading him in the direction of the crew's quarters. They were on the third deck down. It was very low. The placed reeked with the smell of dirty, unwashed bodies. Norman was feeling seasick. He dashed to a porthole, but threw up before he got to one.

'That's the first thing you can do is clean that up,' said Mongo.

There were rows of rolled up hammocks and Mongo took Norman to one by the porthole.

'This is yours. It's all the space you get. The shit-houses are at the end and there's a bucket so you can get some water if you want to wash. It's seawater, mind. The galley is at the other end and you will find the tables there and eating irons. Here are the clothes you got to wear. They should be clean – the last bloke who owned them drowned.' He laughed. 'Get changed now. Go on, don't be shy, we all got one of those dicks, get changed, and hurry up. I got work to do.'

Norman did as he was told.

'Right come with me. If you got any questions ask. If you don't do as you're told you get the whip, it's not nice getting the whip. Ah, here's the boatswain. Mr Masters. Here's Norman your latest volunteer,' he laughed, handing him over.

Mr Masters was a big man with black hair which he wore long and tied back, a round sea-burnt face, and a big pimply nose. Most of his front teeth were missing except one.

'Right, Norman, there's a bucket and soap. Get some water and scrub the deck, and I want to see my face shine in it. Now get going.'

'When do we eat?'

'You'll get bloody fed when you've done some work. Now get moving.'

Norman got some water from over the side and started scrubbing.

'Not like that – put your back into it, lad. I can see I got to keep my eye on you. You're going to be a lazy bugger. Think yourself too good to be a seaman? Well I'll show you.'

He kicked Norman up the arse. 'Now bloody get to work,' he barked.

After Norman had spent two hours scrubbing the deck, his hands were raw and blistered and his knees and back ached.

'Right, join those others I want a sail brought in.' Norman went and joined a group.

'Grab hold of the rope and pull hard when I tell you. Ready, steady, pull ... pull ... pull.'

Norman was feeling crippled and ached all over. He had never done such hard work. All the men were tired after that and sat down for a blow.

'Hard work isn't it mate,' said a little Welsh fellow. 'Where you from, boyo?' he asked.

Norman smiled at him. 'I'm from England and have come to Australia to live. I was going to university when I got snatched to work here.'

'Oh, you will get used to it. We got three others like you. We can't get the crew. Nobody seems to want to work, so we have to snatch them.'

'Will I get off?'

'One day, can't say when though. Some of them have been on years,' said Taffy. 'They grow to like it. You might be the same.'

'No hope for that, the sooner I get off this tub the better,' said Norman.

'Right, all hands on deck. We have to reef the sails, there's bad weather ahead. Up the rigging you go lads and reef in the sails.' The ship had three masts and two jib sails. Each mast carried a main sail and a top sail.

'Now you will see what hard work is really all about. Come on, follow me and climb the rigging,' said Taffy.

'I can't, I'm afraid of heights. I'll fall.'

'Come on, you will be alright just do what I tell you,' said Taffy.

'No, I'm frightened.'

'You better do it, Norman, otherwise it could mean the whip. Don't worry, it's not stormy, just don't look down.'

Norman stood on the ship's side and followed those in front of him. Taffy came behind him. Step by step they gradually ascended the rigging to the cross spar.

'Follow what the man in front of you does. Place your feet where his have just been. Don't look down. Go out along the crossbeam. Right stop, fasten the sails.'

Norman carried out all of Taffy's instructions.

'Right, now replace your footsteps and follow me.' Once more Norman obeyed Taffy and eventually found himself down on safe ground.

'Well done, we'll make a sailor of you yet. Come on, it's time to eat.' All the deckhands jostled down the steps onto the mess deck and took their seats.

'Sit by me,' said Taffy.

Two crew members at the end of the table went and got the food and plated it up, then sent it hand by hand down the table. It consisted of a chunk of bread and a thick slice of pork. This was followed with a mug of watery beer and an apple. They mostly ate in silence.

'Right, that's your lot till tomorrow. We don't get overfed on here, Norman my lad. Come on, it's getting dark; we will go on deck for a sing song.'

All the hands sat around in a circle and smoked their pipes. They were dressed pretty much the same with baggy trousers and thick woolly shirts. Hardly anyone wore a hat. It seemed the different nationalities stuck together in groups, and didn't mix.

In the night the wind got up and the crew were roused from their warm hammocks to go on the cold, windy deck and adjust the sails again; some needed hauling in; others needed to be set up. It was very tiring at three in the morning. Their clothes were wet through when they finished. Most never bothered to get back in their beds but sat up talking. At six it was the start of the day. Some men had a wash; most didn't bother.

'Come on, Norman, that's the mates' whistle and it means we all got to muster on deck ready for the assembly where they tell us what we got to do.'

Norman went along with the others. He thought about home and his family and wondered if they realised he wasn't at college as they expected him to be. One didn't have time to get bored. Time flew by. A week had passed very quickly.

'We got the worse weather to come,' said Taffy. 'We go round the Cape of Good Hope. It can be hell then. So don't think its all plain sailing,' he said with a grin.

Norman was starting to realise that life on board wasn't so bad when one got used to it. Men can be funny creatures when bunched together for long periods and the *Sea Vixen* was no exception. There was a big Swedish fellow – nobody knew his real name, everybody called him Hans – who took a dislike to Norman for no apparent reason. He would bump into him, knock him and pick arguments, getting him involved. Hans was also a bully and ruled by fear. None of the crew liked him. Norman had never fought in his life, and when one day Hans pulled a knife on him Norman was petrified. There were no ship's officers around, just the deckhands.

'Come on my little English pig, come and fight with a real man,' said Hans, menacingly swapping the vicious knife from one hand to another.

'I can't fight, I don't know how to,' said Norman, with his back to the bulkhead. 'I have no knife.'

Hans threw his knife and it quivered at Norman's feet.

'Here, use my knife. I have another,' he said, pulling one from his belt. The crew were getting excited and egging Norman on; some taking Hans's side.

Hans was a very big man .Norman estimated him at nearly twenty stone. He had short blond hair and blue eyes. He wore a spotted bandana round his head, which made him look a bit like a pirate. On his body, he wore a hair shirt and beeches held up with a wide leather strap.

'Come, you not a pig, you a little chicken,' said Hans, getting impatient.

Norman wished someone would appear and stop the fight. He bent down and picked the knife off of the deck. He was, by token, accepting the duel. He was now entirely on his own. Hans circled Norman, taunting him. The crowd knew that there was no intention to kill Norman, unless it was an accident; they were quite happy to see blood. The first to draw blood was the winner. It was an accepted rule.

Hans lunged at Norman, who being lighter on his feet, manage to avoid him and the knife passed through Norman's shirt, missing the skin of his arm. There was a gasp from the crowd.

Hans lunged at Norman, who being lighter on his feet manage to avoid him and the knife passed through Norman's shirt, missing the skin of his arm. There was a gasp from the crowd. Norman wiped his brow. He knew that more than his honour and status as a man was at stake and although only a lad he had accepted the challenge. Some of the crew were running a book as to who would draw blood first. Once again Hans circled and made another lunge at him which he managed to sidestep. Norman had a plan, if it worked. The big Swede was ready to end the fight, it was getting boring.

'You ready to die now, English boy?' he said.

Norman threw his knife and it quivered in the deck. Then taking on the boxer's stance of the Queensbury Rules he raised his guard and, with two well aimed blows, placed one on the big Swede's nose making it gush with blood, and the other to the point of the chin, knocking Hans out cold. The crowd cheered Norman as the winner and Hans became the laughing stock.

The crowd were changing money between themselves as they had won or lost on the fight. Those who backed Norman came over and congratulated him. Taffy came over.

'That was a good fight, Norman. I knew you would outwit that big Swede. I won a few pounds as well.' Norman sat down on a box, and put his head in his hands. It had all been very stressful. He was shaking.

'Don't worry, Norman, that's normal. You will feel alright in a minute. You have made your mark on this ship. No one will mess with you again.'

Norman smiled at his friend. 'Thanks Taffy, I don't know what I would do without you as a friend.'

'That's alright boyo,' he said, as he walked away.

When Hans came to after five minutes, he came over and stood in front of Norman. At first Norman thought the big man wanted to continue the fight.

'It was good fight, yes? You not English boy, you are English man.' He laughed. 'You and me now lifetime buddies. Anyone hurt you, they answer to me.' He held out his shovel-sized hand. 'Shake hands, Norman.'

Norman obliged, he was glad he had made friends with Hans.

Norman had gained respect from the crew and they were helpful and no more bother. But Norman still wanted his freedom to go home, which was going to be a long time coming.

8   *Rustlers*

'ALRIGHT,' said Beatrice, 'I will contact the University. I know he will want to come back for the funeral.'

It took several days before Beatrice got a report from the University saying that, although Norman had deposited his belongings in his rooms, there had been no sign of him since.

'I don't understand it dear, whatever is Norman up to? We haven't heard from him and nor has anyone else. I am very worried about our son's welfare and want you to do something about it, Charles.'

'Like what, my dear. Where do I start?' said Charles.

'I suggest you try my stepsister Betty. He said he intended to make it his priority to visit her as he knows no other person in Victoria.'

'I will leave this afternoon, my dear. Let me have her address.'

Charles found the residence of Betty and her daughter with little trouble. Unfortunately, although she was pleased to see him, she could throw no light on what had happened to Norman since leaving her house. In fact she added that she thought it strange as it was a month ago, and he gave the impression that he would take up her offer of kindness and return to visit her very quickly. Charles returned home very worried. Knowing his son as he did, he knew that Norman was a responsible person and would have kept in touch because he wouldn't want them to worry.

Beatrice broke down when he gave her the sad news and she feared he was dead as she could see no other explanation for his disappearance without trace. They thought of every possible reason why he had vanished, but could come to no satisfactory conclusion. They put pictures of him in the paper and contacted the police; all to no avail. As time went by, they stopped crying and accepted the inevitability that Norman had vanished, but until they received definite proof he was dead, they lived in hope that one day he would turn up.

Alex's funeral had gone ahead with very few mourners. Betty wasn't there because no one had contacted her in the sorrow of his death; it hadn't crossed anyone's mind. It left a gap in the family with his passing away, and Charles was desperate for some new staff. He enquired in the nearest town and advertised in the local paper; but all to no avail. It meant extra work for everyone until new farmhands could be found.

It was Bruce who first spotted strangers approaching the farm.

'Daddy, come quick. There are two horsemen riding this way,' called Bruce.

Charles, who was shaving some wooden poles, looked up to see what his son was shouting about. Sure enough, two horsemen were cantering their horses in no great rush towards his farm. They dismounted outside the residential area and showed politeness by tying their horses to a hitching rail, and walking towards where Charles was standing, waiting for them.

'Good day, can you spare us some water? We have both emptied our billycans and still have a way to go.'

'Certainly. Come and rest a while,' invited Charles. 'Bruce, go and get these lads some drinks and ask mother to rustle up some grub.'

'That's damned decent of you, cobber,' said the older, taller one. Both of them gave the appearance that they were farm workers.

'Are you by any chance looking for work?' asked Charles, once they had refreshed themselves.

'That's where we are heading now, to a sheep farm about ten miles from here. We heard they were short, and you are as well?'

'I just lost my top shepherd. Got bitten by a funnel web and died.'

'Sorry to hear that. It's quite a rare thing but usually fatal. Can you take the two of us on, only you see we're inseparable, we're brothers?'

'Of course I can. What do you specialise in – cows, or sheep?'

'We can handle either,' said the tall guy who seemed to be the spokesman of the pair. 'We worked on several sheep farms in the area but we ain't never been ones for holding down long-term jobs.'

'Not a very good recommendation is it,' said Charles,

'Do you want us or not? Tell you what. The lambing season is coming. We will work six months and if we like it here, and you like us, we will stay. How's that for a deal?'

'Sounds good to me. The wages are fifty a month, plus food and bed. The crew hut is round the back. What are your names?'

'As I said, we're brothers. I'm Bob and this is Jaz, only everyone knows him as Bluey.' Charles shook hands with them,

Bob was tall and thin and if it was possible to vouch for a person's honesty and integrity by their facial features and smile, then Bob appeared to be completely trustworthy. Charles reckoned it beat all the paper references in the world. He was tall and thin, carrying no extra fat but one could see the muscles and sinews moving beneath his checked cotton shirt.

Blue was the younger of the two and Charles didn't think he was much over twenty. His features were pretty much the same as his brother's but he appeared to be the thinker of the two. He didn't say a lot but didn't seem to miss anything either.

'Well, they look two fine lads,' said Charles to himself as he strolled into the house and saw Beatrice standing there, just waiting to question him about the two farmhands he had taken on.

'So you have found your new farmhands then, dearest,' she said. 'Are they good?'

'They appear to be. I don't think I have made a mistake.'

Mary had also been standing there watching all that had been going on, and had formed a few opinions of her own.

'I like the young one, what did he say his name was, Bluey?' said Mary.

'Oh, so you have taken a fancy to him have you, young lady? Well, just remember you're only nineteen,' said Beatrice, in a kindly, motherly way.

Time passed uneventfully on the farm. The lambing season came and went, the two new hands proved themselves worth double what they were being paid. They were hard grafters, and very versatile. It was also important that they got on well with the other farmhands; which they did.

Bob and his other hands rode to the top pastures to check the flock and count them. They had split into two groups to assist with counting and getting an accurate total

'What was last month's numbers, Mikano?' asked Blue, as he rode up alongside him.'

'Close on two thousand, but I think were missing a couple of hundred this year.' The sheep up here on the hills were left pretty well to themselves. There had been very little trouble over the years. Dingoes or wild dogs were the main problem, and they had to be shot regularly, but otherwise there were no natural predators.

'Then we're five hundred short. Someone has been rustling our sheep. Ride back and tell Charles he will want to see for himself.'

Mikano, who took his orders from Blue, turned his horse around and galloped off down the hill leaving Blue alone with the remaining hands. Two other riders of theirs were about two miles away over a ridge, out of sight. Blue got off his horse and went and looked at the fences. He could see where the wires had been cut to facilitate the rustling. He also noticed the many hoof marks in the soft earth.

One of the hoof marks was different: not only did it have a nail missing, but part of the horse's shoe had a big dent in it which was very noticeable and showed up as a gap in the hoof mark. Blue noted this and would be on the lookout for a hoof mark like that. He had a smoke while he waited.

It was about twenty-five minutes later that Charles, Mikano and Bob came racing over the brow of the hill to join up with Bluey.

'You sure of your figures, Bluey?' asked Charles.

'I am that. I been looking forward to a big head count this month after lambing and now we're down by about five hundred sheep.'

'I've been suspecting rustling for some time,' said Charles, 'but had no proof. They were always so careful.'

'Well, they're not now, boss. Look, you can see the damage they done and the hoof marks.'

'They will hang for this if we catch them,' said Bob, who had taken Alex's place as the head shepherd.

'We'll catch them, boss, don't worry about that. Me and the lads will do some night patrolling. We will need our guns, because they will be armed, that's for sure.'

'OK, but don't fire unless you have to. I don't want a range war,' said Charles.

'No fear of that boss,' said Bob, smiling at the other crew members.

When they got back to the farm, Bob got all the men together.

'OK, tonight, we will patrol in small units. I will do the first with my brother and Mikano. We don't want too many up there as it will give the game away. You will soon hear if there is any gun play and when you hear it, come and join us.' They all nodded their agreement and understanding. Once the sun had gone down the three men nominated got their horses ready and rode up to the high pasture land. Luckily it wasn't a cold night and there was plenty of moonlight. They didn't want to end up shooting each other in the dark. They picked a spot which was a depression in the hillside. It would give them some cover and they knew they would have sufficient warning if the rustlers did come, as it was not a quiet exercise rounding up sheep, especially at night.

It wasn't till midnight that their own softly murmured conversation was interrupted by a man coughing some distance away from them. They tethered their horses so they couldn't run off and, lying flat on their bellies, they approached the rustlers. Each of the three had a revolver in their hands; they had to be prepared for the worst. As soon as they could see the rustlers pulling down the fences they knew they were dealing with the right crowd.

'Stop what you're doing and get off our land,' shouted Bob. The reply was a pistol shot fired at him which appeared to go wide of its mark.

'Don't make us shoot, we don't want trouble. If you leave quietly right away, that will be an end to the matter,' shouted Bob. Another two shots were fired at them.

'Come on lads, there are only two of them,' shouted the leader of the rustlers, firing another shot at Bob and his men.

'Right men, return fire,' said Bob. It was then he realised Mikano was not with them.

'Where's Mikano?' said Bob, in an anxious voice.

'He must be back at the horses,' said Blue, searching the darkness for their friend.

'Keep low and fire some shots at them,' whispered Bob. 'I'm going back to see to Mikano.'

Bluey fired off five shots at no one in particular as he couldn't make anyone out.

Bob was soon back at his side 'Mikano has been shot. He caught a bullet in the shoulder. It's bleeding badly, but otherwise he's alright. He's staying with the horses.'

'Poor devil,' said Blue.

'I know. This is getting serious, I will send for the constable when we get home and tell him the facts,' said Charles. The rustlers had left the flock empty-handed this time. 'We will keep a permanent guard up here, Bob, until this crowd of rustlers are caught.'

Once the shooting had started, the other half of the crew who were on the farther side of the hill came round and joined them.

'Bob, I want you to leave a guard up here tonight and every night. Understand?'

'Yes boss.'

'Jim, Shorty, Mike, Go down to the bunkhouse, pick up some tucker and your bedroll, and come back up here. I will stay here with Blue until you get back.'

*

Charles went into town in the morning to report to the authorities the fact that they had been rustled, and had made a contact with them the previous night. He also reported the fact that one of his men had been wounded. The constable on duty took notes from Charles, and said somebody would be calling at the farm to have a look at the evidence. Charles had to make do with this for the moment. He hoped that the rustlers wouldn't return in which case it would mean a shooting match.

Meanwhile Bob and Blue rode back to where the rustling took place. Bob searched once again for the distinguishable hoof mark with a piece missing from it. Sure enough, it was there once again, so it was the same gang of rustlers.

'Life is certainly tough out here, Charles,' said Beatrice. 'It's so short. One day you're talking to someone and the next day they are dead. I don't think I will ever get used to it. There's still no news of our son. What can have happened to him, Charles? I'm sure he would have contacted us if he was able to; which means he might be retained against his will, or dead. Somehow I have a feeling he is still alive,' she said, as if talking to herself, expressing her inner feelings.

'May God look after him wherever he is,' said Charles.

The constable rode out to the farm next day.

'Hi there, are you Charles Redlock?' he asked, as he dismounted.

'That's me constable, and this is my wife Beatrice.'

'Please to meet you, ma'am. My name is Toby Trucker. I have just been made Constable. I hear you have had one of your men murdered by rustlers, is that right?'

'No, not murdered. He was wounded in the shoulder by the rustlers.'

'We haven't had rustling of sheep for years out here,' said Toby.

'I know only too well. I been here longer than I can remember,' said Charles.

'There have been many changes since then. This was all scrub and grass and was infested with Abbos when I came out here in fifty-three,' said Norman. 'Built the whole lot on my own with a bit of help from friends.'

'That was before my time, sir, but I know what you mean, and I admire you for it,' said Toby. 'Christ, it's hot,' he added, wiping his head and neck on his neckerchief.

'It certainly is. Would you like a beer?' asked Beatrice, who had come out to greet the constable.

'Sure would ma'am,' he replied.

'Come into the house,' said Charles.

Toby was a short man of medium build; certainly not overweight; not many people around the area were. His hair was dusty brown, as was his skin; he had obviously worked the land before becoming constable. He wore a large, wide-brimmed hat which helped to keep the sun off, but there was no solution to the thousands of constantly irritating flies.

'Nice to be in the cool again,' said Toby. 'You been out here long, ma'am?'

Before Beatrice could answer Charles jumped in. He was expecting a few searching questions from Toby.

'This is my wife Beatrice. We have only been married seven years. So when we got married we brought her son and two daughters out here with us.'

'My, that's quite a family.'

Beatrice noticed that Charles had included Mary as being one of her girls; that was smart thinking on his part. It appeared to Beatrice that this was a police constable with a keen eye, who would pick up on mistakes.

'So tell me about the rustling,' he said.

Charles gave him all the details, including the injury to Mikano.

'Can I see the area? Is it far from here?' asked Toby.

'No, come on I'll take you,' said Charles.

Together the two of them rode out to where it had all taken place.

'This isn't the first time then,' said Toby.

'No, it's at least the second, if not more. I have been short staffed, and suspected some sheep were missing for a long time, but wasn't able to do much about it. They take about five hundred each time. Bob, my foreman said there were six of them and they opened fire on my men.'

'Did your men reply?'

'Yes, apparently Blue fired six shots from his revolver – not at then but in their general direction to scare them off.'

Toby and Charles dismounted and examined the soft ground.

'I see there is a horse's hoof with a piece out of it. It shouldn't be hard to find the horse that belongs to if he comes into town,' said Toby.

The constable took all the details he needed. 'Don't take the law into your own hands, Charles,' he said. 'I will handle this.'

'We have got to protect ourselves and our property,' said Charles.

'I know, but don't go out of your way to hunt them down. Protect yourselves by all means.'

'So what are you going to do, Constable?'

'I assume you don't mind me carrying out my investigation on your property, but I intend to get me a tracker, and see where those rustlers went to.'

'I see, well that will be a start. When will you start on that, tomorrow?'

'No, I have some other work I have to finish first of all, but I'll be out one day this week. I've got to get back to town now, see you soon.' He mounted his horse, waved, and rode off.

'Ha, can't see much good coming from that visit,' said Charles, plonking himself down in a chair.

'Well, we just can't ignore those rustlers; surely we are still going to patrol the flock at night dear?' asked Beatrice.

'Yes, of course we will my dear. I'm not going to let a load of bandits ride roughshod over me. No, we'll keep on patrolling. I will instruct Bob what I want him to do.'

Saying this, he got out of his chair and went over to the bunkhouse. 'Is Bob around?' he called.

'No sir, he's back up on the high grass mending the fences,' called out an old hand, who was fixing a bridle.

'Thanks, tell him I want to speak when he comes in.'

It was much later in the day that Bob came and knocked on the door.

'You want to speak with me boss?' said Bob.

'Yes Bob, we had the Constable out here today wanting to know all about the rustling. He was certainly very keen. He went to look at the fences to see where it all took place, and he found that hoof mark you saw. He warned us not to get involved. He said we could protect what was ours but not to go seeking them out; a factor I am in favour of.'

'Right boss.'

'I still want you to patrol the fences at night until this lot are caught.'

'That's fine, I mended all the fences – well, me and the boys did.'

'You have done a good job, Bob, keep it up.'

That night Bob, Bluey and the boys were on site ready for the rustlers if they turned up; and sure enough they did. However, they didn't get the chance to tear the fences down and rustle any sheep because the lads fired their pistols in the air and chased them off before they had a chance. Nothing more was heard of the rustlers for two weeks or more. It seemed they must have gone elsewhere and left their ranch alone.

That feeling of complacency was unwarranted, because it was two weeks to the day that Bob was lying in his bunk when something caused him to open his eyes. He checked his pocket watch and it was 2.30 in the morning. He lay there for a moment listening to the sounds of the night when he heard whispering along with the jingle of a horse's bridle. He raised himself up to look out of the window and the night sky was lit up by the fire that had been started in the hay barn.

'Wake up, wake up,' he yelled. 'The hay barn is on fire, get up, all of you and help put it out.'

Immediately the crew jumped to it, got dressed and ran for the barn. As the arsonists were leaving, Bob fired two quick shots at them and hit one in the arm. The horses that were stabled in the same building were going wild with the fire.

'Go and release the horses,' shouted Bob.

Charles came out to help, quickly followed by all the household and servants. Everybody was lending a hand.

'Form a chain of buckets and get the mobile fire extinguisher out of the tackle shed,' he shouted.

Men were running everywhere. Luckily the horses were all shooed out and they didn't need a second invitation – they were terrified. There was soon a steady row of buckets being emptied on the fire but Charles could see they wouldn't win. The tinder dry wood and the hay were burning out of control.

'Control the fire, Bob,' shouted Charles. 'We won't win trying to put it out.'

Bob told the men to let the fire take its course but to ensure it didn't spread and was put out properly. It was dawn by the time the tired crew were satisfied the fire was out. They were tired and dirty; in fact everyone concerned in putting it out was dirty and exhausted. It had been a frightening night.

'Tell the boys no work till noon, Bob.'

They were grateful for that news. After breakfast Bob and Charles went and viewed the damage done. The building would need to be completely rebuilt. All the hay was gone, as was the tack for the horses. It was going to cost a lot of money to rebuild the barn and restock it.

'Say, boss, look here. It's the same gang again. It's about time they reshod their horses because they leave this distinctive trail every time, it's always the shoe with the piece missing out of it.'

'Well, they haven't caught the owner of that horse yet, I reckon he is a phantom,' said Charles and they chuckled with him. Just then, Bluey came over, carrying something.

'What you got there Blue?' asked Charles.

Blue held out to him the horseshoe with the piece out of it. Only it was attached to a metal bar like a branding iron would be. Charles looked at it and handed it to Bob.

'We have been hoodwinked, boss. There hasn't been a horse with a duff hoof but these rustlers have made sure they imprinted the sign of it every time they made a raid.'

'You mean like a brand name?' said Charles.

'Yes, that's right. So we would be looking for a horse and owner who didn't exist.'

'Very clever, well they must have dropped it so that's the end of their little game.'

'It won't stop them, boss. They will be back of that I'm certain,' said Bob. 'They haven't finished with us yet. They are out to see us go under.'

'Well, we must be on our guard and give them a rousing welcome next time they come. In the meantime I'm going into town to report the fire,' said Charles.

9 *Shipwrecked*

WHEN CROSSING the Atlantic Ocean one can experience every type of sea condition from complete lulls to raging monsoons. It's very much the luck of the draw and the time of the year which will determine the voyage of a sailor; especially one who is at sea for the first time, as was the case of the kidnapped Norman Redlock.

He was by now a very seasoned sailor. His philosophy was 'If you can't beat them join them.' And as he always tried to do his best at everything he undertook, it soon became obvious to his superiors that here was a man who could easily climb the ladder of promotion as a seaman. He didn't know all the ropes, but found he was enjoying the life of being a sailor. He wasn't frightened to ask questions and learn all he could of the ship and sailing her. His cheerful personality won him many friends, though there was a contingent that didn't like the cocky upstart, as they called him, though his fear of heights always made him very careful when told to climb the rigging.

They were in mid Atlantic one night when a terrible gale blew up. It was in the early hours of the morning and Norman was asleep when he felt someone shaking his hammock.

'Come on, boyo, the bloody boat is sinking,' said Taffy.

'It's what?' said Norman, leaping out of his hammock and getting quickly dressed. There was no sign of a gale when he went to bed at ten o'clock; he wasn't due on watch until three in the morning. Up on deck the wind was howling like a prairie dog. The timbers were creaking and the sails were in danger of being shredded if not drawn in and reefed.

'Taffy Norman, Hans, Egbert, go up the rigging and secure the mizzen sale,' shouted the boatswain.

The team leapt into action, and taking great care with each step, they climbed the rigging and walked across the spar, hanging on like limpets to the wet, coarse sheets. The gale was trying to dislodge them and they couldn't communicate in the noise of the wind.

On top of all this, the ship was diving into atrocious waves which swept across her decks, taking everything that had not been made secure into the sea, including the sailors. The helmsman was tied to the helm, and felt very relieved that he was. In fact there were two of them. It needed two to hold the wheel steady.

Suddenly, the rope that Norman was standing on to pull the sails in broke; he lost his footing, but managed to cling onto the sail sheet he was pulling in. This was all that prevented him falling and smashing into the deck, thirty foot below.

'Help me,' he screamed with all his might above the wailing of the fierce wind. It was only seconds between life and death. He hadn't the strength, or the leverage to pull himself up, and in his mind he prepared for the inevitable, and horrible death awaiting him. The deck was thirty foot below him and if he missed that he would end up in the vast cauldron of saltwater which was bubbling like a stew pot.

Suddenly a huge hand grasped him round the wrist and gently hauled him back onto the cross spar. All eyes below had been watching this incident, and thanks to Hans's strength and bravery he had saved a shipmate. There was a loud cheer from all on board. Norman was so grateful to this big strong Swede. He smiled and shouted his thanks. Big Hans just grinned back at him.

Nobody slept that night The gale continued till daylight and the sea had a look about it like the face of a man who has had a bad night on the beer and has drunk too much; his stomach no doubt felt the same. However, by mid morning the sun was out and there was a mild wind which kept the ship on a steady angled keel towards their destination in of Jamaica in South America.

One morning a messenger came on to the crew's deck.

'Is there a Norman Redlock here?'

'Norman, you're wanted,' shouted Taffy.

'The captain wants to see you now,' said the messenger.

'Hello, what have you been up to?' The lads ribbed him, as he made his way up to the captain's cabin. He knocked and entered.

'Sit down, Norman. I want to compliment you on the fine job you have done as a sailor whilst on this voyage. Particularly as you were press-ganged against your will. You are a natural seaman, Norman, and would make a good officer and one day a captain. Would you like me to put your name forward?'

'Thank you, sir. I haven't given it a thought. I have enjoyed the sail and have made some good mates, but as for making it a career... well I don't know. Can I let you know later?'

'Of course you can. Damn sight more interesting than being a lawyer,' he smiled, dismissing him. Norman was still thinking what the captain had said when Taffy came up to him.

'What's he say then, boyo?' he asked.

'Oh it was nothing important, just about shore leave when we dock, that's all.'

'Oh I see,' said Taffy, not believing a word he said.

Norman gave it a lot of thought, and decided in favour of the idea. He would be doing what he enjoyed, on the open sea, with lots of exciting challenges. He sat alone at the mess table. The area was empty. He was alone with his thoughts. Norman was not one to make rapid decisions on such an important matter, but he had to admit he had never had so much fun and adventure in his young life. Did he really want to be a lawyer after experiencing this life? He had never given it a thought before he was press-ganged.

Life steered a person onto his path of destiny, and despite what one did they would find themselves being drawn back onto life's chosen path. All of this as opposed to being stuck with a pile of books in a stuffy law court. It seemed to make sense. Yes. He decided he would make the sea his career. What would his parents say? He was very worried because his parents hadn't a clue where he was or whether he was alive or dead. He must let them know soonest.

Having made his mind up he asked the boatswain if he could see the captain, and was told a message would be passed to the captain. The next day he was told to report to him. He knocked and was invited in.

'Have you made a decision?'

'Yes sir. I want to become a sea captain.'

'Well done, my boy. Being a sea captain is the ultimate gain you will have to make. Like all work, one has to start at the bottom. There is much to learn both at sea and in the classroom. You will have to learn not only how to sail a ship, but also about the weather and currents; and how to handle men and make decisions. Yes, there is a lot to learn; but you should make it in five years if you work hard and are lucky. I will write a letter recommending you for training as a junior ship's officer, and we will wait and see what happens. It won't happen overnight and will mean many years at sea. Learn all you can. I will lend you some books of mine to read and study.'

'Thank you sir, I badly want to get a letter to my parents so they know where I am,' said Norman.

'We will send a telegraph once we dock,' said the captain. Norman thanked him, and returned to his post, deep in thought and excited he had made this very important decision in his life.

It was a warm sunny day, and apart from a pleasant workable sea breeze the sea itself was comparatively calm. They were heading for Jamaica and were in the peaceful waters off the Caribbean Sea. Norman was enjoying this part of the voyage. The ship was idling along towards its destination. Taffy was standing on the bowsprit cleaning seaweed off it when he slipped and fell into the sea. Norman knew where he was supposed to be and when he heard this yell and saw Taffy was no longer there, he realised he had fallen into the sea.

Under normal conditions like that day it would have been no problem to rescue him. But there were two factors which made his recovery difficult. One was that Taffy was not a good swimmer – in fact he could hardly keep himself afloat. Secondly the area was shark infested.

'Man overboard,' he shouted, as loud as he could.

This was taken up right away by other members of the crew, and the ship had to be turned into the wind to facilitate the recovery of the sailor who had fallen overboard. Taffy had surfaced and was some fifty yards from the boat. Norman stood at the ship's rail and pointed to where the man was, so that the recovery boat could find him.

Taffy was splashing and yelling in fear and desperation at trying to keep afloat. Norman was positioned at a spot higher up in the ship, and from this vantage point he saw the distinctive black triangular shape of a shark's fin cutting through the water in the direction of Taffy. He kicked off his boots, and ignoring his own safety Norman dived over the side and swam rapidly towards the approaching shark. This caused the shark to veer away and take a more cautionary approach towards his intended meal.

Like all sailors, Norman carried a sharp knife in his belt which he used for everyday tasks aboard ship. Norman saw a shark's fin moving towards where he thought Taffy was. The ship had stopped by now, and the captain was putting into practice standard 'man overboard' drill, for which purpose a boat was being lowered.

Norman saw Taffy, and the shark. At this point the shark disappeared below the surface, getting ready to attack. Norman also dived below the surface. By now he was only a few yards from Taffy. The shark was circling. Norman recognised it as a Tiger shark, one of the most vicious maneaters in the sea. Norman pulled his sheathed knife from his belt, and swam towards the shark. The shark's mouth was open, ready to bite Taffy's leg off, when Norman lunged straight at it with his knife, the point of which pierced the shark's left eye.

Blood poured from it, and the shark forgot what it intended to do and turned away in pain, leaving a trail of blood flowing behind it. Taffy was drowning, and was sinking deeper into the sea. Norman was desperate for breath. He quickly surfaced, and on doing so saw the ship's longboat alongside him. He took a huge gulp of air and dived below the surface once more, to try and find Taffy, who by now had started to ascend as his lungs were filling with seawater. Norman saw the outline of the Welshman, and swam quickly towards him.

In the distance he could see two more sharks coming closer. He grabbed the Welshman's sparse hair and dragged him towards the rowing boat. He was desperate for air himself, and felt very tired. He could see the outline of the boat above him as he broke surface. Willing hands grasped both Norman and Taffy, while the other sailors beat the water with their oars to frighten the approaching sharks away.

There was much cheering and backslapping for Norman on his timely rescue of his sea mate. The captain came over.

'Words fail me Norman,' he said. 'That was indeed the finest act of bravery I have ever witnessed. Coxswain, give every man a drink of rum. It's not only the Queen's Navy that can toast a victory in rum. Three cheers for a brave man,' he called to the crew, who heartily responded.

Norman was more concerned as to how Taffy was. He went below, and there was Taffy looking none the worse for wear, smiling a semi toothless grin at his latest adventure, and the brave man who had saved him.

'Taffy, are you alright?'

'I'm fine boyo, thanks for saving my life that was a brave thing you did. I won't forget that.'

'It was close. You were only inches away from being a shark's dinner,' smiled Norman.

'Well, he didn't get me, thanks to you.'

An hour later the ship was tied up in Kingston harbour and her cargo of bales of wool unloaded. Taffy was back on duty, none the worse for his adventure. Norman's first concern was to contact his own parents. They must have thought he was dead, as it was nearly ten weeks he had been away from home. He went to the telegraph office and sent a message:

```
I am in Jamaica South America stop I am
well and happy don't worry stop Norman
stop
```

Once Norman had contacted his home he felt very relieved. Norman had become an official member of the crew after his interview with the captain. He withdrew his charges of being press-ganged and signed the ship's register as Norman Redlock, Crew member.

As he was a volunteer now, the ship's captain saw no need to restrict him to the ship when in harbour, so Norman was able to view the town and interesting sites. They stayed there for ten days, and took on board large quantities of green fruit and tobacco leaves amongst other products of Jamaica. Norman was made a midshipman, which was a very junior office post, so that he could learn all he could about sailing the oceans of the world. He intended to stay with this captain and his ship until he qualified. The crew were in good spirits having had a good rest and were still enjoying fresh fruit from the island. Also they were on their way home, because most of them lived in Australia.

Norman was studying his books one evening by candlelight in his cabin. Nobody on board showed any jealousy towards Norman. In their eyes he deserved all he got, so the little privileges, like a small room to himself, were gratefully received. He was busy making notes. They were expecting a big sea tonight with a strong wind, but were quite confident that they could weather the storm, and had already reefed the sails and made provision to sail through the gale when it struck.

However, the gale they had to contend with was worse than the previous one they had when going there. It blew so strongly that the second mast broke and came crashing down. In doing so it hit the tiller, killing the man handling the wheel. All hands were called to muster. They took axes and hacked at the stays retaining the mast. Eventually the mast was pushed over the side, but the damage had been done. The ship had no steerage and had lost a mast and still the wind blew. The ship tilted to one side and was moving along at an angle, going nowhere in particular. Colin Morgan was the man that died at the wheel. He was taken below, and the carpenter came to investigate the damage to the wheel and the steering gear. His observations did not please the captain.

'We will have to see where the wind and sea takes us, Captain,' said the carpenter. There are no repairs we can do tonight.'

Norman had taken the precaution of wrapping his books in oilcloth in case they had to abandon ship. No man slept that night for fear of what else might happen. The ship was in a mess, with the broken mast still attached to her, and the sails and sheets trailing in the water. The broken mast had caused damage when it came crashing down, damaging the upper deck structure, and wood splinters were every where.

The captain, and the carpenter, together with Norman and the boatswain, were in conference about the situation.

'Well, we can't get far in our present state, and as far as I can tell, we have drifted out of the main shipping lanes further down into the Pacific. I don't know what we will find down there,' said the captain, when he opened the meeting.

'We need a new mast, Captain, and a new rudder and we aren't going anywhere we want to go without them,' said the boatswain.

'Can we fix the ship?' asked Norman.

'Aye, we can fix her if we had the tools, the manpower and the materials,' said the carpenter.

Norman was well aware he was a very junior ship's officer, and because of this he didn't want to air his views openly. There were men at the table far more knowledgeable about the problems, and what was entailed than he was. However, it was obvious they couldn't go around feeling sorry for themselves. They had two options: either make for land, and do what they could to repair her, or abandon ship and take their chances at sea; this was not a pleasant option.

The captain made a decision. 'We will make for the nearest land and repair the ship, no matter how long it takes. That is my final word on the matter.'

There was a general murmur of approval at what the captain had said, but his next words came as a shock to them all.

'Norman, I am putting you in charge, with the help of the carpenter, in getting us ready for sea again. I know it is a big undertaking. You can call on all the help you need. Keep me informed as to progress.'

The other two at the table looked at Norman, congratulating themselves that the captain hadn't chosen them for this pig of a job. Norman was astounded at the gigantic task that had been put on his young shoulders. The captain must have had a lot of faith in him to give him this job. He didn't know where to begin, and knew he would have to rely on Bert Crow, the carpenter, to work together in fixing the ship ready for sea.

The captain dismissed the group and asked Norman and Bert Crow to remain behind.

'You looked shocked, Norma,' said the captain, smiling at him.

'That's putting it mildly sir,' he said. 'I have no skills as a shipwright, or handling men.'

'I chose you because I can think of no one on board capable of getting the men together, to work as a team, in completing this difficult task. I know you can do it, Norman, and I know Bert has all the qualifications and skills we need, so you should make a good team.'

There were two factors that came to help Norman and the distressed ships crew:

Although this was good news, there was another problem, which was the ship was drifting, and unless something happened quickly they would pass the island. It might take weeks or months until they spotted another. The captain ordered both longboats to be lowered with the crews, and that they towed the *Sea Vixen* to the island. The men set to and were soon pulling for all they were worth to drag the heavy ship towards the island. Luckily, they were positioned to the left of the island and the current was pulling them to the right.

Because of this, and the hard work of the crew, they managed to land and ditch the ship central on the beech.

The island was green with vegetation, and the captain guessed it was no more than two miles long .There was a large hill in the centre which was also covered in greenery. He didn't know whether the island was inhabited, but hoped it was as he could use all the extra hands he could get. It appeared to be an ideal spot to carry out the repairs.

Everybody concerned in beaching the ship was utterly exhausted, and lay on the dry, sandy beach to recuperate their strength. The captain called all the ship's crew together, and briefed them on what they intended to do.

'First of all, men, I want you to know I have placed the junior ship's officer in charge of this very big task of getting the ship ready for sea. I want you all to cooperate and obey his orders. Anyone who doesn't will answer to me and the boatswain. Understood?' there was a loud chorus of 'Aye Aye skipper' from the tired men.

The ship was made fast to wait for the next tide when they hoped to get her nearer the beach.

The captain called all the officers together, including Norman. We will have to cut and shape a new mast.

'Impossible,' muttered one officer.

'Nothing is impossible,' said the captain, glaring at the officer in question. 'It will take time and lots of effort. Norman is in charge of the making and fitting of the mast.'

Norman gulped. What a task. How did one set about that? All the officers turned in his direction, glad they had not been chosen for the task. 'You can have your pick of the officers and men to help you and they will be answerable to you alone. Keep me in touch with the progress. Dismiss all of you. Norman, stay behind.

'I have chosen you for this task, Norman, because it requires technical knowledge, common sense and mathematical knowhow, all of which I think you possess. It's not going to be easy, but as you can see, it's a job we have to do or we are marooned on this island. I think I have found which island it is but won't know till later when the sun is up.

Make a good job of this, son, and it will carry a lot of weight for future promotion.'

'Thank you sir,' said Norman with a smile. I don't think anyone was jealous of me having been given this job of fitting a new mast.'

'If you need any help, let me know. Alright, off you go.'

Norman went to his cabin which was rain-soaked. He was looking for some dry paper and drawing instruments so he could work out some calculations. The men were busy ferrying stores to the shore. Many of them thought this was fun. It was like a holiday on a tropical island which they were desperate to explore. It was fortunate that the broken mast was still attached to the ship as this would be a great help in modelling a replacement.

Meanwhile he inspected the stump of mast which remained and knew this would have to be removed. It was no use now anyway, except for dimensions. He knew he had to copy the original mast as much as possible. It was a good job the mast to be replaced was one of the smaller ones, but still essential to the ship's steerage and power; they still had a long way to go home.

It took all day to measure the broken mast remaining in the bowels of the ship, and figure out how to remove it. The men he nominated to help him were very keen and gave some good advice as to how the job might be done. One old chap by the name of Charlie said he was on a ship where the same thing had happened and told Norman how they went about it.

It was evening, and there was still no sign of the three men who had been sent to search for a suitable tree to be used as the material for the mast. Norman told the captain, who instructed that an armed search party be sent out with torches to try and find the men. Six men volunteered, led by a ship's officer. Not Norman this time – he had enough on his plate.

The broken steering wheel and its housing had been removed. This replacement was also a tricky operation; the ship's carpenter certainly had a lot to do. The captain estimated it would take two months to complete the work; not that the men objected very much.

At three in the morning Norman was woken by the clattering of boots and chatter as the search party returned.

'What happened, are they back?' he asked a crew member, in a low voice.

'No, they have been taken hostage and are being held to ransom. There was no time to negotiate,' said the officer in charge of the search party.

'Who is holding them?' asked the captain, coming into the room.

'The islanders, they said they will cut off their heads off if we don't deal.'

'What do they want?' asked the captain.

'They didn't say, I suppose anything we can offer, sir.'

'That gives us plenty of scope. Did you see our sailors, are they well?'

'It appeared so, sir. I saw them tied up under a tree, we couldn't get near them. One shouted, "Get us out of here."'

'We can't do anything till tomorrow. Go back to your beds,' the captain told his men.

Norman lay back on his pillow. How were they going to get out of this one? he wondered. Two hours later Norman awoke, he couldn't sleep so went up on deck. It was a moonlit night. He heard voices coming from shore and looked in their direction. He could see black men with torches moving amongst the trees at the jungle edge. Norman was concerned because he knew there were stores and men on the beach. He decided to wake the captain. He knocked loudly on the door as the captain was snoring loudly.

'Come in,' he heard.

'Captain, there is a large party of natives on the beach in the area where our stores are, and we have men there as well.'

'Is there? Right Norman,' he said swinging his bare legs clear of his bunk. 'Give me two minutes and I'll be ready.'

True to his word he was up on deck with Norman, only this time he had a telescope with him and could make out more details.

'Yes, the bastards are pinching our stores. We will send an armed party to recover them. You stay here in case they invade the boat.' They left at dawn. Norman, as instructed, stayed on the ship. There were only six crew left. About forty minutes later Norman could hear rifle shots and knew then they were having trouble. He felt frustrated at not knowing what was going on, but knew he dare not leave the ship.

There was more sporadic firing, and then a lull. Eventually he saw a lot of men returning along the beach carrying goods that had been stolen from them, and through his telescope he saw that the other members of the crew were there with them. He was pleased because unless they could work with the islanders he doubted that they would ever fit the new mast. He saw they were carrying one man on a stretcher, so they weren't entirely without casualties.

Once the crew were back on board Norman went to see the captain.

'How did you get on, sir?' asked Norman.

'Well, it was touch and go to start with. They had all our men lined up and were preparing to chop their heads off when we turned up. I lined the men up with their loaded rifles and pistols and when I gave the command they fired above the native's heads. It worked; they ran into the bush frightened. We reloaded and pointed our weapons at them. I then got our best marksman to shoot at a seagull and do something impressive. So he shot this bird flying overhead and it dropped from the sky, dead, at the chief's feet. He was most impressed.'

'We approached each other and I handed him a gun as a present and showed him how to shoot it. He was delighted. I then gave them all some tobacco and we had a smoke together. By the end of that time we were friendly and they let us have our men and our stores back. The chief signalled that he and his men would cut the tree down our men had selected to be the new mast, and deliver it to us on the beach.'

'Well done, sir,' said Norman. 'What about the casualty? I saw one man on a stretcher.'

'Oh, he broke his leg last night in the dark, nothing more serious than that.' Even as he spoke, one could hear the isolated rifle shot from the native's camp.

'Well done sir,' said the boatswain. 'It certainly seems to have done the trick.'

The next day, true to their word, they brought the log round and left it on the shore. They waved in a friendly fashion as they departed, shooting their guns in the air.

'That was a close experience. I don't want to go through that again. They meant business when they demonstrated they were going to cut the crew's heads off.'

'I agree sir,' said the carpenter. 'I feared the worst.'

Norman set three of the men to de-rig the broken mast, whilst he and two other men went to choose a suitable tree for a new ships wheel. The old one was smashed beyond repair.

'We haven't thrown the old steering wheel away have we Bert? Because we will need that as a pattern.'

'No, Sir. I had the crew collect up all the bits and put it in the sail locker.'

'Good fellow,' said Norman. I think making the new steering wheel is going to require more skill than the mast.'

'Aye, I think your right there,' said Bert.

They made sure they were armed. They weren't taking any chances; especially with these natives.

They found a suitable tree, about a mile from the shore. It was thirty feet high and the branches didn't start till fifteen of them. It appeared ideal. It was straight and there weren't a lot of other trees stopping it falling. The three of them set to work cutting it down. It was hard work, they were all sweating profusely. After an hour their efforts showed little results. The wood was teak. Norman realised he would have to get the men out here working in shifts.

'We are being watched,' somebody whispered.

Norman turned round and a group of natives, fully armed with blow pipes and machetes, were standing and commenting on their efforts.

Norman smiled at them. It's surprising how disarming a smile can be. Anyhow it had the desired effect; they approached the tree and signalled they would like to have a go. Norman handed one an axe. My, this native certainly knew how to use one He cut twice as many wood chops than the sailors and after twenty minutes gave the axe to one of his comrades to take over.

Even for these men the tree was hard work, and they all decided that would do for today. So, with cheery goodbyes, each party went their separate ways. It took four days before the tree was down, stripped of its branches and ready to be towed to the beech. The natives stood watching with their chief as the sea men puffed and grunted trying to move the tree. Norman signalled to the chief to come to him – which he did. Norman pointed to himself and said his name, repeating it several times and trying to convey to the chief he should tell him his.

Eventually, the chief caught on, and with a big grin, banged himself on the chest and said 'Wango-Bango,' which everybody addressing him abbreviated to *Wango*. The black chief Wango was dressed in nothing but a skimpy loincloth, just enough to cover his credentials. His body was covered with various coloured stripes and from his earlobes hung boar's teeth. However, he had a very cheerful nature and a big smile.

Norman tried to ask Wango to help pull the tree. The chief was no fool and showed them he wanted payment in powder and tobacco. Norman took it on himself to agree and sent a messenger back to the ship to ask the captain to release it to pay the natives. They broke out into big smiles when they had been paid and the entire village turned out to help pull the tree to the beach. It was well worth the payment.

It took another week of chipping away at the trunk to get the same dimensions as the old mast. A week later the new mast was ready to fit. There was still a great deal of work yet to be done. The mast had to be got aboard and lowered into the hole made for it in the deck. Wango was very helpful and the seamen and natives became very friendly. Some of the men showed interest in the girls but the captain said any man trying to achieve sexual satisfaction with a native girl would be whipped.

One day when everybody seemed to be busy, a scream was heard from the jungle near to the native's home site. It sounded like a terribly frightened girl. She came out of the bush and ran into the arms of one of the natives. There was a party of them heading towards Norman's group working on the beach. They were jabbering away, very angry and agitated.

Wango stopped in front of Norman and pointed to the crying girl, and by making obvious signs indicated that someone, a seaman, had tried to rape this girl. They demanded he be punished. Norman couldn't authorise it and tried to calm the aggrieved party down while he spoke to his captain. Norman saw the captain on deck with his telescope to his eye, and he signalled that his presence was wanted on shore. A boat was lowered and the captain came to join the shore party and listen to the accusation.

'Who is the culprit?' he turned, and asked Norman.

'Without doing a roll call, sir, I don't know. I can account for the ones I had working with me.'

'Right, order a head count and roll call,' he ordered.

It was obvious the captain was very annoyed. God help the culprit when he was caught. The roll call was done and one man, Geordie Falmouth, was found missing. This man, because he was always swearing, had been nicknamed by the crew, Geordie Foulmouth.

'I might have known it would be him. Send a party to find him and bring him to me here,' the captain demanded.

An officer and four men set off with the natives to their village to find the villain. He wasn't difficult to find, in fact he came forward as the search party found him. The officer in charge told him he was being arrested and need not say anything yet. He came willingly, with one man on either side of him.

They stopped in front of the ship's captain who had set up a kangaroo-type court on the beach.

'Norman, you will be his defence council; Mr Jordan, you will be the accuser and I will be the judge. There will be no jury.'

The natives stood to the side watching. It seemed unbelievable, but it appeared they understood.

'I will hear from the prosecution first.'

'Sir. I object I haven't had chance to have a word with my client yet. Surely if this court is just, I should be allowed a few minutes to hear his story.'

'Very well, Norman, but don't drag it out. Tell me when you are ready.'

Norman took the accused to one side and asked him for his version of what went on. It was all very straightforward.

'I am ready sir,' said Norman.

'Right, the court is open. I will hear from the prosecution.'

'Sir,' said Mr Jordan. 'Today at approximately three o'clock this afternoon a scream was heard from the lady on my left, and when questioned by her father she said that the accused, Gordon Falmouth, had assaulted her and tried to rape her.'

'How does the accused plead to this charge?' demanded the captain.

'Not guilty, sir,' said Norman.

'I will hear from the defence.'

'Sir, my client assures me he did not intend to rape the lady, but kiss her. He did not touch any parts of her.'

'What does the prosecution say to that?' said the judge

'We maintain that as the defendant admits to trying to kiss her, in this instance that is the same, in this lady's case, as rape. Also sir, you have made it clear that if any of the crew touch a native, he will be whipped. By his own admission he is guilty.'

'Hmm, a very good point, Mr Jordan. Has the defence anything to add?'

Norman was having a quick word with the defendant.

'Yes, sir, my client says he is in love with the maiden and it was natural that he should want to kiss her.'

'Rubbish. He can't love a black girl. Whatever next; never heard anything so ludicrous in my life? These people don't kiss. They fuck yes, but they don't kiss. That's what white men do. I find the defendant guilty and he is sentenced to ten lashes which will be delivered by the boatswain.'

He banged the butt of his pistol on an empty barrel and stood up.

A rack was assembled with wooden spars and rope and the defendant had his shirt ripped from his back and was tied to the wooden rack. The boatswain produced a long wicked cat-o- nine-tails and flicked it in the air to make sure it wasn't tangled. The officer stuck a piece of wood in the defendant's mouth to bite on when those cruel whiplashes scored his back and drew blood. He would carry these scars for the rest of his life.

The boatswain was about to swing the cat when there was a scream from the young girl.

'No! No,' she shouted.

She turned and gabbled to her father. He argued with her, but the whipping stopped before it had begun. Everyone looked at the injured party. What was going on?

'I love him,' she said.

'You speak English,' said Norman. 'How, when?'

'I speak a little, Geordie teaches me. We in love.'

'Oh, no,' said the captain in disbelief. 'I have heard it all now.'

'No hit, he my Geordie,' she said. 'Please.'

'Untie him,' said the captain.

Everybody burst out laughing. Nothing like this had ever been seen on the high seas before.

10   *Rapid Romance*

EANWHILE, back on the sheep farm, life was continuing as normal. Beatrice still couldn't get over the disappearance of Norman. There had been no word; it was as if he had vanished off the face of the Earth. There was no way that she and Charles could possibly guess as to the real reason he had vanished. Despite this Beatrice and Charles hung on to their belief that Norman could take care of himself and would turn up one day.

Charles went into town and sought out the constable. He reported the fire of his barns and the fact that the hoof mark of the horse was a decoy. The constable listened to Charles's story and made a few notes.

'I wonder why this gang has a vendetta against you. After all, there are plenty of other sheep farms to pick on,' said Toby Trucker, the Constable.

'I don't know, but I am not going to sit here and let them rob us and destroy our barns. If this means a shooting match and you can't protect us, then it will have to be. We won't start it, but we will finish it,' said Charles, in a very determined voice.

'Can't say I blame you. If you need my help, call on me.'

'I will, Constable.'

'And thanks for keeping me informed,' said Toby, as Charles shook hands with him, prior to leaving the office.

Bob decided, purely on a hunch, that they would patrol the far side of the grasslands belonging to the farm. This was about five miles from where the first rustling attacks took place. He nominated six men to go with him. This time he left Bluey at the ranch, he usually took his brother along. The Constable was with them tonight. He was invited by Charles to come along. There was no guarantee the rustlers would be there tonight; but they wanted to catch them if they were.

Charles did not want a gun fight, but if there was one he would like to have the Constable along to adjudicate.

The six of them rode as silently as they could to where they thought the rustlers might strike. Two weeks had passed since the barn fire and Charles hoped this might be an end to it. Suddenly Bob held up his hand to bring his riders to a halt. There was quite close the distinctive sound of horsemen who were making their way in the same direction as the farm crew.

The rustlers had no reason to be on the land anyway as it was all part of Charles's registered farmland and nobody should be there uninvited. Bob signalled to his men they should circle the intruders so they couldn't escape.

'Don't fire a shot till they do,' he commanded his men. They nodded to show they understood. They took up their positions, and waited.

'I want to catch them red-handed trying to rustle the sheep,' Bob whispered to Toby. Toby nodded, he could see the sense in that. They needed firm evidence to convict them. The night wasn't very bright. In fact it was a bit misty which didn't help, though it was ideal for the rustlers. The rustlers cut the wires and rode in quietly amongst the sleeping sheep. They were very practised at this.

'Halt. This is the constable. Drop your guns and come out here in an orderly manner,' he shouted.

Two pistol shots were fired in the constable's direction. Immediately the farm crew returned the fire. Two of the rustlers fell from their horse. The remainder galloped off into the night. Bob and his men didn't chase after them. Instead they looked at the two men. One was dead, but the other was conscious and able to talk.

'Tell us what we want to know and you could save yourself from the hangman's rope,' said Toby.

'Go to hell,' said the rustler, defiantly.

'OK, have it your own way. It means you will take the blame for all the gang. Do you think for one moment they would bother to save your life? You're living in fool's paradise if you do,' said Bob.

The rustler who had two bullets in him, one in the shoulder and one in the leg, screamed as the crew showed no remorse when they lifted him onto a horse to take him to a doctor, and then to jail. He didn't say a word as they rode back to town. He was in pain and his mind was confused as to what he should do.

'There is a good chance the gang may try and kill you so you can't tell on them,' said Toby.

'It's more likely they will get me out of jail,' the rustler said.

'Not my jail they won't,' said Toby, with a smile of conviction.

They called at the doctors who, without a great deal of sympathy, managed to probe and get the bullets out. He bandaged the wounds up.

'OK, Toby, you can put him in jail,' he said.

Toby did just that and left him till morning, by which time the prisoner had had plenty of time to think.

'Have you thought about the hangman's rope?' Toby asked the rustler.

'My friends will get me out of here,' he replied.

'What's your name?'

'Jimmy Delores.'

'I've heard of you before. You used to ride with the Pathway mob,' said Toby.

'Fame travels,' he responded.

Toby left him with his thoughts. He sent a telegraph asking the judge to hold court when he next visited Victoria. Toby was alert to the fact that an attempt might be made to free the prisoner. The jail wasn't very secure, and the cages were wood, not metal. They were going to be converted when the new jail was built, but there was no sign of that. If it was an organised raid on the jail then unless Toby was properly prepared it could be a success. He beckoned his deputy, Mike James, to come over.

'Mike, I fear we may have a raid on the jail. See if you can round up four other guys to help man the jail in case they try anything.'

'Sure boss, leave it to me. Are we paying them?'

'Two dollars each a night, that's all we can afford,' said Toby.

An hour later Mike came back to report that he had recruited four reliable men who would be at the jailhouse at six o'clock that evening.

Toby was very relieved to hear this. He would be ready for them now. Sure enough, the men turned up. Three were posted outside, and one inside. That evened the numbers up. It was a long wait, and Toby thought it was all in vain.

At two o'clock in the morning four horsemen rode silently into the town. They had covered the horses' hooves to prevent noise, and the bridles were covered to stop the jangling. All the gang wore black. It seemed they were well prepared for this break. Suddenly the general store burst into flames. The alarm went up and all hands were got out of bed in the town to help put out the fire.

'Shall we go and help, boss?' asked one of the volunteers.

'No, you all stay at your posts and keep alert. This fire could be a diversion set by the rustlers as part of the jail break.'

Suddenly, the four horsemen road up to the jail, firing their pistols. The volley of shots they got in return shocked them as they didn't expect the jail to be so well fortified. Two men let out a yell and fell from their horses. The other two turned and fled.

That night four men tried to release the prisoner and two of them died in the process.

'Well, are you convinced now?' asked Toby, after the failed breakout.

'Yes. What do you want to know?' Jimmy Delores, asked him.

'Tell me all you know about the gang – who's in it? Where do they hang out? Everything.'

'Will that save me from the hangman's rope?' he asked.

'It will go a long way to saving your neck. The judge is here next week.'

'OK, write this down,' said Jimmy, getting prepared to tell all he knew. 'The gang members are Stew Richardson Alfie Dodd's and me; that's all that's left.'

'Why are they doing so much damage, burning barns and rustling the Redlocks farm?'

'They were told that small traces of gold had been found in the river that crosses the farm. We knew Redlock wouldn't sell, so we tried to make him bankrupt. It was our idea to put the infected sheep into the flock two years ago, hoping they would all get infected.'

There was a noise outside the jail. Toby looked up at the jail window. At that moment a hand came through the cell window, held by a masked man who shot the prisoner dead, and galloped off out of town before anyone could catch him.

Unfortunately the volunteers had gone home after the foiled attempt at the jail break, but someone didn't want the prisoner to talk. It seemed that one of the jail breakers had returned to kill Jimmy so he wouldn't talk; but he was too late. Mike ran outside, but in the darkness he couldn't see the killer. The fire across the road was under control and not too much damage had been done because the fire had been checked in time.

Toby knew it would be no use chasing after the killer but in the morning he wrote a WANTED poster for the other two robbers and murderers. Then he posted it up outside the jailhouse.

*

Beatrice looked out of the lounge window of the farmhouse and saw Charles driving in the horse and trap like a madman. It was as if he were being chased by a mob of blood-crazed wild dogs. He pulled the horse to a lathered halt, leapt from the trap and ran into the house.

'Beatrice,' he shouted. 'Look what I have. It's a telegraph from Norman. He's safe and well. I just popped into the telegraph office hoping and curious to see if we had a message, and to my surprise this was waiting for me. It has been waiting a week for me to pick it up.'

Charles was so excited; he just kept jabbering on. Beatrice took the telegraph and read it. Her heart swelled with joy at the wonderful news that their son was enjoying an adventure, the like of which they had no knowledge of.

'Isn't it wonderful news, darling, our son is safe and well.' Her face showed the joy and relief from worry she had endured for nearly twelve months.

'I wonder what he's been doing,' she mused.

'I don't know but I don't mind waiting now I know my son is safe and well.'

She leant over and kissed Charles. He was a good father to his family.

*

Back on the *Sea Vixen* the work was finished. The mast was fitted and the rudder fixed and it had only taken ten weeks. It had been hard and very hot work. They couldn't have managed it without the help of the island's native population. Captain Vic Masters found out the reason why they had such a bad reception when they arrived. The reason was that the last lot of white men to visit the island had killed three of the natives and raped a young girl.

'Would you really have chopped the heads of my men off when we landed?' asked the captain.

'Yes we would. It was only ten years ago we would have eaten them as well,' said Wango. 'Now we are friends.' He smiled, showing off his white sharp pointed teeth.

The old chief spoke good English from contact with traders who visited the island when he was a boy. The white men were welcome to trade and the islanders showed them friendship, as long as they did the same.

'How is it you didn't speak English when we first met?' asked Vic.

The old man had a smile on his face when he replied, 'I am no fool. I let you think I don't understand your language, this gives me an advantage till I want to use it.'

'You crafty old devil. I want to give you all the stores I can spare because of the good work you have done.'

'Thank you, and when are you leaving?'

'I am going to do some sea trials, and if everything is good then we sail from here in seven days.'

'We shall miss you. What about my daughter. She is in love with Geordie?'

'I don't know. We can't take her with us. I think Geordie will have to come back for her one day, don't you,' said the captain, with a grin. The old chief nodded his head in agreement.

They managed to launch the *Sea Vixen* on the new tide. She looked fine after all the work spent on her. The crew and the islanders gave a loud cheer when she floated clear of the beach. The sea trials were a great success. The new wheel worked well and the mast seemed to be better than the original one. The captain called Norman into his cabin.

'Sit down Norman. Will you have glass of port wine with me?' he asked, reaching for the decanter, and two glasses.

'Yes please sir.'

'Norman, you have done a magnificent job in getting the *Sea Vixen* ready for sea.'

'I did the thinking and planning, it was the crew and the natives we have to thank. Everybody was so cooperative.'

'I know I shall be sorry to leave the island. It has done the men good to relax, as well as work. We set sail tomorrow. The sea trials were good and I think we will make Melbourne in two weeks if the winds are kind to us.' said Vic. 'You do still want to study to be an officer, don't you?'

'Yes, sir of course I do.'

'Right, what I want to know is do you want to remain an officially listed member of my crew and sail with me again?'

'Yes, Captain, that's exactly what I do want to do.'

'Fine Norman, I will put your name forward as a junior officer on my crew. Would you like that?'

'Yes I would, thank you sir.'

'Welcome aboard,' said Vic, shaking hands with him. He then handed Norman a refill from the decanter, and wished him luck.

*

The remainder of the journey back to Melbourne was pretty uneventful after what they had gone through. All the crew were eager to get on dry land again and meet their loved ones and friends. Norman was no exception.

It was four days later that Beatrice, who was tidying the flowerbeds in her garden, happened to look up when hearing the dogs give their alarm and saw a buggy coming to the farm and the occupant waving wildly. She put her hand to her eyes so she could focus on who it was, and to her surprise and delight it was Norman. As soon as the carriage stopped she couldn't help but notice that a man had come home in place of her young scholarly son Norman. She ran down the path to greet him.

'Oh Norman,' she cried with tears of joy, 'you have come home at last. It has been nearly twelve months. Where have you been?'

'At sea, Mother, I am a sailor now. I am training to be a ship's captain.'

She was so proud of him. He was tall and tanned by the sun. His hands were large and strong, through pulling on the ropes of the boat. He was broad shouldered, with a handsome, shaven face. His two sisters came running to greet him.

'Oh Norman how wonderful to see you again.' they said; flinging their arms round his neck, and kissing him.

'Come on, let's not waste time, come inside, Norman. You will have plenty of time to tell us what you have been up to.'

They ushered him in and Charles, who heard the excitement, came to join them. He was naturally overjoyed at seeing his son, and felt very proud of him. He had sent a boy away to university and twelve months later he had a sea-hardened man in his home. What a fine specimen he was too.

Bruce was very pleased to see his big brother, especially when Norman gave him some weapons he had got from the natives where he repaired the *Sea Vixen*.

Norman took nearly an hour telling his family about his adventures. They all listened attentively and interjected sometimes when he described some unbelievable incident.

'How long are you home for?' asked Ann.

'I have to report back on the *Sea Vixen* in two weeks' time. How have things been on the farm?'

Charles then went on to bring him up to date with the death of Alex, and the rustling, and the burning down of the barn. Norman listened enthralled at all that had gone on in his absence.

After he had rested, Norman went out to look around the farm and saw the replacement barn which had been built. He was very impressed. He was introduced to Bob and his brother Bluey. He could see they were fine, reliable fellows. Being men of the world they laughed and joked together. He liked them, they were good guys.

Norman spent much of his time studying from his books. Beatrice was most impressed and made sure he wasn't interrupted. Two days later Norman decided to take a ride into town and took Bluey along as company. They headed for the small town of Werribee. It had been a good twelve months since Norman last called in for a beer.

They tied up their horses on the hitching rail and went to the telegraph office. There was a message that Aunt Betsy had died. Norman knew that although it was expected, neither his father nor mother would receive the news gladly and both would be very upset, especially as they were so far away, and he knew they would have loved to attend her funeral. He also knew that they realised when they went to England last year that the chances of ever seeing either his Grandma Sally or Aunt Betsy were very slight.

'Do you fancy a beer, Norman?' asked Blue.

'Where? In there?' asked Norman.

'Yes, why not?'

'Yes OK, only you see, Blue, last year before I went to sea I came in here and all the beer drinkers laughed me out of the place, saying I shouldn't be drinking beer – but milk?'

'You're not worried today are you, mate?'

'No way, lead on.' The two of them walked into the pub and up to the bar.

'Two beers please,' said Blue.

The landlord didn't say anything, but he smiled at Norman, in recognition.

'Hey, it's the kid from the milk farm,' shouted one bigmouth.

Somehow the other drinkers in the bar who had been in before when Norman came in could see the difference in him. He was taller, broader; he was a man, and a man you didn't tangle with. They, without exception, preferred to keep their peace.

'Are you talking to me sir?' asked Norman.

The bigmouth realised he was on his own this time. 'No, sorry I was just joking, no offence,' he said, trying to crawl inside his glass of beer with embarrassment.

'No offence taken,' said Norman, raising his glass to the fellow in salutation. He turned back to the bar.

'Those two men sitting over there together are two of the men that rustled our sheep.' said Blue

'Are you sure?'

'Yes, I saw them twice. I am sure.'

'Don't look at them. I'll go over and get the constable,' said Norman. Acting as casually as he could he left the bar and ran over to the constable's office.

'Constable, I'm Norman, Charles Relock's son. I am having a drink in the bar with one of my dad's workmen, who says he recognises two men in the bar as rustlers of our sheep. Will you come over and affect an arrest?'

'I've been looking for these two for months,' he said. 'They got a brass neck coming in here. I'll come right over,' He snatched a loaded shotgun from behind his desk. The two of them entered the bar just as the two rustlers were leaving.

'Hold it there, you two,' said Toby, cocking his gun.

'The hell I will,' said the tall one, snatching for a long barrel pistol hidden inside his coat. It was instantaneous, him pulling his pistol into view, and Toby firing his shotgun at him. It caught him full in the chest. The rustler dropped like a hot penny.

'Who's next?' said Toby menacingly.

'I am,' said the shorter rustler, pulling his pistol out. 'I know your shotgun is single shot, and you ain't got no more bullets left in it. So now it's my turn,' said the rustler raising the pistol in line with Toby's chest. 'Goodbye const... Blast!' He shouted, as a six-inch blade knife was suddenly seen to be protruding from his pistol hand causing him to drop the cocked weapon on the floor, and grasp his hand in agony.

'Who the hell threw that?' he demanded.

'I did,' said Norman. 'I mastered the art of knife throwing when I was on an island in the Atlantic. But that's a long story and you haven't got time to listen because you're going to prison. Take him away constable,' said Norman, recovering his knife.

Once the prisoner had gone and the dead body removed, you couldn't stop wellwishers coming up and congratulating Norman, and wanting to buy him a drink.

Having got the prisoner locked up Toby came back to the bar.

'Norman, thanks a lot, you did a grand job, and hey, what about that knife-throwing? That was really slick.'

Norman's reputation as a young man not to fool with, soon got round.

One of the first things Norman felt he wanted to do was to revisit Betty and Clare. In fact Clare in particular as he had found her very attractive and had a likeable personality and sense of humour similar to his own. He wrote her a letter, asking if he might call as it would be rude to turn up unannounced. His letter received a very encouraging reply inviting him to their house the following Monday. Norman was there on time, suitably dressed to impress the young lady.

'Come in, Norman. You must tell us what you have been up to,' said Betty, ushering him into the front room. Clare was sitting there very demure and innocent, with her hands in her lap, waiting for him. Norman walked up to her, took her gloved hand and kissed it. He realised that he was being old-fashioned. Courtship had progressed from mother's day. But the present house and company somehow insisted these quaint practices should still be exercised.

'How nice to see you again, Clare,' he said.

She smiled at him. 'Thank you, Norman. My, how you have changed from that meek, demure boy who called on us a year ago. You are truly a man now,' she said with pride and astonishment.

'Come, sit by me and tell me of your adventures.'

Once more Norman recited his adventures.

'And you say you are studying to become a sea captain, how ambitious Norman,' said Betty, entering the room halfway through his talking. There followed a lot of small talk about their families and Norman knew this wasn't the reason he had called to see Clare.

'Clare, would you take a walk in the garden with me as it's a fine warm day?'

She looked at her mother for approval.

'Yes my dear, why don't you. I am sure you have lots to talk about.'

He took her arm and led her into the garden. It was a large garden – too much for Betty to look after – so she must be employing a gardener, he thought. There was a rose-covered bower on the lawn with a seat inside.

'Come Clare, let's sit here a while.' She gave him a demurring smile; this was obviously a new experience for Clare. He took her hand, 'Would you like to walk out with me Clare. I find you very beautiful and would be the proudest man to walk with you on my arm.

'That is very nice of you, Norman. Nobody has ever asked me before.'

'Well?' he questioned her.

'Yes, I would like that.'

'That's wonderful. May I ask you for a kiss to seal our arrangement?'

She turned to face him with eyes shut and lips tightly closed. Norman, who hadn't kissed many girls in his life, knew this could be improved on. But contented himself with pressing his lips against hers.

'That was nice,' he said, courteously. 'Will your mother allow you out without a chaperone?'

'I would hope so, as you are very distant family,' she said with a smile.

'Can I call tomorrow?'

'Yes please.'

'Shall we go into the big city together and have some luncheon?'

'Oh yes please,' she said, her eyes lighting up at the thought of the fun and the freedom on offer.

They returned to the house and Clare told her mother most of what had been said and done together, leaving out the kiss. Betty agreed to Clare going unchaperoned. So they said their goodbyes till next day.

They saw each other every day after that and Norman felt he need look no further for a bride as Clare would entirely suit his requirements. They walked often together, becoming more and more adventurous in their handling of each other as their affection grew. Both of them realised time was short as he was due back to sea in ten days. Their kissing had developed into something quite exceptional. She soon realised how it should be done and they spent a lot of time practising it.

'My darling, I realise time is short and soon I shall have to go to sea. I shall miss you beyond words and yet my body burns with desire for you. I have never made love to another, but how I yearn for you.'

'And I too, my darling. How fast the days have flown and what a transition has passed between us. Dare we attempt to make love together?'

'Your mother is at Woman's Guild until ten tonight, it is only just past seven, so time is on our side. What say you?' Without a moment's hesitation she agreed and took him to her room.

'You know, Mother thinks we are at ballet tonight, so she does not know we are home, and we didn't know ballet would be cancelled through illness, my love.'

They stood together in the candlelight of the room and with in a moment both of them were clawing at each other's clothes to undress. Neither had much idea of the fastenings in each other garments, but within minutes they had both managed to achieve complete nakedness; two beautiful examples of youth and virility stood for a moment in the glow of the fast dying candle glow.

He pulled her to him and crushed their lips together, his hands running down her back, over her bum and round between her legs where he exercised his finger on her tiny clitoris. She in turn was a little slow in examining his body and he had to take her hand and place it on his hard, throbbing knob. He had seen many men's pricks whilst in the navy and realised he had been well endowed with a big one; she grasped it and gasped at it its size. Pulling the covers back he lay her on the cast iron, brass embellished bed. They sank together in the centre. He gazed down at her.

'You are the most beautiful girl I have ever seen and the only girl I want. Will you be my wife, Clare?'

'Yes darling, oh this is madness, it's only just over a week we have known each other and I love you.'

He ran his hands over her beautifully formed breasts, the nipples already standing proud as he bent down fondling and sucking and kissing them. She had a deliciously slim warm beautiful body. She parted her legs and he lay between them. From that moment on she was a virgin no longer. They worked together in rhythm; neither wanting it to finish. Eventually Norman could stand the thrill of the sensation no more and emptied himself into her.

She in return welcomed him and they stayed together for a full ten minutes before the moment had passed and they lay back happy and satisfied. They managed to make love twice more before they knew they would have to straighten the bed out before Betty came home. They got up and tidied the room.

'Oh Norman, that was wonderful. Before you came into my life I never thought ... well I thought I would remain an old maid. My mother never encouraged callers of the male sex.'

'Perhaps we have been hasty, my darling, but we both wanted each other and I will be away from you for weeks.'

'Perhaps I will have a baby, Norman. Would you like that? I know I would. Imagine our own child – someone for me to love when you are miles away at sea.'

The thought had crossed his mind. 'It's all in the lap of the gods,' he said.

Two days later he went back to his ship.

11 *Ann*

WHILE NORMAN was making a name for himself at sea, Ann was also forging a career for herself in nursing. She was nearly two years younger than Norman and, being a girl, she wasn't entitled or indeed considered eligible for a career. Also she was too young to insist on her rights, as she was still a child in the eyes of the law and under parental control for many years to come. And even when she was old enough to think for herself, a girl of Ann's age still had to be steered by parental approval.

Ann took after her mother in her love of the countryside and farming. She had developed tremendously since coming out to Australia. No longer was she the shy mummy's girl that she once was. She had taken on responsibilities of a working man, just like Beatrice had done when she was a young girl. On a place like the Redlock farm, a woman found herself rolling her sleeves up and mucking in with the men on the many tasks there were to do. Because of this Ann had taken onboard many of their skills.

She could: ride, shoot a bird in flight, and fish as good as any man; besides she could cook clean and run a house; so as far as talent went she was streets ahead of the nearest male equivalent.

However, like her mother she yearned for a career of her own and, as her mother was a nurse and there was still very little choice for girls, she chose to be a nurse. Ann had studied the profession, though it was in its infancy then.

Before 1868 when Miss Lucy Osborne came on the scene there was no such thing as nursing. The care of the sick was up till that date taken care of by convicts; usually those convicts who were too infirm to carry out manual duties. There was no care or respect for the sick, in fact quite the reverse, and the nursing staff would very often come in drunk and satisfy their sexual appetites on beds which had not had their linen changed for weeks. One stood more chance of dying inside the hospital than out, they were so filthy and disease ridden.

However, when a protégé of Florence Nightingale came on the scene she turned things round drastically in hospitals. The wards were cleaned, beds were changed regularly, and the whole attitude changed. Nursing had come of age and would never look back.

It was into this modern climate of nursing that Ann was entering. Her mother, Beatrice, had in many ways been responsible for the high standards the hospitals enjoyed. She was going to the newly opened Prince Albert Hospital in Sydney which had only opened the year before in 1882.

Ann found it was all that she hoped it would be. She was made welcome as a student nurse. She was one of the first as it was such a new profession. Many people were waiting to see how they progressed before letting their sons and daughters join the nursing profession. Like her brother Norman she was a glutton for knowledge. She studied hard and learnt and practised.

'I can see your mother in you,' said Lucy Osborne to the young nurse as she passed down the ward one day. 'It's just what the Australian nursing profession wants is girls of your calibre. One day, to her surprise, she was told she had to take her turn in the operating theatre. She had seen the inside of one but had never helped in one. She was made to scrub her hands and arms and put on a white gown. There were four men and three trained nurses and herself. Ann tended to stand back, not sure what she was meant to do.

'Are you new here nurse?' asked a handsome, brown-eyed, male doctor. He didn't appear much older than she was; he was beautiful, even with a cotton mask on.

'Yes doctor, it's my first day.'

'Well, pay attention and you will learn how things are done,' he said, turning back to the fat old gentleman they were preparing to cut open.

Ann moved in closer. She heard the doctor call for various instruments and the assistant nurse helping him usually managed to hand him the correct item when he called for it.

Sometimes he got angry when handed the wrong one. This was one thing Ann was determined to learn, the name of all the instruments in the surgery and what their role was.

The operation lasted two hours and the room was very hot. The doctor was pouring with sweat and a nurse was there just to bathe his forehead so that sweat didn't run into his eyes and blur his vision. When he had finished he stormed out of the operating theatre without saying a word.

Surgeon James Morrison had noticed Ann Redlock. He couldn't speak to her in the theatre but he had seen her and found her beautiful. Ann paraded out of the theatre with the others but not before it was spotless and everything put away. She went into a cloakroom to remove her gown and put on her nursing uniform. As she was leaving the cloakroom she literally bumped into James Morrison, the surgeon.

'Sorry doctor,' said Ann.

'No, it was my fault; always in too much of a rush,' he said with a laugh. They both stood there for a moment, each lost for words, but wanting to say something.

'My name is James Morrison.'

'And I am Ann Redlock. Trainee nurse,' she said shyly.

'Pleased to make your acquaintance Ann Redlock, will you take tea with me after work on the terrace?'

'I would be delighted sir,' she said.

'It's not sir. It's James or Jim – whichever you prefer. Mother always calls me James.'

'Then I will too, James,' she laughed, her eyes twinkling with her vitality and happiness. He was a little embarrassed, not quite knowing how to end this conversation.

'Right then, till four o'clock. Goodbye.' he said, as he dashed off.

Ann watched him go. This was her first date ever, and with a surgeon. What would her mother say? Ann made a point of being a little late for her date. She saw James look at his watch before she made her appearance. He stood up to greet her, and kissed her hand politely.

'My, you are gracious, James. Are we out to make an impression?' she asked with a happy smile.

'Indeed I am. That was the way father taught me to act.'

'Have you have had many lady friends, James?' she asked mischievously.

'Er, no, not many. One or two acquaintances rather than lady friends,' he said. 'How about you?'

'None, up to now?

'What was the problem? Work or lack of opportunity?'

'Certainly not the latter; I lived on a sheep farm with lots of men.'

'I have heard excellent reports from the matrons about the quality of your nursing and your thirst for knowledge. I find it very impressive. It makes a big difference to a surgeon knowing he can depend on those around him.'

'I do my best. How did you manage to finish up here?'

'I spent three years learning to be a doctor and two years being a surgeon. We, that is my bunch, were virtually the first properly trained to an acceptable standard of surgery. I studied in London.'

'Did you really? My mother was a matron at Florence Nightingale Hospital.'

'I can see where you get your nursing skills from,' they both laughed.

'Enough of work. Tell me where your home is?' she said.

I come from the smallest city in England, Wells in Somerset. Do you know it?'

'I have heard of it but never been there.'

'Perhaps you will allow me to take you one day,' he said.

'Perhaps. When is your next operation?'

'I thought we agreed not to talk about work.'

'I know, but I'm fascinated.'

'I have to remove a leg on Wednesday.'

'Can I help? Please.'

'Leave it to me, I will arrange it. Now as I have done you a favour, would you do one for me?'

'Alright. What is it?'

'Come to the theatre with me on Saturday evening? Say yes, Ann.'

'Alright. My answer is yes. I would love to come to the theatre.'

He grinned with happiness. 'I'm so happy, well ... I could cut both that fellow's legs off.'

They both chuckled merrily at this. Ann was looking forward to Wednesday when she would help James. She had learnt all the names of the instruments and was able to recognise them. She had also familiarised herself with the layout of the operating theatre, so it would appear she would be an asset in any operation.

The operating team took up their positions and James checked that Ann was to his left and next to the instruments. Ann had laid everything out as she would need them and was ready to commence. The operation was fairly straightforward as long as the instruments were to hand when needed.

'Scalpel,' called James.

Immediately Ann was there placing the scalpel firmly in his hand.

'Swab,' again it was ready for him.

'Forceps.' Ann grabbed them, misjudged them, and lost the grip. They went clattering on the floor.

'Forceps,' said James once more, angrily this time.

'Sorry, sir,' Ann said.

'It's alright, don't get flustered,' said James.

There was a pause while he worked on the leg.

'Forceps.' Again Ann missed his hand, and they bounced off the patient on to the floor.

'Can't you bloody pay attention and do your job properly. Get out of the way. Nurse Whitstock, come and relieve her.'

Ann turned, and dashed out of the theatre in tears. She had completely mucked everything up. She lay on her bed in her room, sobbing. She knew she only had herself to blame. She had been trying too hard.

When she left her room she avoided James. She couldn't stand the embarrassment. She was sitting having lunch on her own when suddenly he plonked himself down in the chair opposite.

'Can I join you?' he asked jovially.

She didn't look up, partly through embarrassment and partly because she was sulking.

'I suppose so.'

'Sorry about that little outburst of mine in the theatre. It is, I am afraid, an automatic reaction when one is under pressure. Nothing personal. Is that why you're sulking?'

'I'm not sulking ... I am ashamed of my clumsiness. It will never happen again I assure you.'

'Good. Shall I order for us both?'

'Yes please,' she replied. The next time she was working with James in the theatre things went very smoothly. He was pleased. Never again was there cause for complaint and she was very happy with her performance.

'I am going home this weekend to visit my parents. Will you come with me?'

'I don't know. I don't know what to say. It's all so sudden. I mean, going away with a comparative stranger ... Well, you have taken my breath away, James.'

'Oh come on Ann, don't be a fuddy-duddy-doodah. Say yes.' He waited for her reply.

'My answer is yes. Why not,' she beamed at him.

'Good, my mother will love you.'

'On conditions.'

'Yes, what?'

'That next time you come with me to my sheep farm.'

'I would really love to do that.'

So it was decided. Ann and James were constant companions and within the realms of decency, they were walking out together, but were not betrothed to each other.

On their first weekend off together they caught the train to Melbourne where James's parents live.

'My farm is only about fifty miles from here,' said Ann.

'Do you want to go and see them?'

'No, not this time. We will spend time with your parents now.'

Outside the station they got a taxi to James's house. It was a grand affair; built in 1800 in a Georgian style; plenty of windows and smart lawns. There was a wrought-iron gate and a driveway up to the house. Beautiful, well-kept flowerbeds and a gravel pathway gave the house and surroundings that air of being looked after and loved.

A lady and her dog were playing on the lawn and as soon as they saw who it was they came running to greet them. The cab stopped and James, being the perfect gentleman, helped Ann from the carriage.

'What a gorgeous place,' said Ann, in genuine admiration. 'It's so big and spacious. How lucky you are to live here,' she said, smiling into his eyes. He surprised her by gently kissing her on the forehead.

'Why, James, you kissed me. I was wondering how long I would have to wait,' she said, so very happy with him.

Both his parents came to the door to greet them.

'First let me introduce my little sister Sheila, and the hound we call scruffpot.'

Ann gave Sheila a little hug of affection. 'So pleased to make your acquaintance,' said Ann.

'And I likewise,' said Sheila. 'I'm glad somebody has managed to capture my brother's attention, he's been so wrapped up in his work, I thought he would never find a fair maiden as pretty as you, said Sheila holding Ann's hands, and looking at her affectionately.

'And here are my parents, Joan and Harold,' said James, proudly.

'We are delighted to meet you my dear,' said Joan. 'Aren't we, Harold?'

'Yes, indeed we are. And my goodness, hasn't he chosen a pretty lady friend. Welcome my dear, I hope you enjoy your stay,' he said, taking her gloved hand and raising it to his lips.

'Come on. Let's go inside and have some refreshments, you must be thirsty after your journey,' said Joan, who was walking with Ann, while Harold and James brought up the rear.

They chatted away and Ann found that James looked like and spoke like his father. His mother Joan was not a big woman but showing a little late middle-age spread, had mixed grey black hair tied in a bun, and she was dressed in a full-length black brocade dress patterned with silver sequins.

'How long have you known James?' she asked Ann.

'About six months, we work together in the hospital.'

'I see,' said Joan, who quite understandably wanted to know about someone who might one day be her daughter-in-law.

'And what do your parents do, Ann?'

'They own a large sheep farm not all that far from here,' she said.

'Perhaps, we might meet them one day,' said Joan.

'Yes, I'm sure they would like that,' said Ann.

After they had tea, muffins and home-made strawberry jam; James suggested he show her around the house and the area. She knew it was because he wanted to talk to her and she hoped, better still, kiss her; but properly this time, because she was his lady friend not his sister.

Once out of view of the main house James pulled her into the summer house and having sat down put his arm round her and kissed her. She responded ravenously. She clung to him and a warm feeling of physical desire flooded through her veins. She was in great need of his love.

'I love you, Ann. I felt this way as soon as I saw you, but have been too afraid to tell you.'

'Why, James?'

'In case you ridiculed me. I just couldn't believe a beautiful girl like you could take fancy to a doctor.'

'You silly old thing, I love you James,' she purred, looking deep into his eyes.

'Will you marry me?' he begged her, going down on one knee, as was still fashionable.

'If you will put up with a woman who's always dropping things, yes I will,' she joked.

'You have made me so happy, Ann, I am longing to tell my parents. Let's return to the house,' he said.

The two of them, holding hands together, returned to the house.

'Mother, Ann has agreed to be my wife,' said James proudly.

'Has she indeed. This is all very sudden. It's correct to ask the lady's father for her hand in marriage James, not to go blindly getting engaged without them even knowing,' said Joan.

'We are going to see her parents tomorrow. We love each other and want to raise a family.'

'My, you young ones are in a hurry. Your mother and I were engaged six years, and waited three years after that till you were born,' said Harold, shaking his head in bewilderment. 'Rest assured we wish you the best of luck in whatever you do.'

James and Ann left the lounge and returned to the garden. 'Oh Ann I am so pleased you accepted my proposal,' he said, squeezing her tightly in his excitement. 'I was thinking I might lose you to one of the competition. There are lots of eligible bachelors in the hospital.'

'I nearly did the proposing myself, I was getting so impatient,' she teased him, laughing.

'I believe you would have,' he said, kissing her again. She cuddled into him and could smell the soft fragrance of his eau de cologne.

The following morning after breakfast, the young couple hired a pony and trap and went to the station. They didn't wait long for a train, and took a carriage from Melbourne station to the farm.

'I can't wait to see their reaction,' said James, like a thrilled schoolboy. Beatrice was sitting in an armchair on the veranda when the buggy pulled up at the gates. She didn't recognise its occupants at first, and walked towards them to enquire what they wanted, when she heard a very familiar voice.

'Mama! It's me, Ann. I have brought someone to see you. His name is James, and he is to be my husband.' All this was shouted by Ann before they had even got out of the buggy.

Beatrice was very taken back by what she had heard Ann announcing. Obviously the girl was very excited, and not acting very adult about the situation.

'Hello, my dear, this is a pleasant surprise,' exclaimed Beatrice, clutching her daughter in a tight embrace.

'Mama, this is James, he had proposed to me and I have accepted. Isn't he just wonderful,' she said happily.

James shook hand with Beatrice. 'I am very pleased to make your acquaintance, Mrs Redlock,' he said politely.

'Hello, James, I think you have a crocodile by the tail with this one,' she laughed.

I agree, she certainly is very lively. Just then Charles entered the room; he knew there were guests as he saw the buggy at the front of the house. He didn't know it was his daughter Ann.

Hello, who have we here, he said with a smile.

Papa, this is James, we are going to get married.

'Are you indeed? Not as much as a may we get married. You are only nineteen.'

'I'm nearly twenty, papa.'

'You're still very young. What do your parents say, James?'

'A little like yourself, sir. They don't really approve, but haven't said we can't.'

'How long an engagement are you having?'

'We don't want a long engagement, Papa, we want to get married and start a family. Charles looked at Beatrice for further guidance.

'What do you say, my dear?' he asked.

'I don't see how we can forbid them now they have left home. I suggest we consent, and wish them the best of luck,' said Beatrice. The two pairs of eyes of Ann and James looked beseechingly at Charles.

'Alright, you have our consent and our blessing,' he said, with a grin. Ann ran to him, throwing her arms round him, hugging and kissing her father. James, with a big smile, hugged Beatrice.

'What do I call you now, Mrs Redlock?' he asked.

'Call me mother, James,' she said. 'After all, I am going to be your mother-in-law.'

While all this was being discussed Mary and Bruce were standing on the sidelines watching. They hadn't even been introduced yet. Ann saw them standing there, not knowing what to do.

'Oh James, this is my sister Mary. Mary, this is my future husband James.' He took her hand, and raising it to his lips, he kissed it.

'You are even lovelier than your sister said you were, Mary.'

She smiled at his generous compliment. 'Thank you, James. This is my brother, Bruce.'

'Hello, Bruce. Ann has told me what a good sport you are, I'll be glad to have you as a brother-in-law,' said James, shaking his hand.

'I haven't met my new son yet,' said Charles. 'Come over here, James, and let's get acquainted.'

James put on a big smile, and marched across the room to shake Charles's hand.

'Pleased to meet you sir,' he said.

'I'm pleased to meet you, James; I hope we have a long and happy life all together. Welcome to the Redlocks.'

Charles thought James was a fine fellow to be his son-in-law.

All the rest of the day was spent talking, eating and drinking. James was shown around the farm, and said the next time he came, he and Ann would love to go horseriding. Mary felt a little out of it because up to now she had sort of been the Cinderella in the home and was Beatrice's right hand. Still, she was young, and knew one day a young man would enter her life because she was a very pretty girl. Bruce was growing into a fine young man and he seemed much taken to farm life which Charles was pleased with; he badly wanted the farm to continue when he retired, which wouldn't be that many years away.

Ann and James stayed two days with her family before setting off back to their hospital.

'Well, we have achieved what we set out to do,' said Ann.

'Even more my love, because up till this weekend I hadn't kissed you, and now here we are engaged to be married; all in just two days.'

'I know, my sweet, it is all a big rush, and you don't think we have been too hasty?'

'Hasty? Yes. Too Hasty? No. We have done what we both wanted to do. We have our parents' approval, the rest is up to us. I am going to buy you a beautiful ring to seal our pledge.'

'Thank you, my darling,' said Ann, cuddling into him.

The following weekend James took Ann to the jeweller, and together they chose a pretty sapphire and diamond engagement ring. They didn't plan to wait a long time for the marriage as time was precious. There was no doubt that the sex life of the student doctors and nurses at this period of time was far less strict than that of their Victorian parents, many of whom had come from England.

One had to accept the fact that these young people were setting their own moral standards, and were deviating from the frumpy ways of their parents whose moral standards were being discarded by the young generation of Australians.

12   *Marriage*

*A*NN AND JAMES were feeling the need to complete the physical side of their betrothal. Their kissing sessions were lacking something, they knew what it was and the desire both of them felt for each other could not be contained much longer.

'I want you, Ann. My body is hungry for you. Let's make love,' said James.

'I feel the same, darling. I cannot contain myself much longer. I ache for you inside me.'

'Where can we go to be alone?' asked James.

'I have never seen your room's darling. I would so like to see so that I can imagine you curled up in your bed when I am in mine,' she said, with a wicked little grin on her pretty face. James knew what she was leading to.

'Alright, come round tonight. I will pick you up at seven and take you there. Would you like that?'

'Yes please darling,' she said. They had for some time past refrained from working together in the operating theatre as they both thought it might be a distraction.

'This is most unusual my dear,' said James. 'Men are not allowed to bring their lady friends into their rooms.'

'I don't suppose we are the first, James.'

'Hush! Talk in whispers, so we are not heard. Here we are. This is my room,' he said, turning the key and pushing her forward. The room was in darkness. James lit a lamp which showed a typical male study. The room was a tip, with piles of books, piles of clothes, bed unmade; general untidiness.

'It's very untidy, James,' she admonished him, in a whisper.

'I know my love, there just isn't the time. That's why I haven't brought you round before,' he said, straightening the bed out and remaking it. He hung some clothes up and sorted out some books. Soon the room was more to Ann's liking.

'Let me take your coat,' he said removing it, and stopping to kiss the nape of her neck as he did so. She turned, and disregarding the coat, which fell to the floor, she flung her arms round him and gave him a strong kiss. He ran his fingers down the back of her dress and unhooked the fasteners. She helped slip it over her shoulders and let it fall to the floor. She pulled her underskirt down; and James, as if he had been practising it all his life, eased her out of her drawers, which she had carefully made sure were worn over her suspenders so they would slide off easily. It was only moments later that the two of them were lying naked, clutching each other, and preparing themselves for their first passionate lovemaking.

As one might expect, being the first time it lasted only a few minutes, but they both felt relieved that they had achieved the physical love from each other which they so desired. After a ten minute rest James found the energy to do it again, this time he didn't rush at it and they both enjoyed it even more as they managed to climax together.

'Time I was getting you home, my dear,' said James, after a rather weak third attempt.

'Please, can we come again soon? I did so enjoy our little session,' pleaded Ann.

'You can be certain of that my dear, as soon as I have regained my strength,' Ann giggled at her fiancé; he was such a treasure.

And so on a semi-regular basis they practised the art of lovemaking with no protection and as one would expect Ann missed a period. She didn't mention it to James until she had missed two.

'What are we going to do darling, we aren't even married yet?'

'Well, we have a few choices, we could get married in a hurry before the lump gets very big; or we could have the baby and get married after.'

'What's the third choice?'

'I don't think you want to know.'

'I do, go on tell me,' said Ann.

'We could get rid of it.'

'What do you want, James?'

'I want the baby, I don't care if you do get married with a lump, and we have been betrothed for three months. Shall we bring the marriage forward?'

'I was hoping that's what you would say, my love. Yes, we will do that and we will have our own new baby. Oh how wonderful darling,' she said, kissing him.

James was very pleased at the arrangement and pulled out all stops to arrange a quick wedding.

The first thing was to tell their parents of the forthcoming birth; and the marriage which was to precede it. It was Ann who decided to send a letter to them both explaining the circumstances, and confirming that the whole thing had been planned that way. Both families replied, and to the young couple's amazement, they were both happy with the birth and the wedding, and said they would be there.

The marriage took place and there was little evidence of the baby on the way. It was a happy wedding with one or two friends and family. Ann was sorry Norman couldn't be there as he was at sea.

James was bowled over by the generosity of his parents, who bought them a small cottage near the hospital, as a wedding present. Ann was delighted likewise. Her own parents put five pounds into their account. After the wedding the two of them took a delight in furnishing their little house together, and building for themselves a home for the three of them. Their baby boy came into the world, weighing eight pounds, bright blue-eyed and sound in all limbs. They were two very happy parents and christened their son, Alfred.

13   *Death of the Vixen*

T HE *SEA VIXEN* was sailing to India, and then down the coast of Africa to Madagascar; it would be away for some time. Norman carried Clare's picture with him, and he thought about her a lot. Often as he lay in his bunk he thought of her and the wonderful evening they had together.

Norman was now officially a junior officer under training. He ate in the wardroom with the officers and had his own bunk. It was small but better than sleeping in a hammock on the men's deck. Taffy had reported back to his ship; so had Hans and Mongo; in fact just about all the old faces. Norman liked that. He was happy now. He had said his goodbyes to the farm and they all wished him well. The legend of Norman and his knife throwing would live for years.

Norman was studying hard and applying all he had learnt to sail the *Sea Vixen*. All the officers gave him help. Sometimes he asked for it; at others he didn't; but he was always grateful. He was learning about tides and winds, sea currents and cloud formation. He soaked it up and his skill fascinated those on board. He learnt how to use a compass and measure the angle of the sun. The captain gave him lessons in reading a chart and taking measurements. He also often tested Norman on what he had learnt.

They had completed their voyage to Bombay in India – a country Norman found fascinating. He went ashore and bought presents for Clare and his family. For Clare, he bought a gold necklace; it didn't leave him much money after that. The winds were kind to them and they were making good time. The captain had been warned that there were other dangers en route he might encounter apart from storms. He laughed it off. He wasn't afraid.

They were heading down the coast of East Africa. It was glorious sunny weather and a light breeze, their destination was Madagascar. There were a few ships in sight, which was usual. There was one very fast steam sail boat of a design nobody recognised. It was heading in the direction of the *Sea Vixen*. Nobody paid much attention to it. It was a warm afternoon. Some crew were sunbathing; others below sleeping. There was an officer on watch and a man at the helm; that was all that was needed.

'Ahoy there,' came a voice from a loud hailer. It seemed to come from the steam-powered boat as it drew near. Sailors sat up to see what the noise was and lay back down again. Norman was studying in his bunk.

'Ahoy, *Sea Vixen*, heave to. We are about to board you. If you don't comply we will sink you. We have the means to do that.'

The *Sea Vixen* refused to heave to and it took another shot in front of her bows, narrowly missing the ship's mascot, to make her stop. All the crew, with the exception of those on duty below, were on deck, trying to find out what was going on.

'It's bloody pirates, I tell you,' said Taffy. 'I heard of them, and what they can do to you. Your life is not worth sixpence if they capture you.' As he was the only seaman with any knowledge of the pirates, all the hands were crowding round, asking Taffy questions. He was in his element, letting his imagination run wild with his made-up stories.

'What shall we do, Captain?' asked Silas Watts, the first officer. He was mystified with the situation. He had never come across pirates before, or read a manual on how one dealt with them.

'Wait and see what they want,' said the captain.

'Shall I issue guns, sir?'

'No, let's see what they want. I don't want any unnecessary bloodshed.'

A longboat was lowered from the pirate vessel manned by twelve oarsmen who were heavily armed. The captain had a rope ladder thrown over the side and in a short while all twelve of them were aboard. The first pirate to appear over the side was their leader. He had the facial features of a Chinaman, with narrow eyes and a flattish nose, black hair, dark eyes and broken, uneven teeth. He was no taller than five foot, bare- skinned, in canvas trousers and open-toed sandals. He was heavily armed with two revolvers, a wicked sheath knife with a sawtooth edge. The other members of his gang were an assortment of black men from the East coast of Africa, and more Chinese types, similar in appearance and dress as their chief.

'Who is the captain?' their leader demanded.

'I am.'

'Where are you going, and what are you carrying?'

'We're going to Madagascar, and we're carrying wool.'

'Who owns the cargo?'

'The Melbourne Auxiliary Wool Company.'

'Well we are taking you captive until the Wool Company pay a ransom for you.'

'You can't do that, it's piracy on the high seas. If they catch you they will hang you.' The pirate leader ignored the captain.

'Is this all your men on deck?'

'Yes it is.'

'Have you any women on board?'

'No!'

'You tell the truth, or we cut your balls off.'

'It is the truth.'

'Right, take everyone down below and batten down the hatches. It won't be for long, Captain; we are not far from our hide out.' He pointed to one of his ruffians. 'Take a search party and collect up all the weapons on board and do a search in case there are any more crew hiding away.'

The crew were taken down into the hold and the hatches secured so they couldn't escape. Norman was still in his cabin while all this was going on. He was sleeping having been on watch the night before, and was woken by the noise of all the crew scrabbling on deck, and the shouting. He could overhear what was being said and the captain was speaking in such a way as he was hoping that Norman, who he knew was still in his bunk, could overhear, and avoid capture.

Norman realised he was possibly the only one of the crew who was not imprisoned, so he hid under his bunk hoping this would help him escape detection. There was so much of the ship to search that it was not done very thoroughly; they missed Norman's little bunk altogether. He could feel the ship moving. It was being towed by the pirates. He didn't know what to do but he realised that any hope for the crew and the return of the ship rested with him; he must not be found. The pirates had the guns so there was little chance of an armed escape; he still had his knife and he wasn't afraid to use it if he had the chance.

Night was closing in. Norman eased himself from the very cramped position under the bed, and peered out into the passage way. There was no one about and as the pirates were sure that the captain and crew were locked up they could relax their vigilance. Norman looked out of the window and could see a few lights from the shore; not many. It obviously was not a town or city, but a small harbour commandeered by the pirates.

They certainly had a cheek, taking a cargo ship in for ransom. Did they really think that a ransom would be paid for the ship and the lives of the crew? He supposed it depended on how much money was asked for. Norman was hungry and needed to relieve himself. He had to do something; but realised that it had to done cautiously; because one slip up on his part could jeopardise the lives of all the crew of the *Sea Vixen.*

He tried to formulate a plan. Every idea he came up with seemed unworkable. The lights on the tiny harbour were gradually going out. It appeared the pirate captain was keeping the crew in the hold till morning.

An hour ago he had heard what he took to be the pirates passing food and water to their captives, but they weren't letting them go – not tonight.

Norman checked his pocket watch. It was two o'clock in the morning. Give it another hour, he thought; then he would make a move. The pirates were all a mixture of coloured races, so the whites amongst the crew couldn't impersonate them.

Three o'clock came round on his watch dial, and Norman crept stealthfully from the cabin onto the deck. Staying in the shadows he looked around. No one was in sight; sounds of snoring came from the crew's quarters that were now occupied by the pirates. There was a watchman sitting on the hatch covers, he was the only person in sight, and was probably the only one awake until relieved to take over the watch.

Carefully and quietly, keeping to the shadows, Norman crept up on the guard, who was having difficulty staying awake. It was the worst hour of any watch. Norman didn't rush, but managed to get right behind the man. He placed a hand over his mouth and cut his throat; blood spurted everywhere. The man, who was of slim build, slid into a heap on the deck. Norman dragged him into the shadows and as he did he heard the replacement guard approaching across the deck.

'Hello Winchy are you OK?' asked the man.

Norman didn't want to make the guard suspicious but what could he do? He was in the shadows. He tried to imitate the accent of the black African. The guard was upon him.

'You not Winchy,' he couldn't see Norman's face for a moment. 'Hey, you a white man. I call de boss,' he says at that moment Norman pounced on him and tried to knife him but this is a bigger and stronger man than Winchy.

'I is going to strangle you, white man,' said the guard, gripping Norman round the throat. His lungs were near bursting; he could feel life being choked out of him. It was a natural reaction; he jerked his knee up hard right into the black man's bollocks.

Almost at once he released his hold on Norman's throat. As quickly as possible Norman also slashed this one across the throat. Frantically he searched the men's pockets for the keys, and he found them. Having done so, he opened the hatches and called the crew back up on deck. Most of the men were asleep and even when they woke they did not associate being called on deck at that time of the morning with freedom.

The captain and officers got the crew moving without a word. Silence was imperative as stealth was required to complete this bid for freedom. They locked the pirates in their cabin. There were only about six of them to look after the ship and her crew till they were taken inland, possibly to be sold as slaves.

Vic was surprised and delighted to find the ship's small arms and ammunition stacked up in his cabin. He had them issued to responsible people. He then had the jib sail raised, which did not require a great deal of effort, but had to be done stealthfully and quietly. It was imperative the pirates weren't aroused. The idea was they would quietly slip away from the dock. He had the ropes tethering the *Sea Vixen* to the dock released. All the crew sensed the urgency and need for tasks to be done quietly. It was a ghostlike operation, but slowly the big ship slipped away from its captors.

As she made more progress more sail was raised, so increasing the speed. By now the pirates were aware that their prize was slipping away, and the *Sea Vixen* was being restored to its rightful owners. There wasn't a great deal the pirates could do about it. They let fly with their guns and rifles but in the dark there was no accuracy and the shots went wild. Although the pirates had a boat powered by steam it would need firing up to get the steam up to pressure and by then the *Sea Vixen* would be out of sight.

The two dead pirates were unceremoniously flung overboard. Only when things were back to normal did Vic call all the crew together to praise the skill and daring of Norman. This raised three cheers from the ship's company, which Norman modestly accepted. The *Sea Vixen* had some mileage to make up, so it was all hands on deck and maximum safe speed obtainable. Vic was stuck for words for the fine efforts shown by Norman and wrote a glowing report of his young officer to the Board of Sea Captains about him and what he had done in the past years.

Time passed quickly and Vic often let Norman completely run the ship planning the route and doing weather forecasting. The crew respected Norman but at the same time realised he was only a young man under training.

*

The *Sea Vixen* made the rest of its journey to Madagascar without any more incidents worth recording in the ship's log. The crew had a few days' holiday before continuing to Cape Town. Even the Cape of Good Hope was calm for that time of the year. Norman was looking forward to getting back to his sweetheart, Clare; he wondered if indeed he was to be a father. It was certain he wouldn't know until he arrived home. Then there would have to be a marriage and finding a home to live in. He also wondered how his sister Ann was managing now that she was going to be a nurse. Having had no mail he was completely unaware of what his family were up to.

When he was about to leave South Africa for the journey home there was talk of possible war with the British as they were trying to take over South Africa's goldmines. One advantage of living on a ship was that one was generally out of touch with what was going on in the world. It was only when one got to port that they were able to keep abreast of world politics and how it would affect their livelihood. At the moment all one had to deal with were pirates.

Norman had endured most of what a sailor had to live through in his time at sea; in fact his adventures far surpassed that of most seamen. He felt capable to sail the ship himself. His knowledge of winds, tides and the weather were such that there wasn't a great deal more to learn. What he was lacking was command of men and making decisions that would affect their lives and the safety of the ship.

He knew he had another two years to go before he could go before the board and be assessed as to his suitability to command a vessel of his own. There was always work to do on board and one of the regular tasks was making sure the ship didn't leak. This usually meant sealing the joints between the planks of the deck and the hull. The sun and the sea soon made wooden hulled ship look tatty and unseaworthy.

It was one of those days when the decks needed resealing and a party of men had been designated to see this task completed. Norman had been put in charge of the crew but his knowledge of the skill in performing the sealing and caulking of the deck was one he had yet to learn. However, there were members of the crew who were used to it and they were teaching him. At least now, as a junior officer, he didn't need to get down on his hands and knees and actually perform the work, but he was responsible for it meeting the standard required by the captain.

By the end of the first day half the ship's deck had been done and the crew were resting after their evening meal. There was a strong southwesterly blowing and the *Sea Vixen* was making good speed in a homeward direction.

Norman was tired and had been studying and taking notes for some tests the captain was preparing for him. Just as he was dozing off he heard the ship's bell being jangled loudly and the dreaded word 'FIRE' being shouted throughout the ship. A fire at any time was unwelcome, but on a wooden hulled sailing vessel it was greatly feared. Norman swung his feet to the floor and put his boots and jacket on. Having got dressed he ran on deck.

'Where is the fire?' he shouted to a passing crew man.

'In the galley, sir. Some oil has caught fire and it is spreading.'

'Are the pumps being manned?'

'Yes sir, but the fire is too big for them.'

He saw the captain issuing orders to the crew. The ship had been brought into the wind and was virtually stationary.

'How bad is it sir?' asked Norman.

'It's bad, Norman, and getting worse. The sail locker is close to the fire and we can't get to it. The oil which is alight is seeping down through the middle deck to the hold, so we have fire there as well.'

Sailors were running backwards and forwards with buckets of water.

'Right you lot, form a line, a chain and pass the buckets along it then return the empties and refill them,' commanded Norman.

This was more effective than odd sailors running backwards and forwards with half-filled buckets slopping water everywhere. Mr Harrod the boatswain came up to the captain.

'We can't put it out, sir; it's caught the sail room door. Two men have been injured by falling timbers from the roof. What shall we do?' Norman could see the worry on the captain's face.

'What are our chances Mr Harrod?' asked the captain, very concerned.

'Very little sir, I fear the worst,' he said, wiping black, sooty embers from his face and hair. Smoke was blowing up from below and crew members who were feeling the effect of the heat and fumes from the fire were staggering on to the deck rubbing their tear-filled eyes.

'Prepare to abandon ship, Mr Harrod,' he commanded. He dashed back into his wardroom and gathered together all the charts and navigating items he would require.

'Norman,' he said. 'Get four pistols loaded – we may need them. Issue one to each officer. Make sure we have plenty of drinking water and rations.' He came back out on deck.

'How long do you think we have, Mr Harrod?'

'About fifteen minutes, sir, that's all.'

'Right, *abandon ship*,' he called loudly. 'Make sure you have warm clothing with you men. Lower the boats away – crew overboard.'

The officers were supervising the abandonment of the *Sea Vixen*. Already the flames were coming up on deck and the ship was leaning to starboard.

'Alright Mr Redlock, over the side,' he said to Norman.

Norman did as he was told with a great reluctance as he had grown to love his ship. Most of the boats were standing off waiting for the captain to give his directions. The *Sea Vixen* was burning furiously now. The dry tar saturated timbers were readily being gobbled up by the flames. It had all happened so quickly. Norman checked his watch. Half an hour ago he was reading a book. Norman noted he had Taffy and Hans the Swede, in his boat, plus several other reliable crews he recognised. The captain's boat was close by.

'Where are we heading, Captain?' asked Norman.

'As luck would have it we're slap bang in the middle of the Indian Ocean. There is nothing south except the Antarctic. To the west is Australia, and there are two small inhabited islands of Reunion and Mauritius to the north. I think that's our best course, all keep together and we should be alright.'

The men started opening the ration packs and water.

'Ration the food and water,' shouted the captain.

'Did you hear that lads. We have to ration the food and water. Mr Harrod take charge of the rations. We may be at sea some time. Everybody is to have two ship's biscuits and half a cup of water a day.'

'Is that all? We wont live long on that,' moaned a seaman.

'It's better that and arrive alive than twice that and not arrive at all,' said Norman. 'Whatever you do don't under any circumstances drink seawater. It will make you go crazy.'

'What else is there to drink?' bellowed, a big fat fellow in a black shirt.

'Drink your own piss,' said Norman.

'What if we can't piss?' yelled another

'Then drink your best friends.'

They all laughed and pulled faces at this.

'I assure you the time could come when you will be glad of your mate's piss.'

They wouldn't believe it. Norman thought the men had it in their heads that they would be on solid ground by tomorrow.

There was a sail aboard every longboat, so they hoisted that, in fact all the boats did.

'Did you scupper the *Sea Vixen* before we left her, Mr Harrod?' asked Norman

'Yes, I made sure plenty of sea water was pouring in. I expect she's in Davey Jones locker by now.'

'She was a good boat; we had some great times on her.'

'Aye, we did,' all the crew muttered their agreement.

The food was served out and stored away under the boatswain seat. Norman had a loaded pistol just in case of trouble. There was a heavy sea that night and they lost sight of the other boats. By dawn Norman's boat was all alone on the

Indian Ocean. All eyes turned to Norman. How was he going to get them out of this? All the maps and compasses were with the captain's boat.

'What will happen now sir?' asked Taffy.

'We are not lost yet my hearties,' said Norman. 'I shall find North and we will find our way to land. We know we don't want to go south, so we will head West-North-West; and hope to find those islands the captain is heading for.'

'How will we do that without a compass?' asked Mr Harrod.

'By my pocket watch,' he said, taking it out of his pocket and winding it up. All the crew looked on, confused, as if watching a magician.

'I point the small hand at the sun and divide the angle between that and the minute hand that gives me north.'

'Ingenious,' said the boatswain.

'Are you sure?' said Hans.

Norman didn't answer. 'Hoist the sail, and set a course in that direction,' he said, pointing with his outstretched arm. 'It will be tricky because we will have to keep checking the angle as we have no landmarks, but tonight we can steer by the stars,' said Norman.

The hot sun poured down on them. Everyone was thirsty. Norman tried ways of entertaining his crew; making each one tell a story, and the next day each one would sing songs. He even had questions and answers; anything to keep them awake and alert. The danger was if they went into a slumber brought on by lack of vitamins they might easily die.

Bertie Drewly started gibbering incoherently one morning. He thought he could see his mother's house and wanted to walk to it. It was as much as the crew could do to hold him down and stop him capsizing the boat. The boat wasn't going anywhere fast anyway. There had been no wind for a day, the sea was as flat as a bath full of water. But the sun kept pouring down.

'Now all of you men pay attention,' said Norman. 'We are going to have to reduce the rations especially the water. We must make it last as long as possible.'

Those that were conscious moaned about this.

'How many days have we, Mr Harrod?'

'Four days at the most,' he replied, through terribly cracked sundried lips. That night one of the crew died. They had been at sea in the longboat for three weeks. That day they had made no progress. There was no wind, just boiling hot sun.

Norman had the sail taken down and used as a sunshade. They couldn't all get under it at once so he made them take turns. Those that were conscious were drinking there own piss; the little that they had. The delirious man who died was Hans, the big Swede. Norman was sad to see him die; he had been a good friend. A prayer was said for him before he, too, was heaved overboard. Norman wondered if they were going to survive. He was feeling the heat and loss of water and food like the rest.

That night Norman felt pressure on his leg, and awoke to find Taffy, the little Welshman, who was a close companion of his in the early days and was now out of his mind. He had grabbed one of the young crew members and, holding a knife to the frightened man's throat, demanded extra rations from the few that were left.

The noise woke the remainder of the crew, who seeing what the situation was tried to calm Taffy down and make him see sense. But he was adamant that he would have extra rations even if it meant taking another man's life. Norman could see the look in the Welshman's eyes. He was not conscious of what he was doing.

'Come on now, Taffy. Don't be silly we only have a few days' rations left; we can't give you any extra. The feeling of hunger will pass,' said Norman.

'I want food otherwise I cut this man's throat.'

Norman pulled the pistol from under his coat where he kept it, and pointed it at the Welshman.

'If you don't let that man go and go back to your seat I will shoot you, and I will shoot to kill. Make your mind up. I will count to three – *one*' (immediately the crew backed away from Taffy) '*two*.' Norman could see the sharp blade had already drawn blood on the crew member's throat. He couldn't take a chance on the Welshman seeing sense as he was not compos mentis and was irrational. '*Three,*' he waited another second or two, and then fired the pistol.

The bullet caught the Welshman in the throat. As he collapsed in a heap he fell overboard. The poor captive was weeping with relief that his life had been saved.

'You had no choice, sir,' said Mr Harrod. 'I will vouch for you.'

'Thank you Mr Harrod,' said Norman, reloading, and putting the pistol away out of site.

It was the end of the week. Nobody spoke now, each man content with his own dreams and thoughts of home. They had been at sea for four weeks. The last water and biscuits had been shared out. Another man died through drinking seawater. The boat was half full. Half full of near dead men. Through the hot afternoon everyone was asleep. Norman knew their end would come mercilessly this way. They would die in their sleep. One of the crew tried to get up for the toilet. He was very weak.

'A boat, a boat,' he croaked. He shook the others.

There was indeed a boat. It looked like a naval vessel and was heading in their direction. Soon everyone was up and awake. New life had been born into them. The ship had spotted them and signalled they were coming to help. A grey-coloured vessel with a smokestack and sails came alongside. It was a South African patrol boat that had been sent to find them. The crew of the naval vessel helped the *Sea Vixen* crew on board; much to Norman's relief.

They received them well and made them comfortable. Norman asked if any of the other boats had been found, and was relieved to hear that his was the last one to be recovered. They were taken back to Cape Town where he met up with the remainder of the crew. They were accommodated in a small hotel until a ship could be found to get them back to Australia. Norman reported the shooting to the captain and had to write a report about it. There were no repercussions, as there were plenty of witnesses

'What are you going to do with your life now the *Sea Vixen* is no more, Norman?' asked Vic Masters, the captain.

'I really am not sure. I might join the Australian Navy as opposed to the Merchant Navy. I am sure I have exhausted every avenue of adventure any merchant seaman could find in two years at sea.'

Both men laughed heartily, and agreed that Norman had had more than his share of adventures.

14 *Boer War*

ALFRED WAS FOUR when the Boer War broke out in 1898. He was developing into a fine boy and was dearly loved by his parents and grandparents. It came as a shock to James when he heard that Australia was not only involved in the Boer War in South Africa, but that Australia was sending a contingent of doctors and nurses to help their British allies out there.

'I have been asked to volunteer to go to South Africa to help our English allies, my dearest. I would like to go but realise I am a family man and can't just go off on a whim. What are your views on the matter?'

'I, too, have been asked to volunteer to form a contingent of sixty nurses to help the wounded. The nurses are terribly understaffed. I really feel I should go, but like you my dearest, and even more so, have family responsibilities to look after our home and our son. What shall we do?'

'Do you want to go, Ann?' James asked, holding her hands and looking her squarely in the eyes.

'Yes, it's what I always wanted,' she said.

'Well, Alfred is nearly five, hardly a baby any more. I feel sure my parents would look after him for us. Shall we ask them?'

'Oh James, it would be wonderful if they would foster him for twelve months, I'm sure it will be over by then, plus the fact that I expect we can serve together.'

'I will telegraph them right away,' said James, heading towards the door of their cottage.

They had a reply next day, saying the grandparents would be delighted to look after Alfred while they were serving their country; and they could bring him along when they were ready. Ann and James both gave their names as volunteers for the Boer War; there was no enlistment or conscription. They were gladly received, and within a week had received their enlistment orders to embark to South Africa. They were both to sail on the *SS Euryalus* from Melbourne There was to be a contingent of Bushmen infantry accompanying them. Despite the seriousness of the occasion Ann couldn't help but feel excited. The war had already started in South Africa and there were many troops out there.

Much to both of their concerns they were not able to travel as a married couple and, even worse found that they were serving in different areas of the war. They managed a tearful good bye as James's contingent was driven away to a site up country. Ann was astounded at the conglomeration of men and equipment filling the port and surrounding country side. The nurses stayed together because to get lost in this mêlée of life, horses, ships and men would possibly mean one would be lost forever. Later that day they were to be moved to Beira on the East Coast of South Africa. When they arrived it was to find they were living in tents.

She heard to her relief that James had been posted to the Cape Town General Field Hospital. She wasn't too far away. It might be possible she could meet up with him. The wounded were soon coming into the small field medical unit, where she was employed in patching them up and, if the injury was serious or life-threatening, they were sent to the hospital where James was serving. The tactics of the Boers soon changed so that instead of fighting an open war they resorted to guerrilla tactics and hit and run raids. They were good fighters, but so were Ann's Australian countrymen.

She had letters regularly from James and she did manage to see him at least once a month. There were also lots of letters from home saying how proud they were and that young Alfred was doing fine but was missing his mum and dad.

One day James was asked to go into the bush part of the country where a man was trapped and his legs were trapped under a vehicle. They would it feared; need amputating in the field which was not easy. He left with the staff and surgical equipment he needed to do the operation in an area off the beaten track. The man was a black man and a general's driver.

It seems that he was driving the general to a secret place for a conference. Suddenly he was blown out of his horse-drawn vehicle by an explosion – either it was an artillery shell or some type of mine. The general was blown clear, but the vehicle had come crashing down on the driver's legs, trapping him. The general was soon whisked away his bodyguards who were bringing up the rear. As for the poor horse, he was killed outright in the explosion.

James enjoyed this type of operation. It was so different from a stuffy fly infested tent, working in poor light and extreme heat. On arriving at the scene he quickly assessed the situation and which was the best way he could carry out the operation with the least pain to his patient. He had the area cleared so that he could operate.

Next, he had a screen set up to shield the surgeon and patient from the glare of the sun. He laid out his tools, and was about to start when he felt the need to relieve himself. Excusing himself from the nursing staff with him, he went into the long grass for a pee. A Boer marksman, having heard the explosion and knowing there was something going on in the clearing, had come to investigate. He settled down and awaited the moment when he might find a target. When he saw James having a pee, he shot him in the head.

Ann was having lunch when she was called to the matron's office. The Boer War was not easing off, but the enemies attack techniques had changed; they using more sniper attacks, and not revealing themselves to the enemy.

'Come in, Ann, and sit down. I am afraid I have some very sad news for you. Your husband has been shot in the head. I'm so sorry.'

'What! Is he dead?'

'I suppose so, I don't know, though it's quite likely. You must be brave, it's war, and these horrible things do happen.'

'Oh my James, my poor James,' she sobbed. 'What am I going to do without you?'

'Once the funeral is over you may return home to Australia where you belong. I don't think you will want to stay here, will you.' Matron was very cold, and matter of fact

'Yes matron I do matron, at least I can visit his grave,' she said, wiping her tears away. What a shock. What a terrible nasty shock. She felt so sorry for his parents, they would miss their son so much, and yet he died doing what he wanted to do. He didn't suffer. If only they could have said goodbye; made love for one last time. Now Alfred was without a father. The poor little lad was just beginning to realise what a father was; and starting to have fun with him.

'Where is James now?'

'He is in the General Hospital. You can visit him there. Would you like to go today?'

'Yes please, matron.'

'I will arrange transport for you.'

Matron left her alone to reconcile herself and try to come to terms with her loss. Ann made her way back to her ward and although still a little weepy, she managed to perform her duties. Her heart was heavy with grief. She and James loved each other so much. He would be a terrible loss to her.

Early in the afternoon Ann was told transport had been arranged and she was taken to the hospital where James had been taken. It was early evening when she arrived at the hospital. On arrival she enquired about her husband's condition and a steward told her that her husband had been taken straight from the battlefield to the little chapel reserved for officers.

She was immediately taken to the chapel where James had been laid out. He lay there with his eyes closed. He was dressed in the uniform of a major. He looked so smart, so at peace with the world; it was hard to imagine he was dead.

Ann spoke a few words to him of farewell, and then she leant over and kissed him. Suddenly she saw his eyelid flicker. She jumped back with fright. Was it her imagination? Or was it a reaction after death? She didn't know, but hoped that he was still alive, which was now a priority.

'James! James!' she said with urgency in her voice. 'Can you hear me? It's Ann. Please say something. Give me some hope that you're not dead.' She shook his shoulder. She saw movement in his chest. She ran from the chapel shouting hysterically 'Doctor! Doctor! Come quick. My James is not dead.'

A doctor stopped her mad rush down the ward.

'Quiet please, men are ill and some dying.'

'It's James, my husband. He's in the chapel, but he's not dead. I just saw him moving. His eyelid moved and he breathed. Oh please, come quick, doctor.'

'Are you sure?' he asked, thinking she was mad.

'Yes, I'm sure, come quick. The urgency in her voice made him follow her to the chapel. They stood at the door traumatised; James was sitting up.

'James,' she screamed, 'you're alive. You must have been concussed not killed.'

He rubbed his head. A deep furrowed grove where the bullet had hit him reminded him of the occasion when he was shot.

The doctor, who couldn't believe what he was seeing, quickly moved towards James.

'How you are, old chap? We were sure you were dead. You stopped breathing. You gave every indication of being dead.'

'Well, I'm not, thank goodness. I'm groggy, and starving,' James replied.

'Oh James, darling, how wonderful. I am so happy,' said Ann, tears streaming down her face. She put her arms round him, and they kissed. He swung his legs off the table.

'Don't move I will get some bearers to carry you. Please stay where you are, Major,' asked the doctor.

'You poor darling, I can imagine the sorrow you must have gone through when they told you I was dead. What time is it?'

'Three o'clock,' she replied.

'That means I was shot at ten this morning. Luckily the bullet didn't penetrate. Everyone thought I was dead, and I wasn't checked out properly to see if I was. I was then brought here and placed in the chapel. I wonder how many other men are buried when still alive.'

'Oh don't say that darling, it's horrible.'

'Are! Here are the bearers,' said James.

The men settled James on the stretcher, and took him to a ward where he was to be fully examined. Ann walked by his side holding his hand. She felt she had been reborn. How unbelievable, her James was alive. Would he have lived if she hadn't visited him when she did? She doubted it.

James stayed under observation for three days before being released, and allowed to continue his work as a military doctor. Ann continued with her duties, and it wasn't very long before the pair of them were united, and back home in Australia.

When their parents heard of James's return to life, they found it hard to believe, but were so relieved to have them both home. Alfred was over the moon with joy at having his parents home. News travelled fast and for a few weeks James was the toast of everywhere he went.

They agreed that at the time it seemed a good idea to serve their country, but it made them realise also how foolish they were to risk everything, as they had done, and they vowed that they would always live for each other, and never volunteer for anything dangerous like war again.

15 *Heartbreak and Tragedy*

I T WAS SIX WEEKS before a boat could be found to take them back home. Norman was impatient to find out how Clare was. As soon as the ship docked he made his way to Clare's house. She answered the door, showing off a big tummy. He flung his arms round her and hugged her and told her how much he loved her and had missed her. Betty came to the door; she wasn't so enamoured to see Norman as Clare had been, and she made it quite plain she thought Norman had taken advantage of her daughter before going to sea.

Norman was thrilled to know he was going to be a dad. 'When shall we get married?' he asked her. He wasn't too sure about these things.

'I think we ought to wait till the baby is born and then get married, Norman; that's what mother thinks as well.'

'Well, fine, I agree to whatever you say. Oh I have missed you my darling and I know our romance was short and was a rushed one, but I had to get back to sea.'

'Don't worry about it. The important thing is that you and I knew what we were doing, and Mother will just have to go along with it.'

'When is the baby due, my love?' he asked

'The doctor says in six weeks. What do you want a boy or a girl?'

'I don't mind, Clare, but if it's a girl she must be as pretty as you,' he said, kissing her.

'Can I take you to meet my mother and take your mother along too?'

'Is it far?'

'It's about fifty miles. We could go by train.'

'Alright, I will ask her.'

Betty agreed and they set off two days later for the sheep farm.

'I have never been on a sheep farm, Norman. Is it a big one?'

'As far as I know it's big. I haven't really compared it with another.'

'I shall be pleased to see my stepsister Beatrice. I have no other relatives. Did you know my father John has died? I got a message from Newcastle of his passing.'

'I'm sorry, Betty,' said Norman.

They got to the farm late afternoon. Beatrice was so pleased to see them all and to put names to faces. She and Betty took to each other like first sisters; both felt they needed each other. Beatrice was in fits over her Norman getting married, and with Clare going to make her a grandmother. Charles came in with Bruce, who was over five foot tall now and filling out like a real farmer.

Norman had to spend the evening going over all the exciting things he had done.

'What are you going to do now that you have no ship?' asked Charles

'I don't know. I haven't discussed it with Clare.' They both looked at each other and knew this was a problem they had to sort out. Norman did not want to relinquish his life in the navy.

Two days later they returned to Melbourne. Norman was staying with Betty and Clare.

'Well, you two young people have to decide what you are going to do with your lives,' said Betty, on their return home. 'Norman, you will soon have a wife and child to keep, and I expect a few more children to add to this one, so you will have to find work.'

'Betty, what you say is true. Clare and I have spoken about it and she is in agreement with me continuing my life in the navy while she brings up the children – at least for the first few years.'

'You men have got it made, haven't you?' she said sarcastically.

'We are going to find a house of our own,' said Norman.

'You don't need to go to all that expense, this is a big house. You can all live here,' said Betty.

'I think it will be better if we have our own. It can be nearby.'

'As you wish,' said Betty.

'I am going to Sydney to the naval recruiting offices to see if there is any work.'

Norman took with him all the papers and recommendations from the captain of the *Sea Vixen*.

He pushed open the large glass-panelled door and walked into the hall of a greystone built building which had a brass plate on the wall outside which stated that these were the British and Australian Navy offices. Norman wasn't sure which door to knock on, but his mind was put at rest when a naval officer came out, saw him standing there bewildered and asked him his business, and how he could assist.

Norman gave a quick outline of his past life and handed his references to the officer who invited him into his office. The sunlight illuminated the large, dark, oak-stained panelled office with its two button-backed armchairs and large kneehole desk. The smell of cigars hung in the air.

'Take a seat,' said the officer.

'I am Captain Noble, seconded here from the British Navy, basically to assist the building up of Australia's own independent navy.' He looked at Norman's papers. 'And are you Norman Redlock? Tell me about yourself, Norman.' Norman went back to the beginning of his life, right up to the present time.

'Sensational. You have had more experiences at sea than I have and I have been in twenty-five years. I see you have some excellent references,' he said, reading through the papers. 'I will take some details and we will get back to you. I feel certain there will be a commission on one of the Admiralty's ships, and then it is up to you how you progress from there. How old are you now?'

Norman told him. He stood up shook hands with Norman and showed him to the door saying he would be in touch. It was as he was leaving the naval recruiting offices that he bumped into Victor Masters, his old captain of the *Sea Vixen*.

'Hello, Norman, what a small world. I see you have just come from the Royal Navy offices. Are you thinking of joining them?'

'Yes, I was. I am getting sick to death with being on land.'

'How about joining me as my first officer? I have a new ship, its steam and sail and we will be sailing the route up to India and China. I have got most of the same crew.'

'That sounds wonderful. I think I would really like that.'

'She is owned by an English company and compared with the old *Sea Vixen* she is luxury; hot and cold water, and a bath.'

'It sounds first class. When do you want my answer?'

'We sail in ten days' time, so I need to know by the end of this week. Here is my address.'

'Don't bother. I have already made my mind up. It's yes, Captain, I would like to sail with you.'

'Shake hands on the contract, Norman,' said Vic, extending his hand. They shook and sealed the contract.

After they had parted Norman walked home deep in thought. He had taken on a task without consulting Clare. It wasn't the way he wanted to do things. He wondered what her reaction would be. Still, he needed a job and the sea was what he knew best, so it was an obvious choice; there was no going back. The baby was due next week. He was looking forward to being a father, though Clare had been having some bad pains lately, and loss of blood.

Betty had said it was normal, and not to worry about it. Clare was sitting in the kitchen when he came home, she was rubbing her belly.

'Are you alright my dear?' he asked.

'Yes, I think so. The baby is moving about so much I fear he will fall out on the carpet,' she laughed.

'That's every sign it will be a boy,' he said hopefully. There was a small room in Betty's house that had been designated as the baby's room when it was born.

'Where have you been?' asked Clare.

'To the Royal Naval offices to see about a commission.'

'What did they say?'

'They seemed very impressed with my papers and references and said they would consider it and let me know.'

'Oh, the pain, I think I need to lie down,' said Clare.

'Shall I get a doctor? It's too close to the baby being born for anything to happen,' said Norman, who was very concerned.

'No, I expect I will feel better after a rest.'

'I have more to tell you my dear.'

'Tell me later Norman. I must rest now,' she said, as she shut her eyes and tried to sleep. Norman closed the curtains and left her alone. He felt lost. He didn't know what to do. He was so at home when he was at sea that he was bored and frustrated on shore. He was certain that he was going back to sea. He slumped in an armchair; Betty looked at him from across the room.

'How is Clare?'

'She is resting. I am concerned for the welfare of our child.'

'What about Clare; she's the one who's suffering and in pain.'

'Well I'm worried for them both.'

'Are you still going to sea when it's born?'

'Yes I am, we need the money,' he said which wasn't exactly true as his mother and father had plenty, but Norman was not one to sponge on them.

Suddenly there was a scream from Clare's room. The two of them dashed up to her to see what was wrong.

'The baby. The waters broke. It's coming,' Clare screamed. 'Get me a doctor.'

'I will get the doctor,' said Norman.

'There isn't time,' said Betty. 'The baby is coming.'

'What can we do? asked Norman. He felt so helpless.

'My God, the baby is the wrong way round and has the cord around its neck. Get the doctor, quick, hurry.' Clare had passed out, the baby was stuck. Betty was frantic. She knew she shouldn't meddle, there was nothing she could do; yet she felt she had to do something. They couldn't wait. The doctor or a midwife could be ages. She bent down and tried to turn the baby herself but it was stuck fast. It was the cord that was causing the trouble.

Twenty minutes later Norman came pounding up the stairs.

'I can't get a doctor, but a midwife is coming,' he said, puffed out with exertion. The lady's head appeared in the bedroom.

'Let me have a look at her.'

'Oh my dears, it's hopeless. She needs a doctor and an operation. There is nothing I can do.'

'How long will the baby live like that half in, half out?'

'Can't say, could be for hours. It's the mother I'm worried about. Look at the amount of blood she's lost. I have left a message for the doctor to come urgently and a medical wagon to take her to hospital. That should be here soon. Keep her wrapped up warm,' said the midwife.

The next to arrive was the medical wagon pulled by a pair of sweating grey mares. Two burly men came and called upstairs.

'Come on up, quick,' called Norman.

The two men put Clare on a stretcher, and as gently as they could, put her in the wagon and galloped off to hospital.

'I am going to the hospital,' said Norman.

'I am coming too, she is my daughter after all,' sobbed Betty. The two of them were directed to sit and wait. There was nothing else to do.

Norman was praying hard for his girlfriend and baby to be safe. The hospital was busy, so many people with cuts and broken bones. There were sounds of crying and screaming from all directions. A man in a white suit came through the swing doors. He looked around. When he saw Betty and Norman he came over.

'Are you the father?' he asked Norman

'Yes I am how is she?'

'I am sorry to tell you the baby has died; in fact the baby was dead before it arrived here. We have done our best.' Betty burst out crying.

'And its mother – how is she?' asked Norman.

'She is still alive, but very weak. We don't know whether she will pull through, she has lost a lot of blood,' said the doctor.

'Can we see her?' asked Norman.

'Follow me,' said the doctor.

Norman took Betty's arm to comfort each other, and together they went to see their loved one.

16 *Mary*

MARY REDLOCK had adopted her surname as a result of her step-parents snatching her from the prison authorities years ago. She felt very much part of them and loved the Redlock family as her own. Apart from Charles and Beatrice, who were getting elderly, she and Bruce were the only two without a career. She had been Beatrice's constant helper, but she didn't want to grow into an old maid. She wanted to travel and meet people; and she wanted to get married.

She often thought back to as far as she could remember to the days when her real parents were alive and free. As far as she knew, her father might still be alive, but it was doubtful, after living under such harsh prison conditions. She had a distant image of her mother in her mind who had died when she was only four.

Her mother's name was Girty Hamlet. Her parents, who were quite well off in those days, had been accused of not paying taxes, and embezzlement of funds designated for the poor, and stealing a sheep; the latter was true; they were desperate. The judge had taken their house and property and any money they had. Having made them absolutely destitute, he banished them to life imprisonment in Australia. Mary, who's registered Christian name, was Ethel (which she hated) was three when the family left England. Her mother Girty Hamlet had died through an illness she had caught on board ship. The conditions on board these prison ships were deplorable, and it was little wonder she caught a fateful disease.

When they landed, as she was still a child, she was put in care of a big fat coloured woman to look after her while her father was employed on slave labour. She lived in the prison grounds and was treated terribly once she was able to walk and talk and do light duties. She was clothed in other children's rags. These children had died there, and there was a big selection of clothes; though all of them were little more than rags. Her food was basic and had few calories or body-building vitamins. The room she slept and grew up in was an old coal-store, the dust of which was still everywhere. She had a wooden bed with a rope mattress on which was a very stained cloth cover, and she had a pillow and two blankets. She was always itching and scratching and breaking out in sores; but so was everyone else, so nobody bothered.

She remembered one of the prison guards had brought her a doll for Christmas one year; funny how little acts of kindness like that stayed in one's memory. She had one child to play with, he was an English boy named Steven, she couldn't remember exactly, but thought he was a year older than she was. Mary always had a cold and a runny nose, her teeth were falling out and she was waiting for her seconds to come through. Life was very boring and she was pleased when they took her along to help clean the passenger ships from England. She couldn't do a lot, but a bit of light cleaning, dusting and picking up rubbish were tasks she had been given.

She was ten years of age when she was smuggled off the *SS Great Britain,* by the Redlocks. She hadn't seen her father, except once – about two years ago he was being whipped for not carrying a big bale of hay, which was too heavy for him. He didn't know she had seen him. She wondered if all her life was going to be spent like this; surely not.

She had never been to school, didn't know how to read or write, or anything else for that matter. The decision to try and escape from the rut she was in was done on the spare of the moment; there was no planning involved. It was pure devilment which made her do it really; the coast was clear (not literally) so she dived into a linen store and hid away in the darkness. She had no plan of action. She didn't know whether she would be missed, but having made the move she was determined to try and escape from prison, and this ship she was on.

Seeing there was nobody in the corridors of the first-class deck she dived into a room which had Laundry on the door.

The events that followed were beyond her wildest imagination. They fed her, washed her, and dressed her in nice clothes. They even cut her hair. Mary was lost for words. What wonderful, kind, helpful people they were. The only moment of doubt was when the father entered the room and was made aware, by the woman Beatrice that they intended to smuggle the girl ashore as one of their girls.

The scheme was unbelievably simple and because of that she thought it might come off – which it did. Her heart sank when the soldier stopped them on the gangplank and grabbed her by the shoulder: she was sure the escape had been discovered. However, when it was just because she had dropped her doll, her heart rate returned to normal again.

It took a little while to get to know the family, and their names, but they treated Mary as one of their own, and she became a sister to their two children Norman and Ann. Her new father and mother were kindness itself, understanding what she had been through, and a determination that she would never go back to that life. It was thanks to them and their care and attention that she managed to survive the killer disease of consumption. She remembered it all so very vividly.

Beatrice taught her to read and write and she eventually caught up with the other two. They all got on so well together and then she was blessed with another brother whom they called Bruce; he really was a treasure. It was time now she felt to stretch her wings like her brother and sister had done, and see what was on the other side of the hill.

*

'Father, I would like to do something with my life,' said Mary one day when she was feeling very lonely and disillusioned.

'Like what?' asked Charles, putting down the book he was reading.

'I don't really know. I only know that I am nearly twenty-five, single and have no career. I want to remedy both of these situations.' It was as she was talking to her father that Beatrice walked into the room and could see there was some tension in the air

'What is the matter, Mary?'

'I was just telling father that I want a husband, and maybe have a career.'

'Quite right to darling. So you should. Have you any thoughts on the matter I remember when I was your age I was a nurse in the Crimea.'

'I think I would like to follow in your footsteps. It is an honourable profession.'

'Your sister Ann has done very well. Contact her. I'm sure she will help to get you started.'

'She is coming home this weekend, have a talk to her then my dear,' said Charles.

'What is Ann doing now, Mother?'

'I don't know exactly, but after James was nearly killed in the Boer War she went back to the hospital and is now a matron, she tells me,' said Beatrice.

'I hope they bring my grandson Alfred with her this weekend. It's his birthday. How old is he Charles – eight?'

'Who? Alfred, yes I think so,' he said, being more involved in his book than conversation about family matters.

At the weekend Ann and James came to the family home as arranged and brought Alfred with them. After the usual family greetings Beatrice brought up the subject of Mary wanting to be a nurse.

'My dear, that's no problem. I will have the forms sent to you. I don't see any problems. In fact, I could try to get you on my ward so we could be together. Would you like that?'

'Yes I would, thank you dear sister.'

That's how it was left. Two weeks later Mary was summoned to an interview with a board from the Victoria Hospital. She was very nervous as she sat before these very austere-looking men and women who would interview her. As it happened, the interview was very short and her sister's excellent work and references stood her in good stead.

'Have you a birth certificate?' asked the Administrator.

'No ma'am. It was lost years ago.'

'You will have to get a replacement before you can become a nurse. It's the only way we can tell who you really are.'

As Mary left the interview she realised that she would be found out to be a liar as she hadn't mentioned the fact that she was not a Redlock by birth, she had not been officially adopted, and that she had been snatched from one of Her Majesty's Prisons. All of this would go against her. The authorities were bound to find out, and Charles and Beatrice would get into serious trouble. There was nothing else to do but abandon the plan of nursing and seek some other profession, but what?

She was very sad and tearful not knowing what to do. She walked the streets of Melbourne and knew that, whatever happened in life, she would have to have a birth certificate; even to get married and draw a pension, or any state aid. What was she to do? She knew she could go back to the farm and live the rest of her life there, but she was officially an unregistered person, *persona non grata* unless she released all the details of her past. She decided to return to the farm where she had a home and was loved.

Beatrice could see there was something wrong with Mary when she came in. She looked very disillusioned and tearful.

'Mary, my dear child whatever is the matter. How did the interview go? When do you start as a nurse?' she asked. Mary sat down and sobbed the story out to her parents who listened and understood the situation. Mary was right; she couldn't claim to be a Redlock by birth, or by adoption.

'What am I to do, Mother? What is to become of me?' she sobbed.

They couldn't provide an answer. Mary was determined to make a life of her own away from the farm irrespective of having no birth certificate. After a sleepless night she had made her plans and would reveal them at breakfast next morning.

'Mother I have given this matter a lot of thought and have decided to leave the farm and this comfortable secure life, and try another avenue of employment in the big city. I am sure if I persevere I will find something.'

Beatrice looked across at Charles, who shrugged his shoulders as if to say it was her decision, there was nothing either of them could do about it; she was a grown woman. So, the following week Mary kissed her parents goodbye, and Charles took her into Melbourne.

'This is most unusual, Mary, are you sure you are doing the right thing?'

'Yes, father, it's what I want to do. I will stay at The Royal Hotel and find a job. Please let me try.' Her eyes filled with tears.

'You know you have a home and money with us. You need want for nothing.'

'I know, father, but I want to grow up and meet people. Don't stop me.'

Charles took her to the hotel and settled the first month's rent with the hotelier. He had a word with them and explained the situation, leaving his forwarding address if the hotelier should need it. He kissed Mary goodbye and drove off back to the farm.

Mary took the key to her room and went to it; her cases were brought up by the bellboy. She looked around at the furnishings and fittings and they were to her liking. They consisted of a large double bed with heavy drape curtains, a dressing table and armchairs. The whole room was very tasteful and even had electric lights, which was something they hadn't yet got on the sheep farm.

She hung up her clothes and went downstairs for dinner. She felt very conspicuous sitting at a table alone; apart from a couple of business men, everyone else was paired off. She enjoyed her meal of smoked mackerel, followed by boiled ham and tongue, and a sponge pudding dessert. As she walked back to her room the proprietor of the hotel came up to her and introduced himself and his wife as Thomas and Mildred Spanaway. Mary wondered for a moment what could be the reason for the introduction, but within a minute, it all became clear.

'Miss Redlock, please excuse my wife and me for interrupting your train of thought, but your father told us the reason why you are in the city; that being to find work. Though I understand there was plenty to do at your sheep farm. Would you care to come through to our lounge, we have a proposition to put to you regarding employment?'

'That's very kind of you sir, and Mrs Spanaway. Yes I will come and hear what you have to say.'

They led her through to their very comfortable lounge at the back of the hotel. Mary had a chance to take in her surroundings and the hotel owners. Tom was a small, bald-headed man with a bit of a paunch. He was dressed in a three-piece pin-striped black suit with gold watch and chain. He wore a flyway collar and bow tie, with very shiny black shoes. Mary thought that the precision in which he dressed himself so immaculately was a reflection of how he ran his life and business.

Mildred was a tall thin lady; her nose seemed a little short for her long, pinched face. She had jet-black hair, which she had roller-curled around her head, it was held in place with pins. She wore a full length, part silk, part brocade dress. It was cut to show the upper part of her bosom, around her neck she wore a necklace of jet, and sapphire-coloured stones.

'Would you care for a glass of port, Miss Redlock?'

'Please, call me Mary. I hate formalities when not called for,' said Mary, accepting a glass of port.

When they were all three comfortably seated and the small talk settled, Tom made his proposition.

'Mary, we need a secretary and receptionist, and we have talked about it and feel that you would fit the bill admirably. Have you ever considered hotel work?'

'No, I never have. I thought it was a role always taken by men; like most of the good jobs are.'

'Hear, hear,' said Mildred.

Tom looked at her disdainfully. 'Be that as it may be. Would you consider that type of employment?'

Mary quickly made up her mind. 'Yes I would be grateful to consider the job and the remunerations that go with it.'

'You can stay here as part of your salary if you want to.'

'That will suit me perfectly. When can I start?'

'How about tomorrow?'

'That's fine. I will join you straight after breakfast.'

'I will arrange the wages with you tomorrow, Mary,' said Mildred.

'Good, that's fine, thank you both for considering me.'

When she went up to her room she was in a happier frame of mind than she had been for a long time.

Next day, after breakfast, Mary reported at reception and Mildred started showing her the routine, and she worked with her for the first three days until Mary felt competent to handle reception herself. Mary liked the work. It was so nice meeting people and helping them with their problems, and she met so many interesting people.

Mary was not overly attractive. She was five foot two and a little on the podgy side. She wore her long brown hair in a bun, and she found the need to wear spectacles because her eyesight wasn't so good. Her dress sense, however, was right up to fashion and her one luxury was clothes. Her stepmother had made sure she had a good education. Though not to grammar school level, it was sufficient for her to be able to hold down a receptionist's job.

She was at her desk shuffling through some papers when the desk bell rang to draw her attention. Standing at her reception desk was a tall, handsome man in a long cloak and top hat. He was round-faced and had a bushy, droopy moustache, so popular in those days. The only trouble was it made men appear much older than they were.

'Oh, good morning sir, I'm sorry I kept you waiting,' she said with a smile.

'I would like a double room with bath if you have one,' he said.

Mary checked the rooms' availability list. 'Yes we have one sir; it's on the first floor, overlooking the harbour.'

'That sounds ideal. I will book it for a fortnight,' he said.

'What name is it sir?'

'Major Foolproof,' he replied.

'Fine, if you will sign here sir,' she said, turning the register round to face him. She noticed there was going to be only one occupant of the room.

'Just yourself sir?' she asked.

'Yes, it's just for me. I like a lot of space.'

Mary liked the look of him. He had a charming smile with white, gleaming teeth, and he looked so handsome and dapper.

'I will have someone bring your bags up sir,' she offered. 'Do you want to see your room?'

'Not if you recommend it,' he said, smiling once more.

Mary thought no more of the matter until later that evening after dinner he came over to the desk again.

'Please, excuse my very forwardness in asking this but are you married or betrothed?' he asked.

Mary look up a little amazed at his forthright manner. 'As a matter of fact I am neither; not that it is any concern of yours, sir,' she said, going into the back office to cool down and hide her blushes.

'What's the matter Mary?' asked Mildred, on seeing her so flushed.

'Nothing serious, it was just a very nice gentleman enquiring into my marital status. It was an unusual question to me, and I was quite taken aback.'

'You're not shy are you, Mary?'

'No, but apart from the farmhands and my brothers, I have had no dealings with men. That is one of the reasons I have found a job in the city, hopefully to expand my social life and meet a future marriage prospect,' she said.

She went back into reception. The gentleman was gone but when she came down to work in the morning there were a dozen red roses waiting for her, with sincere apologies from Raymond Foolproof, and a request that she have dinner with him at a nearby restaurant. She showed Mildred.

'It's up to you, Mary. You will have to make the move one day.'

Mary left a message accepting the invitation to go out to dinner with him, and waited for him to appear in person, or to leave a time and date. As it happened she was in her room that evening when the telephone rang, and it was him.

'Hello Mary, may I use your first name?'

'Yes, of course,' she replied warily.

'I see you have accepted my invitation to go out to dinner, is tomorrow night too early?'

'No, that would be fine.'

'I will meet you in the foyer at 7.30. Will that suit you?'

'Yes fine, I will look forward to it. Goodbye Raymond.'

As she put the phone down, she realised she had used his first name. She felt daring. She hardly slept that night. It was her first date. What was she to do? Did she kiss him first time? She didn't know.

'Just go and enjoy yourself,' she said to herself.

She eventually fell asleep at three in the morning.

Next day the hours seemed to drag by. She could have finished work at midday but decided to carry on, helping the time pass quicker.

At five o'clock, despite Mildred telling her all afternoon to quit, she went up to her room, bathed and changed. She waited until it was exactly seven thirty before leaving her room. It was her day off tomorrow, so there was no rush to be up early.

Raymond was standing patiently waiting for her. He took her right hand in his and kissed it.

'Good evening Mary, you look absolutely beautiful. Shall we go?' She gave him a lovely smile

'Thank you, kind sir,' she said politely. 'I am ready to go.'

'Fine, I thought as it was our first night out together we might go to somewhere where the food is excellent, the wine refreshing, and the atmosphere stimulating. Do you prefer French, English or Italian, my dear?'

'I leave the choice entirely to you,' she whispered.

'Good, then it will be French.'

They climbed into their carriage 'La Petite Aubergine'. 'It's a little cold tonight,' he said to the driver. 'Are you warm enough, my dear?'

'Yes, I'm fine, thank you,' she said.

After a ride of about ten minutes the cab stopped. Raymond being the perfect gentleman assisted her from the carriage and, taking her arm, they walked into the small French eating house. They were greeted by the patron who showed them to a discreet table in the corner where they would be able to see all that was going on, but at the same time have privacy.

'This is wonderful, Raymond, thank you for bringing me here.'

'The pleasure is all mine, you look divine.' The wine waiter was hovering. Raymond took the wine list and chose champagne. He didn't consult her. He took the main menu and opened it.

'Shall I choose for both of us? If there is something you don't like we can change it,' he said with a grin.

Once they had their wine they began exchanging information about their lives; what they had done, where they had been. Raymond learned that Mary was very new to being taken out and he presumed very new in every aspect of boy and girl relationships, of which he was very well knowledgeable and experienced.

Raymond made a charming escort. Apparently he had been married, but his wife died seven years ago of dysentery, caused by drinking dirty, infected water from a pond where they lived. He said he had no children.

Mary asked him what he did for a living and it seemed he was into banking and high finance, all of which Mary found very intriguing. Mary didn't tell him how she came to be involved with the Redlock family, only that she had come over here from England with them, and that she had a brother and sister. They finished their bottle of champagne and Mary was feeling a little light-headed, being unaccustomed to drink; but she had enjoyed her evening immensely. So she had no hesitation in accepting his invitation to go the theatre later that week.

'That was a lovely evening, Raymond. Thank you for inviting me.'

'I can't wait till Saturday when we go and see Swan Lake. Have you ever been to see a ballet?'

'No, I have so much to learn.'

'I will have great pleasure in teaching you, my dear,' he said, rising from his chair to indicate that it was time to leave. Mary followed suit and they made their way back to the hotel. On the Saturday they went to the ballet and then to see some plays. This was followed by a music festival and concert. Mary was taking it all in, and wondered why she was so lucky in being his lady friend.

*

One evening, as they were coming home in a carriage he kissed her. As one might expect, her kiss was only an amateurish indication that she didn't mind, and eagerly sought more and better of the same. In fact. Mary was at an age when she should have been fully experienced in sexual pleasures. Raymond found her very responsive and explored her willingness to proceed further to a mutual climax.

'Mary, would you come away with me for a short holiday? I feel we ought to know each other better and have fun doing it. What do you say?'

'Yes that would be very nice. Where do you suggest?'

'I have a little cottage along the coast. It's beautiful at this time of the year.'

'Yes, fine. Name the day and I will arrange some holiday,' she said.

He checked his diary and suggested the following Monday. Mary agreed and went to ask permission to take a break.

'Well, Mary, this young man is certainly making an impression on you isn't he.'

'Oh Mildred, he is so very nice and kind. I have never been treated like this. I am looking forward to a few days together. He is so kind and considerate.'

'Just take care of yourself. I know you are grown up but there are some wicked men in this world.'

'I will, but I know Raymond isn't one of them.' She ran upstairs to her room. At last life had found her a real handsome man with whom she knew she would be happy. True to his word, Raymond had a sweet little thatched cottage on the side of the bay in a small fishing village about twenty miles from the city. It stood alone; their nearest neighbours lived about fifty yards away.

The little cottage had been well looked after, with a decorative, floral garden in front and a similar-sized garden at the rear, with floral borders and a little lawn. At the end of the flowerbeds was a small selection of fruit trees and fruit bushes; all of which had been well maintained. There were two living rooms downstairs, and a scullery. The white walls had been freshly distempered as had the ceiling. A pair of wicker armchairs were on either side of the open fire, which somebody had thoughtfully lit the fire, and stocked the larder for their arrival.

'Oh Raymond, this is wonderful,' she said, throwing her arms round his neck, and giving him a big hug.

'I would spare no expense for you, my darling. As long as we are together I will see you have the best of everything.'

'You sit down, Raymond, and I will prepare us some lunch.'

'Not too much. I plan to cook you a dinner tonight, Mary, one that you will remember for ever.'

'That will be lovely, I look forward to it.'

After their meal they both went for a walk around the village and the harbour. That evening, true to his word, Raymond spent several hours preparing and cooking a superb three-course meal for them, washed down with a bottle of Chablis. Mary was feeling a little light-headed and was only too pleased when he suggested they sit together on the settee. He had cleared the table and the washing up could wait till later.

They sat cuddled up together, their faces illuminated only by the light of the wood burning fire, which spat and crackled, sending showers of sparks up the chimney. He undid the buttons on her blouse and slid his hand in and onto her firm, round breasts. This is what Mary was in need of; this is what she yearned for. She didn't restrict his probing fingers and hands but encouraged him, assisting, where necessary, their eventual dual nudity.

There was very little foreplay on his part and Mary was new to this lovemaking and went along with his suggestions, enjoying the sensation in her loins and the desire for what she knew was coming. It was the first time she had held a man's pride and joy in her delicate fingers, she stroked it and ran her fingers over the big red knob at the end. She was a very willing lover, and wasn't shy to his suggestions, and exploratory foreplay. Their inevitable union together was as smooth as if had been rehearsed a dozen times. Raymond's experience in the art of lovemaking was unhurried and very fulfilling for them both. She moaned with contentment as they climaxed together, clutching his back to ease the sensational pleasures she was experiencing. Eventually, the two of them separated; and lay side by side recovering their breath.

'Oh, that was divine. To think I have been missing it for all these years,' she said, leaning over and kissing him. If I hadn't met you darling, I might never have known true love.'

'The night is young, that was only an undress rehearsal of better things to come.'

They both laughed their heads off.

*

During the following three weeks of their holiday at the little cottage Mary felt she had been lifted to a higher level of life. It was a strange sensation; but she felt she was viewing life from a new dimension; something that she had never experienced before, and she loved it. Living with a man and loving him, learning each other's likes and dislikes, and tolerating each other's funny ways was the recipe for love and marriage, thought Mary.

He was so attentive to her; nothing was too much trouble. She thanked the Lord that she had found the love of her life at her first dinner date. Even going back to the hotel seemed to take on a new dimension. She felt she was a lady of society. It was difficult for her explain to anyone.

'Where are you going to live, my love?' she asked Raymond when they got back to the hotel.

'Oh I will stay on here until I find a place that suits me. How do you fancy a nice cruise on the Med or somewhere?'

'It sounds delightful, but I am a working girl, remember. I have already had far more holiday than I have earned,' she said.

'Right, I will make enquiries,' said Raymond. 'No rush – we will go when we are ready.'

'Thank you dear. What a wonderful idea,' she said.

The following day he was sitting in the sun lounge, looking very despondent. Mary went through and spoke to him.

'Why are you looking so glum, may I ask?'

'It's my bank in South Africa, they have telephoned me to say that due to a new currency rate of exchange my account will not be in my new bank for a month; which means, in effect, that although I have a fortune in Africa I have hardly anything over here for four weeks.'

'That's no problem, my love. I have more than enough for both of us,' said Mary.

'What about the cruise? We will have to cancel that.'

'No we won't, I'll pay for it and you can pay me when your money comes through.'

'That's awfully decent of you, my dear. I feel so embarrassed taking money from a woman, I am not even related to. Will you marry me, Mary? I know it's short notice but we could use the cruise as our honeymoon. What do you say?'

'It sounds wonderful to me, but why the hurry? I mean we could have our cruise and then take our time to get married.'

'Whatever you say, my dear,' he conceded, returning to the financial pages of the paper. That would have been fine but for the fact that a week later Mary found that she was pregnant.

'Darling, despite what I said the other day about waiting till after the cruise I have changed my mind now. I find I am pregnant with your child. I don't want a big wedding; there will be plenty of time for that later. Do you agree? It means we will have to bring the marriage forward,' said Mary, absolutely delighted that she was to be a mother.

'Well yes, I suppose so. I too am ecstatic at being a father, but I feel so embarrassed being short of money darling.'

'I will have £1000 paid into your account. It's no problem. I will telegraph father and have it arranged.'

'Won't he mind? He doesn't even know me.'

'It's my money. It was given to me when I was twenty one.'

'If you say you want a small wedding, then I agree, whatever you say. I will arrange a small service in that little village we stayed at, and we will go on our honeymoon from there. Does that suit you?'

'Yes, that's what I want. I don't want a load of fuss. I mean it's our wedding after all, isn't it my love.'

And so it was decided. Mary had Thomas and Mildred Spanaway, the hoteliers, as her guest and Raymond had a local couple they had met in the village as his best man.

'I'm sorry it's not what one would normally expect for a wedding, but it's what we both want Mildred,' said Mary quietly, in confidence.

'What about your parents, do they know? Have they met your future husband yet?'

'No Mildred, they don't know.'

'Are you inviting them?'

'No I'm not, for personal reasons,' said Mary, embarrassed at the question. She knew she was doing wrong in not telling her parents what she was doing, but she was frightened now that she was pregnant. She decided not to tell them till after the honeymoon was over. Raymond didn't question her decision.

'Like you say my dear, it's your wedding. You have who you want to it, thanks for inviting us along,' said Mildred. 'Oh there is one thing, Mary. I don't like to mention this, but your husband to be hasn't paid for his hotel room yet.'

'I know, he told me. It's embarrassing for him but his bank in South Africa have said there will be a four week delay till his money comes through. He has plenty. I am subsidising him till then. Don't worry I will look after it. You trust me, don't you?'

'Of course I do, Mary. Sorry I mentioned it.'

As there were only four of them at the wedding, Mary decided to wear a white brocade, sequined dress, with a small hat and veil. Raymond was smartly dressed n a new dark suit with a maroon waistcoat and a top hat. He carried a black ebony cane with a silver and ivory top.

The wedding breakfast was held at their hotel. Mildred had a small room set aside for the occasion and a really superb meal was laid on for their guests. Mildred thought it was such a shame that Mary was having such a skimpy and hurried wedding. She blamed Raymond for getting her pregnant. With his experience in life he should have been more careful. She put the reason that Mary's family weren't informed, or invited, down to the fact that the poor girl was embarrassed at what she had so recklessly done, and perhaps thought they might try and persuade her to abandon the idea.

However the ceremony and breakfast were quickly over. For what it was worth, it was a complete success. Everybody enjoyed themselves, and the following day the couple set off on their cruise. It was a sailboat, which they found much quieter then the steam-driven vessels which had just about completely taken over by now. They had a luxurious twin cabin with a porthole. It was just like a hotel room. The food was scrumptious and plentiful, as was the alcohol. It was just divine to sit on the deck in a reclining chair, soaking up the sun and digesting a good lunch.

This was what living was all about, thought Mary, and on top of that she had a lovely husband whom she could show off to the others on board. Both of them were blissfully happy. Raymond was much more cheerful and less stressed now that Mary's money was in his account. He felt so embarrassed being short and not being able to pay his bills. Mary paid off his hotel bill, but he was quite willing to do it himself.

One evening after dinner Ray said he would go up on deck and have a cigar whilst Mary was finishing her coffee. When she had finished she joined him. He was resting on the ship rail, gazing into the sea.

'Come here my love,' he said, indicating a space next to him. She came over and put her arm round him and they kissed fondly on the lips.

'Come stand by me here, my love,' he said.

It was a fantastic evening sunset. The sky was on fire. She looked about her.

'It's so out of this world. One feels as if one was on Mars, which I know is impossible.'

She turned around to view the other direction, and in doing so made the access gateway in the ship's rail swing outwards, as it had not been secured. Because of this, Mary felt herself falling backwards into the silent dark ocean. She screamed with fright.

A hand grabbed at her chest and clutched a handful of her evening brocade frock. At the same time she managed to grab the ship's rail. Together this was sufficient to stop her falling any further. Raymond took her other arm and the two men recovered her, hauling her on board. She was shivering with fright. A crowd had quickly gathered and when hearing what had happened were very concerned as to Mary's condition, and scathing at the ship's officer who had so negligently allowed the ship's rail to go unsecured.

'Are you alright?' Raymond asked, flicking his cigar ash over the side. 'My dear, that was a close call, you could easily have been killed.'

The man who had actually saved her had vanished into the crowds on deck. A ship's officer came up and enquired if she was alright and was most apologetic on behalf of the ship's company.

'I had been round only two hours ago and checked all the gate safety pins to ensure they were all in place. I found every one correct. Somebody has removed the pin in between times. Why?' he asked nobody in particular, from the crowd gathered round him; who indeed showed they were very concerned.

'It nearly cost my wife's life,' said Raymond, livid that such a thing could happen on a cruise. 'Come on, let's go back to our cabin, where you can rest and recover after your ordeal.'

He put his arm around her waist and guided her back to their cabin.

'That was a close shave, darling, I nearly lost my new bride. Thank heavens that man acted so quickly. We don't know who he was, do we?'

She was too shaken to speak. A porter brought her a chilled magnum of quality champagne, courtesy, and with apologies, from the captain. The ship's doctor called on her to check she wasn't in shock and suggested she should rest. The remainder of their cruise was trouble-free, and apart from the near disaster, Mary had a wonderful time.

'I really must take you to meet my parents. I don't know what they will think of me. Their youngest daughter going off, and getting married, and getting pregnant; and all in the space of eight weeks.'

'I know. It is unusual, but we are unusual lovers, aren't we darling,' he said.

Mary was so happily married; she had a wonderful, handsome husband. She saw many a woman casting an envious eye in his direction, but throughout the cruise Raymond had eyes only for his bride – well, that was the impression he tried to make. Mary noticed women tittering between themselves whilst glancing at Raymond. She guessed what they were saying; but he was all hers, so they could take their eyes off.

They took a carriage from the docks to their hotel. Raymond would share Mary's room now as it was designed to accommodate two people.

'You go up and unpack, my darling, I must have a word with Mildred,' said Mary.

'Fine, don't be long. I want us to have a bath just like we did on the boat.' said Raymond as he hurried towards the hotel stairs.

She waved her hand at him as if to send him on his way and tapped at Mildred's lounge door.

'Come in. Oh Mary it's you. Come in and shut the door and sit down.'

'Why? What's wrong?'

'We have had the police round while you have been away.'

'What did they want?' Mildred looked at her husband, who nodded his head for her to continue.

'Apparently, your husband is a bad one. He's wanted for forgery and embezzlement; also he's on suspicion of murder.'

'Murder! Who has he murdered? I find this all very preposterous. They obviously have the wrong man,' said Mary indignantly.

'That's what we thought, until they showed us his picture. Look at him,' said Mildred, handing Mary the picture the police had left. Mary looked at it. He was younger, and apart from the beard there was no mistaking him.

'They said they would be back. They have been searching for him for years. His real name is Stanley Granger, and he has been married twice before. Both times his wives have been wealthy, and have died under suspicious circumstances.'

Mary broke down and started to cry. Mildred left her to get her relief the best way she knew how; if it was with tears, so be. She sobbed for five minutes, then reconciled herself, and put the matter into perspective. She had made her mind up as to what she was going to do. Several pieces of the jigsaw were already in place.

'Phone the police, now please,' she asked Thomas, as she dried her tears. He left the room and went to phone. Mary remembered the incident on the boat and how she nearly drowned. She related it to Mildred.

'What shall I do?'

'Well, you can't go upstairs and face him with it, and you certainly can't act as if everything is normal. I should stay here and wait for the police,' said Thomas, returning from the telephone. 'They will be here in minutes.'

True to his word about five minutes later two of them appeared in the lounge.

'Which room?' said the sergeant.

'Sixty-nine, first floor,' said Tom.

Five minutes later they were back.

'Missed him. He's escaped by the fire escape,' said the sergeant. 'That's typical of him, always one jump ahead of the law. He must have seen to police wagon through his window and taking no chances he done a runner,' said the senior of the constables

'There is a little cottage where we stay, he might have gone there. I know he has some clothes there, this is the address,' said Mary, as she handed it to them, and they left straight away. Mary had a cup of tea with Mildred then went upstairs. Raymond's suitcase lay on the bed, unlocked but not unpacked.

She didn't know why she did it, but with tears of unhappiness pouring down her face she started unpacking his suitcase. It was only when she got to the bottom of the case she found the missing locking pin to the gate on board ship. She knew then that he had unsuccessfully planned her death.

Mary was devastated and heartbroken when she realised how Raymond had tricked her. He had taken everything she had to offer, with no intention of marrying her – in fact, he was already married. Now he was a hunted man, wanted for murder, amongst other crimes. She didn't think she would see him again, unless it was in court.

She went back downstairs to see Tom and Mildred. They invited her into their lounge, and were sorry for the state she was in.

'What am I to do Mildred? I feel devastated. I daren't see my parents and tell them what's happened. What do you advise?'

'Tom and I have been discussing the problem and trying to find a solution. Firstly, we think you should stay on here just as you were before you met Raymond.'

Mary nodded her head in acceptance of that idea. 'What about the baby? I don't want his baby now, I couldn't love it.'

'We can understand that Mary, there are two alternatives. One, have it adopted, and two, have an abortion. Who said you're pregnant anyway? Have you been to see a doctor?'

'No, should I?'

'You poor girl, don't you know anything about life? Go and see a doctor right away and have the pregnancy confirmed. How long is it since you last had a show?'

'This is the third month.'

'Well, it's still worth seeing a doctor.'

'What about the marriage?' she asked.

'Don't concern yourself about that, Mary. The marriage will be null and void as he is a bigamist. Don't be so trusting next time you meet a young man,' said Tom.

'I don't want to meet another, I don't trust them,' she said.

'Don't worry, Mary, you will get over it. There are millions of nice men to choose from.'

'Oh, I nearly forgot. I brought this down to show you,' said Mary, handing Tom the rail securing pin from their ship.

She told them the whole story. They couldn't believe the cowardly act he had tried to perform in getting Mary killed, so he could benefit from any inheritance she might have been entitled to.

*

Mary went to see a doctor later that morning. It appeared that she might have had a phantom pregnancy; but there was nothing in the womb now. It could have been an early miscarriage, brought on by some sudden mishap causing shock. He said it was very mystifying, but she definitely wasn't pregnant. Mary was greatly relieved, and felt that a great burden had been lifted from her shoulders. She returned to the hotel smiling and a lot more cheerful.

'I want to start work this afternoon Mildred, may I?'

'Of course, if you feel up to it.'

She had just taken over the reception desk two hours later when the two constables came back to the hotel.

'Thanks to your help we caught your husband,' one said.

'He's not my husband, he belongs to another woman,' said Mary, indignantly.

'Yes, of course. I'm sorry for the mistake.'

'Perhaps you would like to add the charge of attempted murder to the list you already have,' said Mary.

'Go on, tell us about it,' said the taller constable, taking out his notebook.

Mary quickly related her experience on board ship, and proved it by producing the locking key from underneath the reception desk.

'Are there any witnesses?'

'Not really. The man who actually saved my life vanished into the crowds, and we never saw him again.'

'Would you recognise him if you did see him?'

'No, unfortunately I wouldn't.'

'May we take this pin, we will need it for evidence. Also we would like a proper signed statement from you. Will you do that for us?'

'Of course,' said Mary.

At the end of the week Mary went to Redlock Farm to see her parents.

'I don't believe it's you, Mary. Do you realise it's nearly three months since you went away. What have you been doing my dear?' asked Beatrice, after giving her daughter a big hug.

'I'm sorry, Mother, but time just flies by. They gave me a reception job at the hotel. Tom and Mildred are very nice and friendly, and then I went on a cruise. That's what I wanted the money for,' she lied. 'Apart from that nothing really exciting has happened.' She managed to hide her blushes.

'Your father wanted to come and visit you, to see if you were alright, but I insisted he leave you alone to find your own way in life. No sign of any romance yet, my dear?'

'No Mother, though I have been out on several dinner dates. I haven't found anyone yet who suits me,' she said with a smile. She felt so guilty at not telling her the truth.

Charles came in and nearly crushed her in his delight at seeing her again. Once more she had to face the inevitable barrage of questions, all of which she parried satisfactorily.

'Are you staying long, my dear?' asked Beatrice.

'Yes, till Sunday. I have to be back at reception on Monday.'

Bruce came stomping in from the farmyard. He seemed to have grown another foot since she saw him last. He was a handsome chap, and he wasn't short of girlfriends, he said.

'What's the news on Norman? I seem so out of touch.'

Norman is at home nursing Clare. You know she lost a baby don't you?'

'Yes, that happened before I left home,' said Mary

'Well, apparently, Clare has complications, and is still bedridden. Norman won't leave her.'

'And Ann, what's happened to her and James?'

'Ann is expecting another baby. She and James are still working at the hospital. James is having bad headaches from the bullet wound in the Boer War. He is thinking he may have to give up doctoring altogether. His father Harold has died of consumption; he was coughing blood at the end. There was nothing they could do for him,' said Beatrice.

'That's sad news,' said Mary sympathetically.

*

A little later they sat down and ate lunch together.

'So is Norman going back to sea one day?' asked Mary.

'He wants to but he can't until Clare is better. He must be short of money, as he's not working,' said Charles.

'He was going to sea with his old captain of the *Sea Vixen*, but that all fell through when Clare was taken ill,' said Beatrice.

'What's wrong with her, exactly?' asked Mary.

'They don't know, she can't walk, and has to be fed. Luckily her mother Betty is at the house.' added Beatrice.

'Is there something you haven't told us, Mary?' asked Charles, as he lifted up her left hand to see it properly.

'No Father, why?'

'Because you have a white ring mark on your wedding finger, burnt in by the sun, but no wedding ring?'

'Don't be so silly, Father, you are suspicious, aren't you. I wore a dress ring of Mother's on that finger for years until it got too tight, didn't I Mother?'

Her mother had to agree this was correct, though she also had her doubts, like Charles.

'We are having one of those new telephone gadgets fitted. I expect you have one at the hotel, so we can keep in touch,' said Bruce excitedly.

'Are you? Yes, we have one at the hotel, Please contact me when you have a number,' asked Mary, happy to change the subject.

She spent a pleasant weekend with her parents and brother, and when she opened the hotel on Monday morning her first guests were the two constables.

'Good morning, Miss Redlock,' said the shorter of the two, remembering she was no longer married. 'They have had the trial of Raymond Steele, alias Major Foolproof.'

'Have they, already?'

'Yes, and he's cunning and only got six months for bigamy. The other cases couldn't be proven to the judges' liking.'

'What about his trying to murder me?'

'Inconclusive evidence,' they said. 'Mind you, he had a good defence lawyer.'

'And the pin? What about the pin from the ship's rail?' she asked.

'They said it could have come from any ship. In fact, he said it was a souvenir from one of his earlier cruises.'

Feeling very disillusioned, Mary thanked them, and continued with her duties.

*

Matters stayed like that for some time, and nothing of any consequence happened. Mary was so depressed. She had placed all her faith in one man, who had robbed her, embezzling money, and had tried to drown her at sea. She wondered if she would ever trust another; having been let down so badly. If she could find the evidence to convict him she would. Why should he get away with it?

Her parents had their telephone fitted, and she was now able to communicate with them. How it all worked puzzled Mary. She wasn't short of invitations out to dinner, and dances, and accepted those that sounded promising, and fun. It was three months later, one warm afternoon in late summer, that a very distinguished man came into reception and requested a room. He was dressed in a three-piece suit – which seemed ridiculous considering the temperature – plus one of those new-fangled bowler hats. He certainly looked a professional man.

'Good afternoon, may I have a room with a double bed, overlooking the harbour if possible?'

Mary checked the availability. 'Yes, we have one sir. For how long?'

'Oh, five days should do, thanks,'

'That's twelve shillings sir, including dinner.'

'Yes that's fine.' He gazed at her for a moment. 'We have met before, haven't we?'

'I don't think so, sir,' said Mary. She had heard this familiar line as a way to getting an introduction.

'No, I'm being serious. On the cruise ship *Collumpton,* about three months ago. I never forget a face.'

'Did we speak?'

'No, you were just about to fall into the sea, when I grabbed you.'

'No! Not you? And you didn't stop, but disappeared into the crowds on deck.'

'That's right,' he said with a smile, revealing a full set of brilliantly white teeth.

'But why? We all wanted to thank you – me especially.'

He didn't answer, but took a business card from his top pocket and handed it to her to read: CHIEF INSPECTOR ARCHIBALD TREMBLE.

'You're in the police? What, the English police?'

'Yes, I was following a suspect on that boat and could not afford for anyone to know I was a London police inspector. It would have given the game away.'

'I see, well thank you for saving my life, Inspector.'

'It was my pleasure ma'am, perhaps we may talk again later?'

'Alright Inspector, sign the register please, and here are the keys to your room.'

'Thanks,' he said, picking up his small suitcase, and running up the stairs.

He had made quite an impression on Mary, who having not yet got Raymond out of her system, found this rather alarming. Just then Mildred came out to reception

'Who was that?' she asked.

'An inspector – "Chief Inspector Archie Tremble from the London police",' said Mary, reading from the register.

'Do you know him?' asked Mildred.

'No, he just happens to be the man who saved my life on board our cruise.'

'Well, I never did,' said Mildred, taken aback by this story.

'What's he want here?'

'I don't know, he said he would like to speak to me later.'

'I bet he would. You just be careful young lady,' warned her friend.

'Yes, Mummy,' replied Mary jokingly. She couldn't help but smile at her friend's words of caution.

Mary was so busy in reception that day that she didn't have time to think about the police inspector. It was only later in the evening, when she was getting ready to hand over to Mildred, that his name cropped up again, when he suddenly appeared at her desk.

'Would you be so kind, assuming you have nothing better to do, to sit and have a few words with me this evening?' he requested.

'What are they, police words?' she asked.

'Of a sort. No, but honestly I would very much like to chat with you. Would you do me that honour?'

Mary didn't reply, but glanced at Mildred, who had just walked in, and introduced the inspector to her friend.

'I have just asked this very nice lady to sit and talk with me. I would be delighted if you would join us, perhaps to act as a chaperone,' said the inspector.

'I'm sure that won't be necessary, Inspector, as Mary has been married before, and is no stranger to male company.'

'Yes, of course I forgot. So Mary, will you sit and talk with me for a while this evening?'

Mildred nudged her friend, hoping to make her say yes. Mary took the hint and accepted Archie's invitation.

'I just have to finish a few things and I will join you, Inspector.'

'I'm not on duty. Please call me Archie.'

'Very well. I will be with you soon, Archie,' she said with a smile. Ten minutes later the two of them were seated, each with a glass of port wine.

'Did you find who you were looking for on our ship, Archie?' she asked as an opening gambit.

'I found him alright; it was the man you were married to.'

'Never! Are you sure?'

'Oh yes, he's wanted by the English police, as well as the Australian and American police.'

'Did you know I found the missing securing pin in his luggage when we got home?'

'No, we might get a conviction on that.'

'We tried and failed. The judge wouldn't accept that as evidence.'

'Have you still got the pin?'

'Yes, why?'

'Would you let me borrow it, as I have an idea?'

'I will go and get it,' said Mary. She was back in five minutes.

Mary told Archie most of the things about her life, and Archie did the same about his. He had been married, and had a grown up son. His wife died in childbirth, and he had been so involved in his career that he had never married again.

'I like you, Mary. Will you come for a walk with me tomorrow?'

She found his invitation quite acceptable, because she felt at ease in his company and found him very sincere and refreshing to be with. He was eight years older than she was. After the experience with her previous husband, she was very wary of men. However, life was passing her by, and she was getting older; besides she and Ray did have lots of fun together, until he tried to kill her.

She quickly made her mind up. 'Yes Archie, I would be delighted to walk out with you. I am free from tomorrow afternoon.'

'It looks to be a fine day. Shall I meet you here at two?'

She agreed, and stood up to leave when the phone rang .The call was for her. She said goodnight to Archie and took the call. It was from her mother.

'Hello, Mother, what's the reason for this late call?'

'Mary, I have some sad news. Norman's lady friend, Clare, whom he has been nursing, had died. Norman is very cut up with grief. He tried so hard to save her.'

'Oh, I'm sorry to hear that mother, what's Norman going to do now?'

'He says he's going back to sea, and will spend the rest of his life there.'

'I hope he finds what he's looking for at sea, Mother. I'm sad for him. I do love my brother.'

'I know. How are you coping now?'

'Fine, I will visit you shortly, Mother, goodnight.'

*

Mary and Archie became good friends and found great pleasure in each other's company. Despite this, Mary was very cautious, and wanted to be certain she had found the right man this time. Mildred, was suitably impressed with him, and tried hard to assure her friend that he was a good marrying sort.

Raymond was due out of prison from his bigamy charge. Once released, he would be hard to trace, Archie knew this, and was making every effort to get his man. It was six weeks after his first meeting with Mary that Archie told her he had some good news.

'Come on then my dear. Tell me, what's this good news?'

'Well, before I say anything, I want your assurance that you won't take it out on me if I get a conviction on Raymond Foolproof. Even if it's one that puts him away for a long time.'

'Do you really think you can, Archie? No I wouldn't object.'

'That's fine, I don't want to say too much just yet but you will definitely be wanted as a key witness, if we can get this to court.'

Two weeks later, Archie told her that the trial was the following month, and told her she would be required and would receive official notification. The relationship between the two of them was such that they avoided being apart whenever possible. They had not made love yet, but had kissed many times. Archie wasn't ravenous for sex, like her husband had been; it made a nice change. Mary was quite happy to let nature take its course in their relationship; though she knew she was falling in love with Archie.

Just as Archie had said, Mary received a summons to attend court. The case against Raymond Foolproof was that of 'Attempted murder of his wife Mary'. She was quite shocked to find that Archie had been able to make a charge stick, whereas previously the judge wouldn't even let it go to court.

The accused pleaded not guilty. However, the evidence against him proved conclusive and he was found guilty and given twenty-five years in jail. It was all over in two days. Archie was beaming when he came out of court.

'That was wonderful, darling. How did you manage to get the judge to change his mind and allow him to be put on trial?'

'It was all to do with the locking pin from that gate.'

'But the judge knew about that before,' said Mary, a little confused.

'I know. But what they didn't realise was that on the *Collumpton,* each individual gate locking pin in the ship's rail is individually fitted. I don't know why, but because of this, the pin that your husband removed matched the same gate on the ship. You see it has a number, and the ship's rail lock has the same number; they match, so he must have removed it and put it in his case where you found it.'

'I'm hungry, let's go and eat,' said Mary, taking his arm. The two of them walked off into the distance, happy in the knowledge they had a conviction on the man who had tried to kill her, and that their friendship would certainly result in marriage in the very near future.

17　Bruce's Story

BRUCE REDLOCK was celebrating his twenty-third birthday. His parents were passing on a lot more of the farm responsibilities to him as they were getting older, and not so capable of getting around with the inflictions of old age which were gradually encroaching on what had been a steady, though demanding way of life.

There were also all these new wonders of science. There was now talk of something to replace the horse and possibly, some type of gadget that would fly across the sky like a bird. To Charles it was more than he could take in. Let the young folk figure it out, was his view. He was going to sit back and enjoy the latter years of his life. It was the same with Beatrice. So much had happened in her life that she had no real regrets; apart from the loss of loved ones. Charles was quite happy that Bruce would inherit the farm one day; after all, he had put more work into it than any of the other children.

Norman was captain of his own ship, and even he was thinking of retiring. He never married after the loss of Clare and his son. He thought of Ann and her life as a nurse, the near loss of her husband James and how they were well blessed with two children. Charles was pleased with the way things had mapped out for the family, and looked forward to a happy retirement with Beatrice.

Then, of course there was Mary. Although not a blood relative she was nevertheless included as one of the family, with equal rights. It was unfortunate that Charles was unable to legally adopt her, and she had no birth certificate. By what she said in her letters and phone calls she seemed to be enjoying life and had found a male companion who was a police inspector. His name was Archie and apparently he had recently proposed to her, an offer which she had accepted.

Bruce rode into town on his horse. He wanted to see a solicitor about some land dispute and look around the few shops that had opened up. He saw a notice that there was to be a barn dance that coming weekend and made a note of the details. Bruce didn't get out much. Usually he was too tired, but he felt he could do with a few beers and a couple of the farm hands would go with him for company.

He entered the office of Wentworth and Smith, solicitors, and went up to the desk. A charming young lady was acting as receptionist. Bruce found her very attractive and realised there was more to life than sheep. She stood about five foot four, and was of medium build with auburn hair in a permanent style of curls, which were very much in fashion these days.

'Hello, I'm Bruce Redlock. Mr Smith is expecting me, I have an appointment,' he said with a big inviting smile.

'Alright Mr Redlock, I will see if he is free,' she said, returning his smile.

Two minutes later she reappeared. 'He will see you now, Mr Redlock,' she said. Bruce went into his office, shook hands and sat down.

'That's a pretty young woman you have in the office,' said Bruce.

'That, Mr Redlock, is my daughter Sheila, who has come over from England where she has been living with her estranged mother. I have given her employment in the company.'

Mr Smith knew the Redlock family and their good reputation in the sheep business. He had no hesitation in helping his daughter get acquainted with one of their fine lads.

'Would you like an introduction, Mr Redlock?'

'I certainly would, sir, when we have finished business.'

'Of course,' he said, picking up a file on his desk. They sat and talked through the problems that Bruce had to solve and eventually reached a satisfactory conclusion.

'Thank you, Mr Redlock, you can leave the details with me and I will have the papers for you to sign in a week,' said Mr Smith, as he showed him to the door.

'This is my daughter, Sheila,' said Mr Smith, pointing to her.

'Hello Sheila, welcome to Australia. I hope I may have the pleasure of meeting you on a more social occasion; like the coming barn dance. Do you intend to go?'

'Perhaps I will go. I haven't finally decided yet, we will have to wait and see Mr Redlock,' she replied in a very teasing, uncommitted manner.

'It's Bruce, Sheila.'

'Alright Bruce.' He bade Mr Smith good day and raced back to the farm, just dying to tell his parents who he had just met.

'Father, I have just met the most beautiful girl in the town. She has just come over from England. She's a real beaut.'

'I have never seen you so enthusiastic over a woman before, she certainly has made an impression on you, young man. Calm down or you will burst a blood vessel,' Charles said with a grin.

'That's for sure. I am going to the barn dance on Saturday and I was going to take some of the lads with me, but I don't think I will chance it. I don't want to share her.'

Charles chuckled at his son's enthusiasm for this young woman. On the Saturday Bruce and two pals went into town. They had a couple of beers and went to the dance. Bruce stood just inside the entrance looking around to see who was there and one certain person in particular. He didn't see her but he did hear a commotion over by the dance bandstand where this big six footer was trying to drag Sheila onto the dance floor against her will.

'I don't want to dance. I have just come off the floor. I want to sit down and cool off.'

'Oh come on, Sheila,' he said, pulling her arm. She was crying.

'The lady says she doesn't want to dance, big fella,' said Bruce.

The big guy stopped and looked round at Bruce. He pushed the flat of his hand into Bruce's face so hard that he fell to the ground with the force of it.

'Stay out of it, sheep herder,' he said, returning to try and persuade Sheila to dance.

Bruce got up. The crowd split as Bruce went up to the guy, pulled him round and punched him on the point of the jaw. The big guy collapsed like a half-full sack of pomegranates. The man was pulled off the dance floor to a corner of the room, where he was left to recover.

Sheila smiled when she saw Bruce. 'Thank you, Bruce, you came along just in time, I have been dancing with that man all evening and he wouldn't let anyone else dance with me,' she said, rubbing her arm.

'Never mind, Sheila, I'll look after you from now on, and you can dance with whoever you like. I am not a jealous person,' he said with a comforting grin.

They had a great evening together, dancing and laughing. Bruce had a marvellous wit and was brilliant company for Sheila. When the dance was finished Bruce walked her to her home and they exchanged a goodnight kiss at the gate. Bruce turned and made his way back to where the lads were waiting with the buggy to take them home.

Suddenly he found himself surrounded by four brash bullies, the big guy he had knocked out being one of them. They were armed with pickaxe handles.

'Oh look, what we got here fellows – the big hero who saves a girl's honour,' said one.

'A proper knight in shining armour,' said another.

'Come on fellas. I will fight any one of you in a fair fight but this isn't fair,' said Bruce trying to reason with them.

'It isn't meant to be, Mister Sheep Farmer. Hell, he even smells like a bloody sheep, doesn't he lads,' said the big guy.

Bruce decided attack was the best form of defence, so he kicked the one nearest him in the bollocks and headbutted the second. He didn't remember much after that because two axe handles crashed down on his skull. As he lay there, those that were able kicked hell out of his body until they heard a noisy group of partygoers approaching, and they fled.

The partygoers stopped and attended to Bruce, bringing him round. He ached all over from the bashing he had taken. Once they got him on his feet, he still felt unsteady.

'Where ya heading for mate?' asked one.

'There is a rig waiting to take me home. If you will give me a hand to get that far, my lads will look after me from there,' said Bruce.

'OK mate, take my arm.' Together the two of them staggered back to the dance hall. Bruce's mates were very concerned when they saw the state of him and vowed vengeance on the gang, though Bruce did his best to persuade them otherwise.

When Sheila next met Bruce he was still covered in bruises. She was very concerned and he explained how it had happened.

'Oh Bruce, it was entirely my fault.'

'Don't be silly, I suppose I asked for it by interfering, but I couldn't let a beautiful woman like you be bullied by him.'

Bruce continued to see Sheila on a regular basis, and it was with much pride he took her to his farm to meet his parents. Beatrice and Charles were taken with her right away, and were very impressed by her beauty and femininity.

'She's lovely Bruce,' said his mother. 'Your father and I do like her a lot. Do you think she is the girl for you?'

'Yes, Mother, but we haven't got as far as that yet. We have hardly kissed.'

'Well, don't lose her, she would be a good catch for any young man, and you know you have some rivals, don't you.'

Bruce courted her every day, and eventually told her how much he loved her, and she replied that she felt the same, so a marriage was arranged. Sheila's parents came out to the farm to meet the Redlocks and discuss the arrangements.

There was a grand wedding. All the family were there including Mary and her husband Archie. He was the latest addition to the Redlock married circle. Straight away, he made a great impression on all its members. He was a really nice guy, and in return was pleased and proud to join the Redlocks. Norman was back on dry land once more and pleased to be able to make Bruce's wedding and catch up on family matters.

'I thought it was never going to happen, little brother,' he said to Bruce, slapping his younger brother on the back. 'It was a good job you made me best man, otherwise I wouldn't have come.'

'It's about time you got married, Norman,' said his father. 'I know you lost Clare and your son, but time is passing and you will still have your memories.'

'Yes I know, you're right, Father, I will get around to it when I leave the sea, but it's not fair on a girl with a family to be left on her own with the uncertainty of where her husband is or how he's fairing.'

'I expect you are wondering what wedding present your mother and I had in mind for you, Bruce. Well, about the cottage we have just completed out the back, which we said was a gift to your grandma to retire to – we told you a fib, because it was built for you and Sheila, so you will have your own place and still be able to run the farm.'

Bruce's eyes lit up with excitement as it was a worry to him how and where they would live. He didn't want his new bride to live in the main farmhouse, which he thought they would have had to resort to.

'Thanks, Father,' said Bruce. 'That is a wonderful present, just what we needed.'

He hurried off to find his bride, and his mother. Sheila was absolutely delighted with her new home, and with cheers of the wedding guests ringing in their ears. Bruce carried his new bride over the threshold, kicking the door shut behind him.

A year later, Bruce and Sheila added a son to the family, whom they named Harry, and eighteen months later a little girl named Rose completed their family. Charles and Beatrice had by now retired from sheep farming. Charles passed away in his sleep a month later. Beatrice was at a loss without him, and spent most of her final days sitting in a rocking chair remembering her past life and all the people she had known who were now gone.

She was very grey and had severe lumbago, her poor hands were twisted and she was in great pain. One evening she fell down the farmhouse steps, having lost her balance. The damage to her hip was irreparable. It was a relief from her pain and misery when she too died six months after Charles.

In both cases the sad loss of their parents cut deep into the emotions of the rest of the family. In retrospect all of them, except possibly Bruce and Harry, hadn't up until then encountered any great loss or hardship; though nobody begrudged them their good fortune.

A piece of land had been designated and consecrated as a family burial plot on the farm. It was a mile away from the farmhouse and a small chapel had been built on the ground. Alex had been the first of the family to occupy a place, and now Beatrice and Charles would be interned in there also. There was no one missing at the funerals. All the family turned up, as did the sheep farmers from farms nearby.

Bob and Bluey had left the farm before the deaths of the Redlocks, but somehow news got through to them and they turned up unexpectedly. Norman was on shore leave at the time, and attended. He had grown a beard now, and his hair was turning grey. He too was ready to finish with the sea, and try and find a home and possibly a loved one on land.

Mary and Archie had decided to join together in holy matrimony. Mary felt so confident in her steady, older, police inspector husband. They were both in love, and Mary was to have two girls by him, which made both parents very happy. Archie bought the hotel off Mildred, and they gave her permission to stay there rent free as long as she wanted.

However, life was never that perfect for long, and so misfortune found a place eventually in the lives of Bruce and Sheila; and the younger generations still had some surprises in store.

Bruce was very good at training or breaking in wild horses. It was dangerous work, and took years of experience to become good at it. Harry just didn't want to know anything about riding a horse. When Bruce first seated him on one at the age of three, he bawled his head off, and would never go on one again. Harry was a disappointment when it came to the kind of son Bruce had hoped for – one who could run the farm when he retired.

There was a new black stallion in the stables who was consistently trying to kick the shit out of the one that he was in. His eyes were like hot coals; they glared at you, daring you to come to close. This stallion hated the human race and had never been ridden by one.

Bruce put a cover over its eyes and a rope round its neck. He tried talking softly to the horse to get it to recognise his voice and stay calm. The horse whinnied – whether in acceptance or denial Bruce could only guess. He opened the stable door and led it out into the pasture. When he removed the cover from his eyes he had a job to hold the black horse back as it wanted to gallop off on its own. If it did, Bruce thought they would never find it again.

It appeared to be a very powerful and fast horse. He had the tack brought out and took the horse into a small breaking enclosure. He tethered it to the railings and climbed on. The horse let out a terrifying scream of objection to a saddle and rider, and was very obstinate when the bit was added. Bruce patted it and talked to it, trying to calm it down and gain its confidence.

When he was ready he slipped the halter and left the horse to its own devices. It kicked and bucked, sometimes coming down on all four hooves together, causing a pain to Bruce's spine. It tried every trick it knew to dislodge its rider. Bruce hung on, never knowing if the horse or he would tire out first.

The pair of them battled it out for forty minutes before the black reluctantly gave in by signalling a quiver down the length of its black sweaty body, and a few snorts of what could be taken for disgust that he had been beaten. Bruce was delighted with himself. This horse had been one of the toughest he had ever had to break in.

A crowd had gathered around the compound where Bruce was breaking the horse, and a loud cheer went up when they realised he had broken its resistance. Someone opened the gate to let the rider and horse out and Bruce took it half a mile at a gentle canter to see how it handled. He was very pleased. He turned the horse round and set off back.

Suddenly a rabbit shot out in front of them, hotly pursued by a yapping terrier dog. The black was frightened, and reared up on its hind legs, intending to fall down onto its back. Bruce was as startled as the horse at first, but from experience he knew what the black was going to do, and if Bruce wasn't quick the horse would land on him and crush him.

He quickly tried to kick his feet free of the stirrups, but unfortunately a piece of leather had come away from the sole of the left shoe which snagged in the stirrup. This meant he couldn't withdraw it from the stirrup in time to jump clear. Bruce was looking up at the sky as the body of the horse blocked it from view as it fell to the ground with Bruce beneath it. Rider and horse hit the ground simultaneously. Fortunately, Bruce was to the left of it, and it was only his leg which took the force of the impact. Bruce passed out unconscious.

The crowd, who had been watching him and cheering him, now came racing across the meadow to see how Bruce was.

'Quick, go and get a cart and some blankets,' shouted Bluey to one of the hands. The horse had got to its feet, and stood there shaking. One of the hands took the bridle and led it back to the stables. Sheila came running across the meadow to see what had happened to Bruce. She knelt down by his side and smoothed the hair from his face. She kissed him, gently calling his name. He stirred and opened his eyes.

'Hello sweetheart. What have I been and done?' he asked, with a little grin of pain.

'Lie still, the wagon is coming and we have already sent for a doctor,' said Sheila. His leg was twisted, and a bone of the leg poked through his jeans. Bruce was taken back to the house but remained in the cart until the doctor arrived. He examined Bruce and diagnosed compound fracture, which could only be repaired at the hospital.

Bruce remained in the cart as it was driven to the main hospital where he could be seen to. He was out of action for three months, and even then he couldn't walk without the aid of a walking stick; his days of horse breaking in were over.

Bruce started training Harry as soon as he was old enough to take on the duties of the farm, so that it would be in good hands for the next generation of Redlocks. However, Harry didn't show the same aptitude and love of sheep farming that his father and grandfather before him had done; which was a disappointment to his dad.

When asked what he wanted to be when he grew up, Harry would say 'a soldier'; though where he got it from nobody knew, as there had been no military personnel in the family since Ann and James went to assist in the Boer War.

18   *Harry*

THE PENDING WAR with Germany was in the news. England and Australia were asking for volunteers to join up. The young men of these countries had never experience war; the last one being so long ago. The thrill of the adventure of dressing up and marching to meet and punish the enemy was enough to stir the blood of thousands and thousands of young men, who thought it would all be over by Christmas. It was – but nobody told them it would be Christmas 1918 – four years later.

Bruce was reading the morning paper at breakfast one morning, when Harry, who had arrived late, noticed the headlines in his father's paper.

'What's that, Dad, are we at war?' he asked, leaning over his father's shoulder.

'It seems like we are, son. We're going to fight that German Kaiser bloke, who has got a moustache and wears a spiked helmet. Apparently the greedy bastard wants to rule the world. But the British won't let him, and we Australians are siding with them against Germany. It should be a real old set to.'

'Do they want volunteers, Dad? If so, I would be interested.'

'Don't be in such a hurry, son; we don't want to see you going off to war, and maybe getting killed.'

'I know, Dad, but I can't just sit and watch all my mates going to join the fight, and not me. Hell, they would think I was a coward.'

'Alright! But I don't want you to rush into anything. Let's wait a week or two and see how it goes. It's early days.'

Harry wanted to join up right away, so it didn't come as a shock when Harry came home the following afternoon to say he had been to the recruitment office and had his medical. Not only had he had his medical, but he had been fitted out with his uniform, and had been accepted into the second reinforcements for the 18th Battalion.

He came home complete with his uniform and showed his dad his documents, an Army Form B103 on which were all his details. Sheila was very upset with her son's rashness in volunteering for the army so quickly. Bruce, on the other hand, understood his son's eagerness to join, despite the advice he had given him.

His son went and dressed in his army uniform, and a lump came into Bruce's throat on seeing his son so grown up and smart. He wore a bush hat with a badge; buttoned-down khaki jacket with large side pockets, belted at the waist; knee-length breeches, long army socks with puttees and black boots.

'I have to be back by tomorrow, Dad, as we're sailing to Gallipoli.'

'Christ, they're not wasting any time are they? Where the hell's Gallipoli?' asked Bruce.

'I dunno. Turkey, I think. The sergeant says the enemy are not expecting us, and it should be real easy.'

'Well, that's good news, son,' said Bruce.

Harry could do no wrong that day. Everybody was nice to him. After all he was a soldier and was going to war. In the morning he said his goodbyes to the family and Bruce drove his son to the station to catch a train to Sydney. Bruce felt very proud of his son as he shook hands on departure.

'Take care, son, keep your head down,' shouted Bruce, with a tear in his eye.

Harry saw some of his mates, and with a cheery wave, he was off. He decided to keep a diary of all that went on and include various pieces in his letters home. It was certainly an eye- opening experience for a young man.

Once in the company of his mates he forgot about home and what they were about to do in the army. The young men were full of life and laughter. To them it was a great adventure. It was simply a case of going over there, giving the enemy a good hiding, and coming back home. He now was the proud possessor of a rifle and bayonet, though he wasn't very proficient in their use, as he had only practised with it for a day before embarking.

'You will get plenty of practice when you get out there,' shouted his sergeant.

The army food was very basic, but there was plenty of it; especially tea and bully beef. The ship was very crowded and the men were kept busy training in the limited space available. Harry kept notes on what they saw and did, and put this in his letters home. It had only been a week since he left home, and he was missing them. He daren't admit it to his mates, but he got the idea he wasn't the only one who missed home and its comforts.

They arrived in Egypt and went ashore at Cairo. Harry and his mates went to see some of the sights. They were most impressed with Egypt. It was so different from what they had expected and had more flies than there ever were in Australia.

They disembarked and stayed there for two months to do their training before moving on to Gallipoli. The enemy they were to take on was not the Germans but the Turks. Eventually they arrived in Mudros Bay which was not pleasant. It was 11 April 1915 .They moved into tented accommodation and didn't get much sleep as an attack was planned for dawn next day.

Harry was attached to 11 Battalion, with two dozen of his mates. It was supposed to be a surprise attack, but straight away it was clear that it was the Australians who were surprised. The fighting was very fierce and bloody, and fifty-seven Australians died in the first assault. Harry's head was ringing from the noise of the gunfire. The sight of his mates falling dead at his side was a terrible shock to the system. When they eventually withdrew, it was a much quieter and morose squadron that returned.

That sergeant who said it would be easy and we would surprise them should have been made to eat his words as it was quite the reverse; they laid on a very large welcoming party. It was so cold at Anzac that he wrote telling them at home that hundreds of Australians were dying from the cold, never mind the military action.

It came as a pleasant surprise when Harry learned that he was to be posted out of Gallipoli and sent to France, where reinforcements were in great demand. The following morning two companies embarked for service in France. Harry didn't realise what a mess he was leaving behind and how many of his comrades would die in Gallipoli. He learned later that by December of that year 7590 of his fellow countrymen had died in those battles.

His battalion were posted to Fromelles, where the battle was at its fiercest. There had been a stalemate of late, with neither side gaining any ground; each side resorting to heavy shell barrages against the other. These were very nerve-racking, and affected the soldiers' mental stability, though the officers would not acknowledge this as an illness amongst the troops. Harry was very tired, and was hating the war. He had been engaged in foot attacks against the enemy, and by some lucky chance he always survived, while hundreds of his mates were killed or wounded.

Harry was taken ill in the trenches and carried to a field hospital; the medical staff thought he was going to die. The hospital was full of wounded by enemy action and physical illness which was also taking its share of life. His ailments were not due to battle wounds, as most were. But he was suffering from some type of gut poisoning where he couldn't keep food down and was getting very weak. All around him were very ill men, many of whom had died. Harry felt he was a coward being in hospital while his mates all around him were dying. But it was the army who put him there.

Harry lay back on the pillow, looking up to the canvas ceiling of the tented hospital. A nurse came to tuck him in and give him his medicine.

'Goodness me, you're a very pretty nurse. You're the sort of girl my mum said I should find as a wife; but I didn't know they existed.'

'Well, this one does, and she is engaged to be married when the war is over,' she said smiling.

'Just my luck to find the prettiest one, and find she is betrothed.'

'Not your day, soldier,' she said, as she walked away.

The Australian nurses did a wonderful job. They worked long hours, and no task was too much for them. So many more men would have died without their help. Conditions in the trenches were atrocious. His mates moaned, which was to be expected. There was a school of thought which said the time to worry was when a soldier didn't moan. If they gave a thought to the fact that at any moment they could die, they gave no sign of it and accepted the inevitability of the situation.

The shelling was sometimes going on day and night, both sides firing over their trenches; funny how one got used to it. Nobody gave a thought as to whether it had any long-term effect on the men. Sometimes the shells landed in the trenches, creating the most appalling devastation. It would kill or wound everyone and everything in the trench would be blown to pieces. The most annoying things were often the little things like the rain. When it rained, the water had nowhere to go but lie in the trenches getting deeper and deeper; one couldn't escape it, even if it came up to chest level.

Harry sat in his trench, cleaning his rifle one bright January day. There were a lot of new men in the trench that day, ready for a raid over the top at dawn the next day. Suddenly something plopped into the mud from outside the trench. It could have been a mortar or a grenade but it didn't explode on impact. If it had it would have taken a dozen men with it.

Without a thought, Harry dived forward; dropping his rifle as he did so. There was a man standing in front of Harry who was unaware of the explosive that had landed as he had his back to it. Harry hit him hard in the back, driving him forward and face downwards into the mud as Harry landed on top of him. At that instant the device exploded, throwing shrapnel in all directions. Luckily, Harry's foot had driven the device further into the mud, so most of the shrapnel had lost its energy.

Harry was pulled off the man whose life he had saved, was placed on a stretcher and rushed away to a field medical unit. The man lying in the mud was the new Company Commander who had just arrived.

'Are you alright sir? I'm sorry about that,' said a very agitated sergeant major, as he helped the mud-caked officer to his feet.

'What the hell happened?' asked the major.

'That was a brave deed that lad did, sir, he saved your life.' volunteered the sergeant major

'Yes I know, Sergeant Major. What is his name?'

'That's Corporal Harry Redlock, sir,' he said.

'Is it indeed? Well, I want to visit corporal Redlock and thank him personally, let me know which hospital he's in and when I can visit.'

'Yes sir,' said the sergeant major, saluting him.

*

Harry came to life in the field hospital ward. He blinked at the light from the sun shining in, illuminating his face. He saw what he thought was an angel. It wasn't, but as near as he would ever see on this earth. A vision of loveliness approached him with a big smile. It was his special nurse; the one engaged to be married to another soldier.

'Hello, Harry Redlock, so you have recovered consciousness I see.'

'What happened, nurse. I don't remember anything except sitting in the trench, cleaning my rifle.'

'You are a very brave man and are being awarded a military medal for your bravery. Do you remember?'

'I do vaguely.'

'Well, you saved the company commander's life by pushing his face in the mud.'

'Did I? I didn't know who it was at the time. My right leg hurts, nurse.'

'You haven't got a right leg – well, that's not strictly true; you have half a leg, we had to amputate it just below the knee.'

Harry pulled up the sheet to see the space where his leg should have been.

'I had a weird feeling, a sort of ache. I didn't realise I had lost my leg.'

'You were lucky. It was touch and go as to whether you lost your life as the poison was spreading through your body and the doctors failed to notice it.'

'You mean the wound went sceptic?'

'That's right, now lay back and rest.'

Harry laid back looking at the ceiling; wondering how he was going to get through life with one leg. Later that week he managed to write a few lines home. He didn't mention losing his leg; he didn't want to worry the family. His leg was paining him. He kept wanting to scratch it, but it throbbed. It wasn't long before his special nurse came to see him, and told him not only the date he was going to be repatriated, but the fact that she was going back to Australia with him; she was to act as his nurse.

'May I ask your name,' said Harry.

'Its Lisa,' she said with a smile.

'Where do you live back home, Lisa?'

'In Melbourne.'

'Hey, I don't live far from there, perhaps we could meet... sorry Lisa. I forgot. I have only one leg now.' Tears of regret came into his eyes.

'I have a boyfriend anyway, Harry, he's in the Nineteenth Battalion. I do hope he will be alright. I have a visitor for you,' she said. She stood aside to allow Major Alfred Morrison to come to his bedside.

'Hello Harry. That was a brave deed you did in saving my life.' Harry didn't know him, only that he was his new commanding officer.

'Don't you recognise me, Harry?' the major asked.

'No sir, should I? I have been told you are my commanding officer, but that's all I know. Have we met before, sir?'

'Many times Harry, the last time was when Aunt Beatrice was buried,' he said, with a smile. 'I am your Aunty Ann's son, Alfred Morrison.'

'Of course, I'm sorry, sir for not recognising you, only I didn't associate you with being in the army.'

'That's alright, Harry, thank you for saving my life. Now you're going home, give them all my love.'

'I will sir,' they shook hands. 'We'll have few beers together when this lot is over Harry.' The following Monday Harry returned to Australia. The sea journey was uneventful. The ship was full of wounded soldiers and nurses plus other people. He was fitted out with a suit of clothes and a false leg which, with the aid of a crutch, enabled him to hobble along. Once he got to Melbourne he phoned the farm and told them he was home and that he was on crutches as he had lost his leg. His parents were so glad that he had come home at all that the lack of a leg didn't upset them too much. A motor car came to pick him up.

'Hi Mum and Dad,' he said, as he struggled to walk up to them. They came hurrying forwards eager to hug him and welcome him home.

'We have a telegram at home telling us of your heroic act in saving your uncle's life. Your aunty Ann is so proud of you and can't wait to thank you, son,' said Bruce, proudly.

'It looks like we have two cripples in the family now,' said Sheila, giving her son and Bruce a family hug. Harry was the talk of the town. So many of the lads didn't return. The fact that he had, even though wounded, was a symbol of what they had gone through. It was as if he was meant to return as a representative of all those that didn't.

Gradually the weeks and months passed and Harry decided to take up a trade as a cobbler. His parents provided him with a little shop in the town and from there he learnt and applied his trade. It took time, but gradually he got better and better at it.

One day he was delighted and very surprised when Lisa walked into his shop. It took a few moments for them to recognise each other; as the meeting wasn't planned.

'Lisa, how wonderful to see you,' he said, shuffling to get off his stool and get round to her side of the counter.

'Its Harry Redlock,' she said, surprised. 'I never expected to see you again. I have just moved up here to stay with my mother, and you live here.'

'Well not yet, I still live at the sheep farm, but I expect I will buy a house in the town one day. How wonderful to see you. Did you go back to the war zone?'

'No they had plenty of work for me at the main Victoria hospital looking after the wounded. I have finished nursing now the war is ended.'

Harry had to know the answer to his next question.

'Did your boy friend come through it?' he enquired.

'No, he died shortly after I left France; his mother sent me a letter.' There was a moment's silence after she spoke, in reverence.

'I'm so sorry,' he said. 'Once you are settled can I show you around the area and take you to our sheep farm?'

'Yes, Harry that would be nice. I will call in here when I am ready; oh by the way, I really did have a pair of shoes that wanted mending,' she said, handing them to him, with one of her innocent angelic smiles.

* 9 7 8 0 9 5 7 2 0 6 1 9 9 *